By David Morgan, the creator of the cult series of 2019 books.

He claims the inspiration for 2019 came from counting squirrels in the park on a long Sunday afternoon

The 2019 Series

2019: The Second Coming

Magick. Is the world changing? A mysterious man with two glamorous assistants launches an organisation promising peace and prosperity. Why do they seek an ancient golden cat? The Omasor Agency investigates, with help from Brick and Blonde, celebrity adventurers.
Book two in the series.

2019: Athens 1 Atlantis 0

Atlantis fought Athens, 11,000 years ago for global domination. Their descendants intend to control the planet again using the Treasures of Poseidon and helped by the Temple Virgins, who are different to other women in interesting ways. Corruption, lust, kidnap, murder follow. Also some bad things. The Omasor Agency gets involved with help from Brick and Blonde, celebrity adventurers.
Book three in the series.
ISBN 978-0-9559767-0-4

www.2019books.co.uk

Also

Amazon Bear Joiner

John Smith is young, rich and bored. What to do with his life? Inspired by his favourite book 'The Exploits of Cadaver Wincepole Gentleman Detective', he sets up as an investigator, employing a sexy young assistant, Eliza. Their first case is to investigate the loss of his parents, killed while exploring in the Amazon. So begins an extraordinary adventure, something far greater than routine murders. With help from two unusual allies, they start to uncover an unearthly mystery. Deception, aliens, bears, monks, trees and a secret sect are all in it somewhere.
ISBN 978-0-9559767-2-8

2019: The Beginning

DAVID MORGAN

Published by

Living Designs Publishing

Campion House, Campion Terrace, Leamington Spa, CV32 4SU

www.livingdesignspublishing.co.uk

Original edition first published 2007 by Exposure Publishing

This extended and fully revised edition published by

Living Designs Publishing 2009

ISBN-13: 978-0-9559767-3-5

This book is for Marie, Chris and the sagacious panda.

1 Prolog

1650. Somewhere in England.

The place of concealment was complete. A cavern, completely lined with heavy granite with six large rectangles forming the roof that was now covered with a deep layer of pebbles and soil and indistinguishable from the original floor of the barn. It remained only to move the final slab to seal the entrance.

James Smith brushed a hand across his brow and contemplated the six men and two women slumped on the floor before him. They were almost exhausted, covered with earth and sweat, their clothing reduced to tattered rags. For five days and nights they had laboured to excavate the cavern, painstakingly loading the removed earth onto the cart each night and scattering it in various hollows in the nearby forest.

In contrast, James felt strong and fit, as he did every day since taking the Blessing.

They had worked secretly, in fear of being discovered by the army that now roamed the countryside killing and destroying wherever they perceived opposition. Smith sighed, very soon the secret would be safe and he would have fulfilled his mission.

He found the gaze of the woman upon him. Elizabeth Beddowes. Unlike the others, her eyes still fired with inner energy although she had worked harder than most. He granted her a smile that she returned, cracking the grime that coated her cheeks. Hanging around her neck was the amethyst rock pendant that she never removed, even when labouring with pick and shovel.

It was time now. He reached inside his leather bag and produced a flask and small silver cup. Rising to his feet he called for attention.

"My friends, we have laboured long and now our work is completed. My gratitude to all of you from my heart and I promise you will be rewarded well. We will celebrate with a toast."

He held up the flask and filled the cup, thanking each by name as they came forward to receive their cupful. The woman was last.

"And you, Elizabeth, I thank you."

She smiled again her eyes fixed to his while she tipped the cup to her mouth.

"Now we rest for one hour before we seal the chamber and begin our journey back to our homes and loved ones."

He sat, closed his eyes and thought of his own departed family. His wife mercifully dead from consumption all those years ago and with sweet irony he could have saved her life with the knowledge he now possessed. Divine fate had intended she perish but the grief had burdened him for too long. He had bedded so many women since then to quench his now unceasing appetite but none had truly satisfied him. As death was now unable to visit through normal channels, he had chosen to make the journey himself to the final portals.

There was one last obstacle to surmount before that final voyage.

Smith blinked his eyes open. Eight bodies lay still. The poison worked rapidly and without pain. He rose to commence the necessary, arduous task of dragging the corpses to the opening and dropping them into the chamber. Elizabeth would be the last.

It was after he had consigned the sixth body to the depths and was turning to reach for the seventh when she stabbed him in the centre of his back. Smith turned more quickly than could be expected, gripping her wrist and twisting the blade from her grasp. Then he struck her with his other hand and she fell backwards, dazed but conscious.

He lifted his heavy leather jerkin to reveal a chain mail vest.

"In the back, the choice of betrayal. I would know how you averted the poison."

His voice remained calm.

She reached into her mouth and pulled out a very thin leather pouch.

'Your venom was retained in this and later consigned to the soil."

He nodded.

"And thus you deceived unto the end."

Elizabeth's eyes still burned but a look of entreaty entered.

"Please join us. Together we will have wealth beyond imagining. And me, take me now as a foretaste of the delights I can offer."

She ripped open her bodice to expose round, perfect breasts and then unfastened her skirt, standing naked before him with eyes wide and lips slightly apart.

Smith considered. He had been a long six days without a woman and it was tempting to have her before she died. It was also dangerous.

He shook his head and grabbing the knife, thrust it towards her chest. She sprang back, clawed his arm aside and began to circle towards the doorway. As he edged round to block the escape route, he saw her glance towards one of the spades they had used.

"I have told the Lord and his men are coming but it's not too late. Look at me for I can be yours."

He knew that she lied. She had sent no messages to Lord Griggan since their work began. But he had not the time for a long and bloody fight. Lowering the knife, he ran his eyes over her perfect body and recalled how his late friend, Grenville Bevill had told of servicing her many times.

"Perhaps I will consider your offer."

He began to unbuckle his trouser belt. She smiled sensuously and moved her hand to caress her breasts.

"You will not regret it."

His trousers fell and he sat down, legs apart. Elizabeth came towards him and stood astride his body.

"My love, I will ride you to paradise," she murmured breathily.

As she lowered herself, he saw her arm reach out for the spade and then pull it from behind her in an overhead swing. He twisted to one side and brought the knife upwards. The spade crashed on the earth behind him, the knife was embedded in her heart.

He stood and fastened his belt.

"You were an evil witch. I still smell the essence of deception on your body. Your scheming was no secret to me and now you shall repent in hell as your penance."

When all the corpses had been pushed into the chamber, he pulled out the empty flask. A depiction on the side, two eagles above six swords. He held it for a moment and then threw it in the hole. The next stage was to use the carthorses to drag the entrance slab into place. Finally, he concealed everything beneath a deep layer of earth.

It was finished. The end was close now. James Smith clambered into the cart and urged the horses away.

The secrets of the Octagon were safe, doubly safe.

2

A year ago. 4.30 a.m. Marseille, France.

The couple left the hotel hurriedly. The night had not been as expected. They had visited the club as usual the previous evening, tight black leather costumes studded with metal under their outer clothing. Met their friends, examined a new selection of whips and thongs on display.

Then the woman had entered the club, moving directly to their table. Unquestionably beautiful with long dark hair and a very noticeable chest. She looked about 19 but spoke like a young girl, giggling and wide-eyed as she conversed. American, from her accent and obviously wealthy, her clothes told them that. Staying at one of the very best hotels. Invited them for the night. 'To become lovely friends with each other', she had said.

Not unusual for them to be asked to spend the night away from home but the question was almost invariably posed by a couple. This one offered money. A lot of money. Didn't seem to understand the value of it in her childish mind. They agreed. Outside, a big car with two heavy men in the front seats. Arrived at the hotel and up to her room, alone with her. Initially, the girl asked them to perform on the bed while she watched. After a few minutes, she joined them. Demanding, insatiable. An hour, two hours. She didn't seem to need sleep.

Then she produced a knife, 'for a new game I've invented'. She began to mark them with it. Tried to resist and she called for the two men. They came immediately. Held the couple while she continued, laughing and singing to herself. Far beyond anything they expected or had experienced before. Finally, she became bored and they dressed quickly and hurried away, blood still flowing under their clothing.

The taxi pulled up in front of them. Jumped in the back, glad to escape. Driver turned to ask them directions. No. He didn't ask anything. Shot them with a silenced pistol. Drove away quickly with two corpses in the back.

The next evening, the large chested girl visited a large house outside the city. Expensive white designer dress, impeccable use of cosmetics. She dutifully accompanied a young, bespectacled man, giving every sign of silent obedience.

They were the only guests at the rented mansion. Live entertainment for most of the evening. Then the bottle was brought to them on a gold and silver tray and the girl waited until the man had finished his drink before lifting her glass. She knew that the liquid contained the Blessing, knew that this was the source of her youth and vitality. She drank it quickly and considered how she would amuse herself that night. Not with her companion. He had never displayed a desire to be close friends with her. She would find others here to play with.

The couple were both members of the Octagon but had very little else in common.

Ten months ago. The Caribbean.

John Porter lounged back on his sun bed in the warm evening breeze. A young, very good-looking man with fair hair, tanned features and athletic body. He picked up the glass that contained the Blessing and smiled brilliantly at the woman sitting next to him.

Mary was equally youthful, long blonde hair cascading over her shoulders. At first glance she looked like a flower child of the 1970's but the demeanour of a much older woman was displayed on her unlined face. She liked John and felt she had chosen well in selecting him to become a member of the Octagon. There had been seven assistants before him, not too many considering she had been born nearly 400 years ago.

This one was different. He lived for the moment, apparently unconcerned with life's trivial concerns although they didn't really have the problems of the vast majority. Mary was immensely rich, building up her assets over all those centuries. Most of the income was from London properties she had purchased cheaply long ago. Their values had now escalated to astronomical levels and the weekly rental income was sufficient to run a small country. In addition, the annual dose of the Blessing guaranteed youth and good health.

An apparently perfect existence.

Mary sighed. No, all was perfect but she still worried. Always had done since her birth in 1619. She looked again at John's handsome, smiling face. Yes, his free going ways raised her spirits now but perhaps it would become boring in time. Then he would have to be disposed of like the others.

She pulled off her bikini and reached a hand towards him. An hour's distraction was needed.

Mary and John were the third and fourth members of the Octagon.

Four months ago.

The large but secluded villa stood in the hills overlooking the East Italian coast, the evening sun catching its white facade. Two people left the car that had just parked on the exquisite mosaic area in front of the house. A slick haired man, immaculately dressed in evening suit, walked from the building to greet them.

"Good evening and welcome. I am your host. Please do not hesitate to ask for anything you require."

He escorted them into the building and through to a central room. It was ornately decorated in ancient Egyptian style with hieroglyphs and coloured depiction adorning the walls. Large multicoloured silk cushions were arranged around a large circle of white marble on the floor, obviously the area designated for the entertainment.

Both visitors were casually dressed. The first was a man who looked in his mid-twenties, medium height with rounded tanned features. The other, a woman of similar age, looked less than comfortable in the luxurious surroundings. She had dark intelligent eyes and untended shoulder length light brown hair. Any casual observer would have found it impossible to believe that they were two of the richest people in the USA.

The man was approached by a pair of dark haired girls, dressed as slaves from the 24th Dynasty, 725 - 715 BC or thereabouts. It may well have also been similar to slave fashion in another Dynasty, or not. Of course being a modern representation, the end result was definitely less is more. With an excess of tactile encouragement, the near naked girls guided him to the cushions.

Meanwhile, two muscular young men in short white tunics met the woman. They displayed another wardrobe assistant's concept of fashion in the ancient Nile Valley and seemed very keen to exhibit their masculinity at every opportunity. She firmly resisted their close attentions and sat uncomfortably on the cushions opposite the man.

"Relax and enjoy, Valla," said her companion.

"Sorry Jim, it's just not my thing," she replied with a shrug.

Valla Toreus was decidedly an academic, the brains behind Jim Fischer's business empire that covered half the world. She had never enjoyed parties and always dreaded this annual event. In practice, her social life didn't exist. She relished her work, freezing out a constant stream of prospecting young hopefuls. Jim was the first and only man she had slept with, more from a sense of duty than for her own pleasure.

Taking the Blessing meant it was impossible for her get pregnant, however many times she made love to him or any other man. Valla knew there were not many years to go before her body could conceive and hoped she would then be ready for motherhood.

Jim Fischer would also have to wait for the same time before he could impregnate any woman but he revelled in this freedom. His wealth and acceptable looks allowed him to churn through an unending supply of models, actresses and almost any other attractive female he felt any desire for. Valla simply considered this as his hobby and genuinely had no objections to his excesses. She had even accepted the somewhat unappealing job of checking the sexual disease status his imminent bed partners, although they both knew that the Blessing made illness a far distant stranger to him.

Valla and Jim were the fifth and sixth members of the Octagon.

The entertainment began. A variety performance that would have sold out a stadium in Las Vegas with world-renowned dancers, singers and comedians performing for an audience of just two.

Jim didn't disguise his enjoyment of the event, particularly the developing attentions of the two girls, but Valla's discomfort increased as the evening wore on.

After the final act, the host reappeared, wheeling a trolley that held a metal tray filled with short, burning candles. He handed an envelope to Jim who quickly scanned the sheet inside and passed it to Valla. She took more time to read and memorise, then folded the paper and placed it on the tray of candles watching it burn and then grinding the ashes into powder.

The host carefully held up a faded bottle.

"And now we have the celebration wine."

He uncorked and emptied the entire contents into two tall tumblers.

"I must apologise for serving in such unsuitable glasses, but those were my instructions."

Jim stood up.

"Don't worry, we understand."

He reached for the tumblers and passed one to Valla.

"To long life and good health."

"Long life and good health," she responded, smiling for the first time.

The toast was the same every year and always appropriate. They drained the glasses in seconds to the horror of their host.

"I trust it was to your liking?"

Jim laughed.

"It was very much to our liking, thank you."

Valla turned unwillingly back to her two escorts and saw Jim departing to another room with his arms around the pseudo-Egyptian slave girls. She sighed. Then she remembered she had brought a good novel to read in her own bed later. A story of alien invaders. She'd enjoy that.

Pietro Von Tarka has irrefutably demonstrated that aliens are already prevalent on earth. At an average height of one tenth of a millimetre, they have naturally gone unnoticed except by certain insects and, of course, their natural enemies, dogs.

Unfortunately humans have been unable to interpret the actions of their canine defenders. As the selfless labrador rushes to sniff round a lamppost, he has identified a thriving colony. The little corgi will often fetch sticks of wood containing a complete battalion of the invaders. Mongrels frequently unearth one of their underground installations in the garden. This diligent work is simply ignored by humanity and even worse, the dog is often told to desist.

Von Tarka's theory also covers the building of their original planetary headquarters, the pyramids of Egypt. He describes how most of the aliens escaped when tomb robbers broke into them, mistakenly searching for treasures buried with human remains.

Many legends are based on episodes from the alien's history. 'Jack and the Beanstalk' describes their first landings on earth after travelling through hyperspace (the Beanstalk) and encountering a race of giants (humans).

From the book 'Careful Where You're Trampling' by Pietro Von Tarka.

The Octagon's final two members sat together in a converted office room at Carney House in England. The young man looked an academic, one who has just left university with an honours degree after painstaking study. Short hair and smart clothes, a fine example of public school education. He sat in front of a computer screen, awaiting the next sentence to encode. Computers were his speciality and he had set this one up with great care. Unless three specific keys were held down when it was switched on, every program, every piece of data on the hard disk would be shredded irrecoverably.

He looked across at the Countess. In just a few years, the two of them will rule the planet and he glowed with anticipation. King of the World, ruler of the globe. That was good and he was ready. At the moment he was just her assistant but when the day came, he had absolute faith in his ability to lead. He didn't find her attractive and she possessed a devious nature that made him uncomfortable. Yes, when they took control, he would find a way to dispose of her and take another woman or women to serve his needs.

Countess Pollan raised her head. She couldn't read his mind but she guessed the thoughts that were passing through it. A silly boy. His skills were useful to her now but she would kill him in 2018, along with the other six current members of the Octagon. Then it would be her choice of the seven to replace them and all the new ones would be totally subservient to her. Only she knew where the supply of the Blessing was concealed and that gave her infinite power. If the other members got together, they could find the hiding place from the clues she had left with them but they would all die well before then. The Countess was 401 years old and she wouldn't allow anything to stop her now she was so close to the event.

3

The Caballini purred through the twisting country lanes like a dark panther in the moonlight. Twisting round in the passenger seat, Victor Vistan reached inside his coat and again checked the McCannin 832 automatic. It slipped easily into his hand, light and powerful enough to stop a buffalo in mid stride.

Two other dark clothed men in the car, his favourite assistants. They were perhaps the two most morbid men on earth, except, of course, for that plumber we all know. This was their fourth mission together with a zero failure rate to date.

"Carney House. Over there."

The driver's gravel voice broke the silence. An elegant country mansion stood back from the road, downstairs windows brightly lit and the beams speared through the frosty November night. It was 9 p.m.

The car pulled into the driveway and coasted to the open tarmac area at the front. The cars already parked there would not have disgraced a Royal Ball. Three attendants stood idly chatting near the doorway and one of them approached, immaculate in grey suit.

"I'm sorry gentlemen this is a private party."

"Thank you, but I'm an old friend of Countess Pollan," responded Victor, handing him a business card that carried a suitable alias.

"I'll just check."

He was lifting his phone from his pocket as Victor shot the dart into his neck. Emerging from the car in a flash, he supported the unconscious body on his forearm while simulating an ongoing conversation, gesturing and pointing with his free hand.

His assistants were already out of the car and strolling towards the remaining two attendants. The shots from their dart guns were inaudible and they quickly dragged the bodies to a group of thick bushes on the other side of the driveway and away from the house.

Victor saw one signalling, palm up. He nodded and waited as they moved to the rear of the building. Then he walked towards the entrance, still dragging the unconscious figure. Victor was immensely strong but his arms were aching as he reached the door. Placing the body in front of him he rang the bell and a few seconds later it was opened by a small blonde girl in waitress uniform.

As he had planned, seeing initially the face of the attendant removed her immediate concern and by the time she realised his condition he had covered her nose and mouth with a cloth impregnated with Carkanal, stronger and faster acting than chloroform. He dropped the attendant's body outside and caught the girl before she fell.

The entrance area was smaller than expected but Victor was pleased to note the quality of the antique furniture, classical paintings and busts that adorned the area. He found a cupboard near to the doorway and pushed the girl inside. No need to tie or gag as the drug would keep her out for at least two hours.

He now had the choice of three doors and listened at each of them. A murmured conversation from the one on the left. He checked the time. His men still had four minutes to clear anyone in the kitchen area and he waited impatiently as the seconds ticked. Then exactly on time, he opened the door silently and stepped inside with the McCannin in his right hand.

Victor hadn't anticipated the grandeur of the large room. It was as if he had entered one of the Royal palaces of Europe. Velvet drapes and gold ornamentation abounded and dominating the room was a large dining table with a large crystal chandelier hanging directly above. He recognised Countess Pollan sitting with another woman and a studious looking young man at the table. Two white-jacketed waiters standing at the far side. His presence wasn't noticed immediately as the light faded towards the perimeter of the room and kept him partly in shadow.

Then he heard one of the waiters shout. The man reached inside his jacket, pulled out a pistol and fired instantly, the bullet grazing past Victor's cheek. He could see the other waiter pulling a gun just as his men emerged from a door at he back, firing in unison. This time they weren't using dart guns. Two white jackets now stained crimson. Only the three diners left, should be easy now.

The eyes and brain operate infinitely more rapidly than movement. Reindeer are good examples. They crouch near water holes hoping to find an unsuspicious rabbit or badger and then pounce with all the gory instincts of a wild carnivore. Nature's predators are dependent on speed of thought beating the escape strategies of their potential meals.

The action had taken just six seconds but the woman diner had already rolled from her chair to a prone position. As if in slow motion he observed the gun in her hand, the flash, the report and the sting as the bullet hammered into him, just below his shoulder. He dropped sideways, squeezing the trigger of the McCannin as he fell. The shot was instinctive and random, it could have gone anywhere. Anywhere this time was the forehead of the studious man at the table. He fell forward smashing into the dishes before him.

Now Victor's men fired off a series in the direction of the woman on the floor who was scurrying towards the protection of a large oak sideboard. One shot took her in the calf in but she still reached safety and kicked the sideboard forward with her good leg to create a protected area. Meanwhile the Countess had left the table and was racing towards a door at the back of the room, reaching it just as a knife embedded in the small of her back. She fell forward, lying very still.

Victor hadn't wanted a gunfight. He had visualised a simple quick robbery with no casualties. Now it was looking like a World War. He heard two more shots and one of his men fell, eyes glazed.

"Dammit!" Victor shouted. This was getting ridiculous.

He jumped behind a large easy chair and tried to line up on his target. The woman had squeezed in behind the heavy sideboard and was firing from the shadows. He loosed five shots into the area, hoping for a hit. His remaining man was edging closer from the other side while he kept her occupied. The situation was under control again. He hoped.

She suddenly bolted from her hiding place firing twice at each assailant as she moved. Victor saw his man fall and another bullet grazed his own cheek. She was making for the door and would have reached it easily if her leg hadn't been hit. And Victor was angry now. Both his men down, both shot by this woman.

Rising to his feet, he squeezed off an entire clip. He couldn't miss and didn't. She fell with blood running across her side and back. He walked over to her, pressed another clip into the McCannin and shot twice more into her head.

"For my colleagues," he said.

In retrospect this action was both unnecessary and a mistake. He felt a sharp pain in his back and when he turned, another sharp pain in his chest. Excluding remarkable coincidence, both were almost certainly caused by the knife held by the Countess. The knife that had been in her back.

He looked at her, puzzled.

"You're dead," he gasped, feeling warm blood oozing from his shirt.

She certainly looked dead, her face only a white mask but he didn't feel too good either.

It was the last thing he said. The last thing he did as he fell was to raise the gun again for one last shot. It hit the Countess exactly in the heart.

In one of the rooms, a grandfather clock began to chime. No one alive in Carney House.

4

Carl Vistan eased his ample body behind the ample oak desk in the even ampler office. The room was crammed with works of art ranging from busts of Nero and Claudius to paintings by the best modern artists, Richelman, Andy Viggor and several others. The insurance value exceeded ten million US dollars, merely a fraction of his total wealth.

His nationality remained a mystery. Rumoured to have emerged from some part of Eastern Europe, he had suddenly become a player in the financial markets, having found he possessed a special talent for buying into and getting out of companies at just the right time. Through various oil deals he had earned a nickname amongst his enemies of 'Oily Carl' although few lived to speak it more than once. He was the father of the late Victor Vistan and he was a very vengeful man.

Perhaps the emotion was the result of guilt. He had never been close to Victor, a child born from a marriage that had finished many years ago. Carl had separated from his wife when the boy was just four years old and had then dutifully paid an adequate monthly amount for their upkeep. But almost no contact. So many telephone calls from his ex-wife to tell him the boy was going with the wrong people, mixing with street gangs, bringing home weapons. Carl had avoided involvement then and later when he knew Victor was running his own criminal operation. A violent, ruthless gang that was associated with a long list of unproven murders and robberies.

Carl was far more subtle. He now specialised in what he called consultancy work, engineering deals between major commercial organisations that pressed the very limit of legality. So different from his son but Victor was still his offspring, still family and today, the desire for retribution burned pale in the small eyes set deep in his round, flabby face.

"Are you sure they are all dead?"

His assistant sat in the deep leather chair opposite. A dour, slab faced man of 45.

"I have visited the hospital and spoken to our police contacts. Everyone died in the attack."

"Then we will kill their families, man, woman and child. They will pay for my son."

"It's strange, Mr Vistan, it appears none of them had any relations."

"Impossible," Vistan retorted sharply.

"I've had four people rechecking the public records, doctors, lawyers, everyone with any connection with the Countess. I'm certain they had no living family."

Frustration burned in Vistan's eyes.

"It's just not possible that all three people would have no living family."

"Countess Pollan was an only child, 34 years old. She looked much younger, probably through plastic surgery. Her parents died over 10 years ago. No sisters, brothers, aunts or uncles. Her secretary was an orphan, 26 years old with no family recorded."

Vistan held up a newspaper when the tragedy was bloodily displayed on the front page and pointed to one of the three faces pictured.

"And the guest?"

"Another orphan who lived by herself. Worked as a freelance bookkeeper. Again no relations."

"Unbelievable."

"It's certainly a remarkable coincidence. But of course it could be that an affinity developed between such people."

"So no relations. Let me think."

Vistan mused, his eyes travelling to the window. His assistant knew when to wait.

Waiting does have the benefit of an implied event to come, even if it's only a new customer. Many years ago an old man stood near a restaurant scratching his ear. The chef noticed him and had a brilliant idea. Instead of the people queuing impatiently outside his kitchen, he would get this man to take the food to the tables. As he would spend much of his time waiting about he thought of a new job title. He would call him a bringer. Incidentally, one place to avoid waiting in is a little town called Vane, rumoured to be somewhere in Missouri.

Vistan's next words set many events in motion.

"You are wrong. The Countess had a relation, a cousin who's living in America."

His assistant understood.

"We'll need to forge papers, birth certificates, other documents. I will start our people working on it immediately."

The tiniest smile of satisfaction crossed Vistan's face.

"I will sell Carney House and every scrap of furniture, every painting, every damn thing in it."

5

The girl who had changed her name from Pat Briggs to Aliane was speaking.

"As most of you will know, Elekkian is the most powerful magick without exception. It has taken me many years to learn the finer points and it gives us the potential to fulfil many of our dreams and desires. Now I have moved to a higher level. With help from my partner, I have integrated the essence of these rituals with completely new practices discovered during my travels in northern India and Tibet."

The girl was young, about 22, with long dark flat hair, and gothic eyes. She wore only a crimson silk robe over an obviously naked body.

Aliane looked at the seven other people grouped around the circular table. Two women in their late 40s and expensively dressed. A young couple, the girl pale and stringy with unkempt long fair hair and her partner, a chubby, dark haired man with half a beard. A very attractive single woman in her mid-20s. A married couple, both of them lawyers, who didn't hide their wealth.

"First we must greet a new member, Stephanie," she continued, nodding towards the single woman who gave a nervous smile.

"Hello everyone," she said in a quiet voice.

Aliane personally checked out any newcomers. This one had told her she was from Canada and currently in England for a long holiday. Staying with her retired parents and not working. Very wealthy. Immaculate dark hair and perfect black skin gleaming with vitality. Elegance summed her up and she could easily have a career as a model.

Aliane genuinely believed in her magickal abilities. From the age of 11, she had studied every book she could find on the subject. She was an only child and had never been close to her parents. Her father had made a fortune from the stock exchange and like her mother, took little interest in his daughters' activities. Two years ago, they had contentedly given her a substantial amount to start her own business without any details of its purpose.

For the first twelve months after setting up the Elekkian group she found herself a magnet for unemployable loafers and a variety of crazy people, obsessed with their own self-importance. Then Paul had come. She didn't know much about his past as he talked only vaguely about several businesses he had started but he soon became her sleeping partner. Within weeks he had forced out all the hangers-on and the group had gradually become a fashionable place for the rich.

He had set up a system that delicately obtained contributions from the members without compromising the group's ethos and their income from the previous year had exceeded half a million pounds. The membership now totalled over 30 but Aliane always restricted the numbers at each meeting and just seven had been invited this time. Part of their finances had gone towards renting their current premises, just south of London. An imposing building with eight rooms, the largest reserved for meetings of the group. The circular table had been custom-made with Aliane's own design etched into the surface, displaying a plan of the spiritual hierarchy that included the names of individual spirits and the areas they ruled.

"For the benefit of our newcomer, I will briefly explain how we work. Any member of our group can send me a particular request, perhaps for additional finances, to resolve a love problem, assistance in overcoming some medical situation or any other application. I then invite selected members to attend a meeting where we endeavour to fulfil the request. As you know, the magick is more powerful when the correct number of people joins together in our supplication to the spirits."

"Tonight, our two friends here have requested that we repair and enhance their physical relationship."

The lawyers each held a palm up with a smile.

"Now I will begin the ritual. I need everyone to concentrate on the task and mentally give support to my words. You represent the seven parts of Sunder-Ka, the portal to the benevolent ones and my assistant will act as the vehicle for the spirits."

Right on cue, Paul entered the room. He was tall, young and muscular with long dark hair that could have been modelled on Rasputin. His crimson robe was identical to the girl except for the size and like her, he was clearly naked underneath.

He moved slowly to the end of the table where the others formed a semicircle in front of him and then looked upwards, lifting his arms. Aliane began to chant words, unknown in any human language, speaking completely from memory. For a few seconds nothing changed and then the mist started to appear. A cobalt blue mist that manifested from nowhere and soon filled the room with a chill atmosphere. Paul was just visible through the haze but his image became less distinct and started to distort, transforming into a mask, a facade of ageless benign intellect.

Then it spoke although not through any mouth. Unintelligible words, but the voice was warm and reassuring. Aliane responded in the same unknown speech and the obscure conversation continued for a minute. The image began to fade, as did the haze and clarity slowly returned.

Paul lay naked on the floor, apparently unconscious. His robe had disappeared.

"Please don't worry, he will recover in a moment," Aliane said calmly.

She looked around the table and found the newcomer's eyes fixed on her. Eyes that had changed. Burning, powerful and frightening.

"I'm afraid you're wrong," Stephanie said. She left her seat and walked to the body.

"Yes, he's dead," she announced calmly.

Horror and disbelief mingled uncomfortably in Aliane's expression. She rushed to kneel next to the still, pale figure and then began to scream. Stephanie ignored her and addressed the others.

"Leave here immediately. I will arrange everything and the police will not trouble you. But this organisation now does not exist."

The room cleared even as she was speaking.

"I don't understand. I don't understand," Aliane sobbed, tears rolling down her cheeks.

"Then I will tell you. This man sells drugs. He was selling drugs when you met him and he's still doing it. You gave him a place where he is safe and also the opportunity to rip off a bunch of the bored and wealthy."

The girl shook her head. "No, no. I don't believe you."

Stephanie sighed. "I really don't care what you believe. These little charades have finished. You worked the old blue smoke trick through the four dummy air con vents I can see in the walls. I guess you have the remote control in your chair, one switch to blow and another to extract. The face image is a hologram projected from the imitation halogen lighting and your man here just dumped his cloak into that little sliding door compartment in the floor over there."

"No, you don't understand. Paul suggested we added these extras but the magick really works."

She looked up and wished she hadn't. Stephanie's face was like ice.

"You wouldn't know magick if it licked your leg. This is real magick."

She gently touched Paul's head with her forefinger. He began to move, raising a shaking hand.

"What happened?"

"Paul, it's impossible. I felt your pulse. You were dead," cried Aliane.

He grunted. Life existed.

Stephanie turned to him.

"You'll be ready to go in a minute. Just simple witchcraft. Real witchcraft."

"I must get him to bed. What did you do to him, Stephanie?"

"My name is Selena Bowman. He sold stuff to a schoolgirl. She died and I was asked to investigate. I wanted to kill him but was talked out of it."

"You're the police?"

"I'm taking him to the police but I'm with the Omasor Agency."

She pulled his robe from the hidden compartment and tossed it to him.

"Please try to escape. The door is just over there."

His eyes flashed to the door then back to her.

"No! Don't run, Paul!" Aliane cried but it was too late.

6

On the outskirts of Warwick, right in the belly of England stands a 300-year-old house, a stone's throw from historic Warwick Castle. It's not clear why anyone would want to throw a stone but the massive grey walls are there if you need a target.

The caretakers, an elderly married couple, lovingly maintained the house and green-hedged gardens in traditional 18th-century fashion. Now approaching retirement, they planned to remain there for the rest of their lives.

In the summer months, some rooms were open to the public and for a small fee they were able to view a display of antiques, ornaments, furniture and paintings. None were particularly valuable or rare but they had a seemingly unending appeal to the day-tripper.

Unknown to the tourists, unknown to all but a select few, the house was also the residence of possibly the most enigmatic person on the planet.

Jerome Jones was one of the richest men in England and certainly the richest unknown man. Supposed to be a recluse, no photograph of him appeared to exist. He was never seen in public, deputising his various business dealings to a team of trusted associates whom he had carefully appointed within an impenetrable array of companies. His primary interest was property and he was reputed to own significant lands, hotels, offices and houses throughout Britain.

Although his face was unknown, his name was recognised throughout the world as the head of the famed and very exclusive detective agency, Omasor. An Agency that could not be hired in the usual sense. Assignments were selected, irrespective of any financial incentive and it was not uncommon for celebrities, millionaires or even royalty to be refused. Omasor also frequently offered their services to people who had not thought of using them. This was not an organisation to be contacted for routine divorce or criminal investigations as it specialised in unusual and often paranormal cases. The only common factor was the success rate. Omasor had reputedly never failed.

In an untidy store room at the back of the house was a shabby wooden door with peeling blue paint. Impossible to visualise the armoured steel backing and the very different world on the other side. Beyond this entrance, a carpeted staircase descended to another reinforced metal door and through that lay an underground complex. An area for living and working that comprised three offices, three bedrooms, a luxurious bathroom and strangely tiny kitchen.

Jerome Jones sat in one of the offices, his eyes lost in a Caribbean beach visible on a massive screen embedded in the wall in front of him. The display was so realistic that a visitor would be certain they were in a beach house on one of the islands, watching the waves slip gently up the sands.

Selena Bowman came through the door. Actually she opened the door and walked through the space created. Tall, elegant and moving with the lithe grace of an Olympic sprinter without the drugs.

"Jerome."

Her smile was like a halogen light but his eyes didn't leave the beach.

"You resolved the Elekkian group?"

"Yes. Trivial really."

"You didn't kill him?"

"No. I did as you asked and left him with the police. But I did need to restrain him when he tried to escape."

"Forcibly?"

"Forcibly."

He paused, watching an old man walking towards the surf.

"Anne South is dead, murdered during a robbery."

Her smile disappeared.

"Details?"

"She was a dinner guest of Countess Pollan when a gang attacked Carney House."

He pressed a button on the console in front of him. The Caribbean transformed to a montage of newspaper reports. She read them rapidly.

"Looks like a straightforward violent robbery. Her death is unfortunate and she was a good colleague. But all the gang were killed. Justice done."

"Anne had been with us for 6 years."

"She had no family. I'll get our lawyers tidying up the details of the inheritance. Looking at these reports, it seems that none of the three people at the dinner had any relations. That is unusual."

"In the last hour, the TV news is reporting that the Countess had a cousin living in the USA."

The woman looked quizzical.

"Suspicious but possible."

At last he turned and looked at her. She had been with him a long time and recognised the expression.

"Something not right. Something about the Countess."

She nodded.

"Yes. I will investigate."

He paused.

"I want Chris Darmant recruited immediately."

She looked doubtful.

"To replace Anne? Is she ready?"

He didn't respond to the questions.

"Our liaison team arranged the transfer this morning."

Selena knew of their close relationship with the British Government. She also recognised when Jerome was not prepared to debate a decision.

"Her file is in my office. I'll take care of it. When does she start?"

"Today. She goes with you on this job."

"In the shallow end."

"No, it's deep. There's something else here. Have you heard of an organisation called the Octagon?"

"Not specifically. Eight sides?"

"Eight members."

"No. Why?"

He clicked the button to change the screen picture.

"The face of the Countess. She always avoided the cameras and any social gatherings. Newspapers got it from a neighbour."

"Ordinary face."

"It's familiar."

"You're not telling me everything, Jerome."

"No."

"As usual then."

"Yes."

A pause before she spoke again.

"One day, I'll get you into bed with me."

He shrugged but no humour.

"I doubt it but anything is possible."

"You must have slept with a thousand other women."

"Yes, I must."

Selena sighed.

"And you'd be one of the most unattractive men I'd ever made love to."

"Yes."

"Is this Chris Darmant a close friend?"

He didn't quite smile.

"I've never met her. Our research indicates she's not a sensual woman. It will take some time before you like her."

"You're the boss. I'll see her today."

"Remember that I'm not happy about the murder of Anne."

"I'll remember."

She left the room. He was bad company today.

She'd miss Anne, but she had seen death before, too many times.

Seeing death is like walking a tightrope blindfold over a flock of alligators floating in a shark infested pool with pointy rocks at the bottom. A little tip here is to grip the rope with one hand and rip off the blindfold with the other. Then take poisoned meat from your backpack and throw it into the waters. The alligators will eat the meat and die, to be consumed by the sharks that will also perish. The mass of bodies will form a safe cushion over the pointy rocks in case of a fall. Then grab the straps of the backpack and fold it over the tightrope. Open your umbrella and the breeze will glide you safe and secure to the other side.

7

From the outside, Warehouse 6 was just another grimy brick edifice in the wrong part of town. A four-storey hulk sitting among a host of identical neighbours but Chris Darmant had been told she was looking at the central hub of an international criminal organisation.

She glanced across at the Officer in charge of the 11 agents, four trained women and seven men who were also trained. They had found cover behind an assortment of dustbins, refuse bags and cast off soft toys in the alley opposite the building. Black woolskin suits provided warmth as well as camouflage in the late evening shadows.

The Officer smiled and held a thumb up to her. Many of his rank didn't appreciate outside interference and Chris was pleased that he seemed comfortable with her presence. Just one hour before, she had received a brief telephone call from her British intelligence chief to join him as an adviser on this job. They suspected that one of the criminal brains she had been chasing for months could be in the building, together with several of his major associates.

"Are you ready?" he whispered.

Chris nodded and reached for the gun holstered on her hip.

He waved a hand and two women sped to the nearest window. Within three minutes the whole team were inside.

The interior was not much different from the exterior. A large storage area at ground level with shabby offices on a small mezzanine at the rear. Filth encrusted the walls and floor giving it a rather unique atmosphere, reminiscent of an elephant's mud bath but without the pleasant aroma. It certainly didn't look like the hub of anything, except maybe a social club for downmarket rats.

Chris watched as he dialled on his mobile.

"The puffins are not in the rookery."

She was close enough to hear the chirpy cockney voice replying.

"I should bloody well think not. They're a sea bird, frequenting places like Norway. What would they be doing in a rookery?"

The Officer sighed.

"I am saying there's no-one here."

"What, in the rookery or Norway? The former is no surprise but I would be amazed if the Norwegians had all disappeared. You could try Sweden. Maybe they decided to move for the improved social benefits. My god, if that's true, the whole country could be overrun with puffins. They could become a major European force. This could be a major threat to Britain. I..."

'Look, is this Cobra Command?'

"Yes."

"This is Boa."

"Ah, right. You should have said."

"We're in Warehouse 6 and there's no-one here."

"That's the answer then."

"What's the answer?"

Chris glanced at the team. Card games had started.

"They gave me the paper the wrong way up."

"So we should have been at warehouse 9?"

"Process of elimination, I'd say, unless..."

'What?'

"Well, it's just possible the pen ran out of ink. So it could be 19...or 61."

"If it was 19, the pen would have run out before they wrote the 9."

"Yes, but not if they wrote from right to left. My God, we may have an oriental mole here in the organisation."

Jack ended the call.

"Ok team, we're going to Warehouse 9."

"Who was that?" Asked Chris.

"The guy who usually cleans the cars but also acts as holiday cover."

Warehouse 9 proved to be the same as it's near neighbour but a little smaller and not so clean. The officer and his team departed and Chris walked back to her car.

She sensed the three men well before they jumped from the doorway. They were just street thugs on drugs but they weren't stupid, circling around her to improve their chances. Solitary young women were a rarity in this area and they closed in for an easy target.

Chris had the choice of shooting or fighting. The night had been unproductive so far and her mood was not the best. The first man received her heel in his groin, the second felt the side of the hand slice across his neck and she saved the short punch for the last. They each booked a position on the floor for the next hour or so.

"Have a nice evening, boys," she called cheerfully, continuing to her car.

Two days later, Chris answered her mobile as she sat in a Fiolla Autopol parked in a side street in Zurich.

"Chris?"

The voice of her direct controller in the hierarchy of British intelligence section CB77.

She brushed a stray blonde hair from her eyes.

"Hello. It's a clear day."

That was the code for an unscrambled telephone line.

"It's okay. I have big news for you. You're booked on a flight to Birmingham in 97 minutes."

"What? I just got here yesterday."

"It's a relocation. Out of my hands."

"And if I say no?"

"Don't think you will. Going up, up and away."

"We'll see."

"You'll be met at Birmingham and there's just one other thing."

"Yes."

"May not see you again. Thanks for the memories."

"Right. Bye then."

Strange conversation. She believed that her work had been satisfactory but it looked like a move to a new department.

Change didn't bother her. She had a seemingly insatiable lust to see the other side of the hill. There had been many hills in her career, some barren and rock strewn but others bright and green with lots of interesting little bushes dotted round. Chris was the opposite of a settling down person. At 25, she had crammed a lot into her life. She lost both her parents in a car accident just before she turned 17, an event that would have undermined most of that age. Somehow she had accepted the situation with an understanding that it was part of a grand tapestry yet to be revealed. She turned to her studies for release and qualified with ease to enter university where she graduated with honours in European Politics. But athletics was her first love. She fringed on selection for the Olympic 1500 metres and ran a few kilometres every morning whenever her work permitted.

Chris was courted by British Intelligence in her final year at university. They seduced her eventually with promises of support and facilities for her athletics training and she had quickly progressed to troubleshooter status, flying to any part of the world where she was assigned. Now she was a veteran of 30 countries, most for just a few weeks collecting information from local agents, body guarding VIPs or investigating potential high-risk terror suspects.

Two years ago, she had been transferred to CB77, a specialised intelligence cell concentrating on stemming the tide of cocaine and heroin flowing into Britain. Her current assignment was to investigate the overseas sources, the supply chain, transportation, routes and methods.

Devotion to the job had shredded her personal life. Her only close male friend was John Porter, a good-looking man she had met at a conference in Los Angeles. She had never slept with him and the affair continued erratically. They met only every few months, usually when business trips took him to England. Other close friends could be counted on the fingers of one hand and if she had a biological clock it was in the shop for repair.

Chris arrived at Birmingham fresh after a restful sleep on the flight and paused before a wall mirror in the washroom. Average height, average body, flouncy short blonde hair and a face often described as elfin with deep brown eyes. Not unattractive, but nothing outstanding. An asset in her job.

The airport was crowded at 11 a.m. Two steps into the concourse and the man was there.

"Good morning Ms Darmant."

He looked like a favourite brother, untamed brown hair flipping around his fresh face and warm friendly eyes. Beige woollen jumper and casual slacks.

"Hello. Where are we going?"

He smiled holding his palms up.

"Sorry, don't know anything. Weather and sport only I'm afraid. Car's outside."

The car was a very unimpressive eight-year-old Ford.

"Can't be ostentatious," he remarked.

After less than 40 minutes of almost no conversation, he pulled into a grimy parking lot in a grimy industrial estate. Paper and waste littered the ground. Skeletons of dead supermarket trolleys lay in piles of black polythene bags. A place to expect metallic vultures, circling their favourite restaurant.

She followed him along a waste covered walkway, kicking empty cans from the path and they stopped in front of a pitted metal door that doubled as a graffiti canvas. Four keyholes, no bells, no signs.

He kicked the door twice and it was opened noisily by a vast, muscular man, T-shirted even on this icy day. He shut the door quickly behind them, sliding two heavy steel bars across and then returned to a shabby desk, newspaper and tea. He didn't speak. The dingy room smelt of dead rats roasted in alcohol and was full of large rusting metal containers that probably contained the deceased rodents.

Her companion seemed quite at ease and guided her across the room to the outer door's smarter brother, also metal but minus the pits and graffiti. Chris waited for him to kick but it slid open smoothly as they approached, revealing total darkness.

Paul turned to her.

"In you go. I hope we'll meet again."

Faintly amused, Chris walked into the blackness.

As she had surmised it was an elevator. As soon as she entered, the doors slid shut and it descended for a few seconds in pitch darkness. About 20 metres below ground, she guessed.

When the doors opened Chris was ready for the brightness, but not for the woman dressed in an ice blue suit. Dark, involving eyes and smooth, perfect black skin gleaming with vitality. She was stunning.

"I'm Selena Bowman."

The appraising eyes were unsmiling.

"Chris Darmant. I was told to report here."

They were in a hotel-like magnolia painted corridor completely devoid of signs or decoration. Chris counted eight doors, all unmarked and Selena led her to the third. Inside was a large beech table four soft brown leather chairs around it. A small cardboard box on the table. The room was dominated by a large window overlooking the Bay of San Francisco. Chris had to move closer to convince herself it was not a window but a high-resolution screen.

"It's live, we have a camera there," Selena remarked casually.

"I didn't know the government invested in this stuff."

"We're not the government."

"What?"

"This is Omasor. All is possible."

"Omasor, the detective agency? But I work for British Intelligence."

"We arranged a transfer."

"You're joking."

"As I said, all is possible. We have what we call a relationship with the authorities. They owe us."

Chris was stunned.

"And if I don't accept the job?"

Selena gave her a sheet of paper.

"This is the offer. Your annual salary is two million pounds."

"Two million? Now you are joking."

"Additionally there is a one off starting payment of a million pounds. We can call it a transfer fee, it's not taxable."

"You're playing a game."

Selena handed her a bank statement. Carter and Cleavers Bank. In her name and the balance showed one million pounds. She was not money motivated but this was something else.

"Do you accept?"

Chris noticed a change in Selena's expression, a look to make a man faint. For some reason she wanted a refusal and that decided her.

"I suppose I must say yes."

"Good, otherwise I would probably have had to kill you."

Selena's smiled but not with the eyes.

"You don't seem pleased that I'm joining."

"I don't make the final decisions."

"Don't you want to interview me or even look at my CV?"

"Nothing to talk about. We know everything about you."

Chris didn't fight that one. She knew Omasor's reputation.

"You haven't told me exactly what the job involves."

"We investigate things. You're an investigator. The working hours and the risks are the same as your previous job."

That's 24/7 and high, thought Chris.

"Okay, suits me. When do I start?"

"Now. We leave in 45 minutes to attend an auction."

Selena pointed at the cardboard box.

"Your accessories."

"I need to freshen up first."

"There is a bathroom here. You just need to think back to find it. I'll return to collect you in 30 minutes."

She left and Chris heard the door being locked.

Her brain was buzzing. An instant millionaire, a cardboard box and an urgent toilet need.

She chose the box.

Two doors away, Selena looked at Jerome Jones on a small screen.

"I'm not sure," she remarked.

"Trust me."

She smiled innocently.

"If she doesn't find the bathroom she'll need new pants."

"She's checking the accessories first."

Selena looked at another screen where Chris was laying out the contents of the box on the table.

Chris assessed the array of items in front of her. A Stellhaus small automatic with spare clips of bullets, several passports with her picture but a variety of names. A car registration number and location with a set of keys .Credit cards and cash in various notes and coins.

She quickly stowed the items in her pockets and now her bladder was complaining urgently.

She examined the room, the table and chairs. Nothing. No buttons, levers. Nothing.

Her eyes drifted to the San Francisco screen window and instinctively began to scan the view. Cars were parked on the shore in the foreground. The picture was so clear she could even see the number plates.

Then she smiled, walked to the screen and pressed her forefinger against a yellow van. A panel in the wall to her left slid open, revealing a luxurious azure tiled bathroom.

The yellow van carried a logo and name. 'Rosa Motel'. The number plate below it was unusual. '10TH SUP'.

There was a note stuck on the bathroom mirror.

'That van was set up just for you. As you're reading this maybe it was worth it. I can be convinced'.

It didn't need a signature. Chris decided the relief of the toilet just exceeded the pleasure of reading the note.

8

Velviva Inc had only two clinics. The original and largest was near Geneva with another in New England, USA. The words exclusive and expensive precisely summarised the business. A minimum fee for a 30 minute consultation was 5 and treatments started at 40. Measurement in thousands of dollars. They sold just one product. Youth. Skin treatments, synthetic and natural anti-ageing remedies and of course plastic surgery.

Velviva's public persona, as it had been for forty years, was Martina Crowne. Now 68, she possessed the face and body of a woman ten years younger. She claimed to have just three current lovers, all under 25, as she was 'cutting down at her age'. This was probably an underestimate as there was an unending supply of avaricious young men volunteering to escort her to all the upmarket celebrity parties on both sides of the Atlantic.

Her sumptuous suite of offices occupied most of the top floor of the seven-storey block in Geneva. Parading across the beech-panelled walls hung a series of portraits dating back 500 years. The earliest was in prime position facing her, an elegant dark haired woman in 17th-century dress wearing an amethyst rock pendant. A name was hand engraved on the original plaque mounted in the lower edge of the frame. Elizabeth Beddowes.

Martina opened a drawer and took out a mirror as she did every few hours. Each day the lines were etched just a little deeper beneath the layers of cosmetics. Age stalked onwards, obstinate and immune to bribery. The one thing her immense wealth could not vanquish. Her soul surfaced for a second, disporting in the flint eyes like a dolphin gone bad. It wasn't attractive.

She spoke to the portrait, another daily habit.

"I have a feeling we are close now, we will find it. We will find it soon."

Elizabeth Beddowes was Martina's ancestor. She had died young. Murdered.

After the death of her mother, Martina had discovered a cache of documents in a sealed box buried in the attic and read for the first time the events of the 17th century. The centrepiece of the collection was the private diary of Elizabeth in which she described how a man named James Smith had invited her to work for the Octagon, a society whose purpose he had never explained. He had recruited many others over a period of 3 months, providing them a small weekly payment together with free meals and accommodation in return for a their labour. The work had been minimal, mainly servant and household duties and most were content in this relative comfort but Elizabeth, being more intelligent and inquisitive than the others, had discovered much more.

It had started when she was serving wine to Smith and noticed documents on his desk. From a brief glance, she just recognised the heading 'The True Intent of the Octagon' and the phrase 'enjoy life to eternity by Gods will'.

Intrigued, she later searched Smith's room in his absence and found papers in the fireplace that had partially escaped the flames. One of the charred pages showed a crest, two eagles above six swords and beneath this a partial sentence referred to something called 'The Blessing' that was imbibed by members of the Octagon every 12 months. Another page carried the words 'The Blessing shall bring perpetual youth and good health'.

She immediately recognised the astounding implications but needed help to progress further. Elizabeth already had a relationship with Lord Griggan, initially by a seduction across a kitchen table three years earlier and maintained by regular weekly encounters. She had become pregnant and birthed a son but had not seen the Lord since, although receiving a small monthly payment from him.

Now Elizabeth decided he would be the best choice to assist her and renewed contact via an exhausting session in the bedroom of his mansion. She told him only that her employer possessed a secret philtre to make a person younger. The Lord already knew Smith and had noticed lack of ageing in his acquaintance. He therefore readily agreed to help her, offering to split the proceeds if she could obtain the composition of the elixir.

Griggan began inviting Smith to lunch out as often as possible to allow Elizabeth time to conduct a thorough search. Frustratingly, she found only one other significant paper. An unfinished note, again rescued from the fire, was headed 'The Ten Constituents of The Blessing that shall be mixed in exact proportion'. The paper was badly burnt and the words barely readable but she could distinguish a list of items beginning 'Malt Vinegar, Parsley, Potato…'. Nine common kitchen foodstuffs were legible but the flames had taken the proportions and also the name of the other, final constituent.

Elizabeth never discovered the identities of the other members of the Octagon but she wrote of her belief that there were eight in number, logically corresponding to the title of the Society. The last entry in the diary related that she and all the others were to go on a journey to undertake an important labour. Smith had told them that they should expect to be away for seven days but would not reveal their destination and Elizabeth noted that she believed this work was the true reason for their recruitment as their other duties had been insignificant. She planned with the Lord that upon her return, they would abduct Smith and torture him for his secret. Leaving her son in the care of a friend, she departed on the journey but was never heard from again.

Various letters and notes written by family members included a testament from her son that described how his mother had 'set forthe with zeale and pietie upon labour most secret'. She had not returned and her body was never found.

Lord Griggan promptly disowned his son as soon as Elizabeth disappeared and when the boy grew to manhood, he had taken revenge on the Lord's remaining family, razing their mansion to the ground and butchering all who fled from the flames.

For the remainder of his life he hunted the members of the Octagon as he was certain they had murdered his mother. However, immediately after her final journey, James Smith and the unknown others in the society had vanished completely. The quest was consequently fruitless and he died with the venom bound within him. He fathered one child who changed the family name to Crowne. Martina was a direct descendant.

The early generations of the family had pursued the search for the Octagon with determination but over the years they had gradually lost the desire to continue although Elizabeth's original documents had been carefully preserved and passed down through the family.

Martina well recognised the potential wealth offered by this age elixir, the Blessing but the primary motivation was her own salvation. Her life was drifting away in a tide of neon and champagne and this was a final opportunity to recover and maintain her youth.

She had shared the information with her daughter, Jessica and for them the quest had become an obsession. They had spent a massive amount in establishing a team of chemists dedicated to evolving and completing the formula. Elizabeth had named nine of the constituents and annoyingly, these could be purchased from the shelves of most large supermarkets. After years of intense research the chemists had identified what they believed to be the optimum proportions and produced a mixture that Martina had named Atlantis Reborn.

This product was desperately sought-after by almost every woman and most men over the age of 35. It was only necessary to drink just a small, diluted amount and within a few days, vital organs and the body metabolism were suddenly 10 years younger. However, the age reduction worked only once, subsequent annual doses simply maintained the normal ageing process but without them the body reverted to its original age within a week.

The tasteless and colourless liquid was simply mixed in a small glass of water, always by Jessica herself and a series of masking agents had been successfully developed to prevent any user analysing the mixture. The only supply was kept securely in a vault in the basement of the Geneva building, guarded by state-of-the-art sensor alarms with a team of armed security men on duty round-the-clock.

Martina had taken Atlantis Reborn herself for four years in a desperate attempt to hold back the dark tentacles of time but having initially returned to her early 50s, she was now again approaching old age. She had decided with Jessica that they would limit the sale of this discovery to a specially selected few rather than issue it on the mass-market. Only the upper echelons of the rich, top movie stars, celebrities, royalty and leaders from around the world. The profits had been immense, raising their wealth to billionaire status.

Mother and daughter were both well aware that they needed the one missing ingredient to fully reproduce the Blessing with its promise of eternal youth. The only source of that information was the Octagon and Jessica personally headed a team of investigators to search throughout the world for the members of the group, concentrating on any individual who appeared to have resisted the march of time. So far without success.

Elizabeth gazed back at Martina from the portrait. She had not known the complete formula but had provided her descendants with this possible panacea.

"We will find it mother, I promise you that."

Her daughter had entered. Tall, slim with dark hair, narrow lips and a defiant chin. She was attractive but something permanently flamed in her deep grey eyes, something dangerous.

"Do you have any news?"

"No, mother. I cannot push the research any faster and I think we need fresh ideas. I'm looking at a new recruit, a professor in the USA who has already worked extensively in the areas of cell regeneration. Her name is Hony Pammican."

"Will she work for us?" Martina asked wearily.

Jessica smiled encouragement.

"Yes, I believe she will be anxious to join our research. I have sent Karmen to bring her here. Don't lose faith, mother."

Martina sighed.

"Life is tedious for me at the moment. Two parties this week and one possible for our treatment."

"Anyone I know?"

"I don't think so, a South African businessman."

"I don't know any South African men."

"No, darling."

Since an unpleasant experience with an alcohol and drug ravaged drummer when she was 17, Jessica had never been comfortable with men. Martina accepted the situation but the episode had left a vicious streak in her daughter. Jessica had subsequently sought out and castrated the drummer but even before meeting him, she had exhibited bouts of violent aggression. Her mother was the only one she listened to now although not always accepting her judgment.

Martina found herself contemplating a future where her daughter inherited the company. She had no other children and it seemed unlikely that Jessica would have offspring, so the family and the quest would end with her. Unless. Always unless.

She sighed and swung in her chair, brushing a pile of magazines to the floor and was about to summon her secretary when she saw a photograph on an inner page that had fallen open. The image focused and unfocused. It was hard for her brain to accept the evidence of her eyes.

"Mother, are you all right?"

Eyes staring she could only point to the photo.

Jessica grabbed the magazine

"What?" she demanded.

"The photo…"

It was a picture of a man surrounded by reporters. The caption was 'Detectives at Press Conference in Murder Room'.

"I don't see. This issue is two months old," said Jessica.

Martina snatched the magazine and pointed.

On a bookshelf to the right of the group stood a small, framed picture. The depiction was just discernible, two eagles above six vertical swords. The sign of the Octagon.

Jessica jumped to the phone.

"Karmen. Get back immediately," she shouted.

Karmen Fidec clicked off her phone. She wasn't going to rush. Jessica's sudden demands weren't unusual, the result of a constant need to assert herself. Anyway, it would take some hours to get back to Switzerland from here in England.

She looked down at the fat man. His face was red, very red and sweat rolled down his forehead, rivulets curving into his eyes. She had used wire rather than rope to tie his wrists to his ankles, forcing him to kneel uncomfortably. The massive stomach bulged forward and his blubbery cheeks were stretched as he looked up at her. Not appealing but begging. He didn't want to die today.

Karmen was a neat, if unattractive package from Russia. Sensible black hair framed a lean face with snake eyes and narrow lips. No problem to communicate with the man as she spoke perfect English with the slightest accent.

"All you need to do is sign the contract to sell the patent to Velviva," she said.

"But it would be the end of my company, my employees. We can't survive without our major product. It took me a lifetime to develop it in the laboratory."

"Then spend another lifetime discovering something else. I'm going to kill you if you don't agree. No one will miss a tubby little chemist. It's unfortunate you have no wife or children. I could have used them to make you sign. Fat men disgust me."

"If you kill me then you'll never have it. I'm the only person in the world who knows the complete formula and process. My lawyers retain the written details but they have instructions to destroy the papers if I die."

"Then no one will have them and your company will collapse anyway. I'm going to give you 30 seconds to sign. Velviva will pay you a reasonable fee and you can move to another country to spend it. A pleasant future or a painful death?"

Desperation in his face now.

"Yes, yes. I'll agree to negotiate with Velviva but the amount is just a tiny fraction of its true worth. It is the finest anti ageing skin cream available, generations ahead of anything else on the market. The profits from just one week sales are far more than your offer."

Karmen smiled as she kicked hard into his stomach. Then kicked again.

"No negotiation. The discussions are finished. I will now conduct some surgery in areas normally concealed by your clothing. You can stop me at any time by simply agreeing."

"No! Don't do this!" He screamed.

She kicked in again, forcing his body over on its back. A painful position with arms beneath him and legs forced to buckle backwards by the wrist-ankle binding. Karmen pulled out of thin knife and sliced open his shirt to expose a flabby chest. Then she began to cut carefully around his nipples.

Screams shredded the atmosphere. Yes, she enjoyed this. Enjoyed the sounds, the trickles of blood. Little tremors ran through her.

"Stop, stop! I agree!" he cried, tears mingling with the sweat on his face.

She continued for another minute. Fresh shrieks of agony. Then she cut his hands free and dragged him to the table.

"Sign these two documents where I have marked and enter the date of two days ago," she instructed.

He picked up the pen, writing quickly and she collected the papers, zipping them into a plastic envelope that she placed in her briefcase. A further 90 minutes before she left, driving away from the isolated wooden chalet in the hills. A chalet that was now on fire.

A comfortable operation, just as planned. The authorities would find that the building had been rented in the name of the dead man inside. One of her people had occupied it the previous week and reported problems with the safety of the log fire. Another in her team would appear amongst the emergency services just to ensure no loose ends. Velviva's phalanx of lawyers would issue a series of statements reporting the distress of the Crowne's on hearing the news of the accident. A tragedy that had occurred so soon after they had reached a most amicable agreement with the chemist.

Now Karmen was heading for the airport, for the first flight back to Switzerland.

9

Hony Pammican held a respected position as one of the senior professors at URCA and had a reputation of steady integrity amongst her peers. Her published work on biochemistry presented gradual advances rather than major breakthroughs in the field.

It was therefore strange that she would be spending a vacation in a camper van with one of her students whose main claim to fame was as backup kicker on the football team. Something in her biological cycle had erupted and she had found herself inviting, even pleading with him to spend a week living and sleeping with her. Hony bitterly regretted it now. He was the most boring man she had ever been with and not much good in bed either.

"What the hell am I doing here?" she murmured softly.

They had parked off-road at the edge of a small forest, high in the Californian hills. Rain dribbled through the trees pattered on the roof and rolled down the windows. She looked across at her companion, sleeping peacefully but noisily and fervently wished she had left him with that little blonde cheerleader who worshipped him like a god.

She sighed. This wasn't the life she'd planned when she graduated, bright eyed, full of energy and new ideas. Then her thoughts were of achievement, discovery, enlightening the whole world of some new concept. Now at 42, with a failed marriage behind her, she was resigned to making the best of a boring job, grinding through the days with a listless listlessness.

Easing gently from the bed, she pulled on pants and bra, jeans and top with the scruffy trainers she usually wore on vacation. After boiling coffee, she sipped from a mug and listened to the rain simpering down. It eased off slightly and she left the van, walking out into the sweet smell of wet grass. Shafts of sunlight glittered across the rain soaked trees and the birds greeted the warmth and light with universal song. This was good. Nature sometimes played her hand smartly, the kings and aces often showing when you least expected.

Hony wandered aimlessly, brushing her hand across moist leaves and found herself at the edge of the forest, some hundred metres from the van. She reached out and touched a huge oak tree.

"Hell, you've been here a long, long time."

No reply from the oak, but someone spoke.

"Good morning Ms Pammican. I'm Karmen."

She whirled round. Emerging from behind a tree was a slim woman, smiling but without the smile. Then she was suddenly aware of another figure with blonde hair standing just behind her. Darkness followed, very black darkness.

Hony awoke feeling good. Her body was buzzing with more vitality than she had known in years. She opened her eyes and found herself on a bed, fully dressed except for no jeans, top and trainers. Leaving the pants and bra.

The room was square and completely unfurnished except for the bed and a table and chair made from solid oak or at least a presentable imitation of oak. There were also a couple of cabinets and another chair and a sofa. The walls were in plain magnolia, certainly not in keeping with the richness of the oak and the bedspread was patched blue and green that clashed appallingly.

She rose from the bed and checked the locked door. It was locked. The only window was an out of reach small skylight that showed just a small square of blue sky. Despite her predicament she felt strangely elated. Excitement had been missing from her life for so long now and at last something was happening.

A tray entered, carried by a young blonde woman. She smiled sweetly and Hony immediately felt comfortable with her.

"Hello, I'm Katya."

"You were outside the camper van. Why have you kidnapped me?"

"Not kidnapped."

"What is this then?" Hony tried to sound irate but failed.

"You are our guest. Please eat. I'm sorry, I cannot answer any questions."

The meal was irresistible. Superb fresh salmon with a sprinkling of lightly cooked vegetables and accompanied by a glass of wine. Katya left and returned a few minutes later with another tray laden with chocolates and coffee.

After the meal, Hony lounged on the bed feeling even better but comfortably tired. Too tired? Perhaps the food was drugged. Sleep drifted over her and the dream began.

She was flying on a magic carpet, floating into a golden bedroom. The four-poster bed was draped with pink and blue lace matched by a soft duvet cover. Then the woman was there, beautiful, long dark hair. So very attractive. Hony reached out to her and they kissed gently. She felt as if her life had been waiting for this one wonderful moment. Paradise found, at last.

Hony awoke on a four-poster bed in a golden room with a dark haired woman lying next to her.

"Is this a dream?" Hony asked.

The woman shook her head.

"Who are you?"

"I'm Jessica."

"I think I want to stay with you, Jessica"

The woman smiled, running fingers through her long dark hair.

"Time to get up, you've got things to do."

10

Outside, the poster oozed formality. 'Auction of the Contents of Carney House'.

Inside, the usual fuzzy murmur of a pre-event filled the large chamber. Numbered leather chairs had been set in rows with each number corresponding to a registration card issued to the buyers. The auction was invitation only and a security team guarded the doors, turning away casual observers. In front of the chairs stood a portable podium for the auctioneer and behind that, the sale items were displayed. Furniture, paintings, sculptures, documents and a variety of household articles were laid out for viewing. Most of the buyers were examining the lots while others talked incessantly to their principals on mobile phones.

Carl Vistan was smart. He had not employed one of the top name auction houses, even though the quality and value of the items would be more than acceptable to them. They asked too many questions, made too many checks on their vendors and he particularly wished to avoid the publicity and chance of recognition at a London venue. He was using a local auctioneer, one he had employed over the years for disposal of a few minor stolen pieces. The auction prices would be lower than in a large city but demonstrating his usual caution, he had traded this for extra security.

Selena Bowman and Chris Darmant arrived a little later than planned. No long conversation on the journey. Almost no conversation at all. Just a brief exchange about their destination.

"You have your card?" asked Selena

"Yes, here. Number 73."

"I'm 74."

"Remind me, what are we looking for?" asked Chris.

"I don't know. Anything or anyone out of the ordinary. We'll split up."

Selena moved towards the displayed sale items while Chris began circulating among the crowd in the seating area. The top buyers were allocated the first rows with the lesser mortals towards the rear. They certainly appeared to be a very exclusive group and she guessed that many applications had been rejected. It was a measure of their influence that Omasor had acquired two seats at such short notice.

Her card, hanging from a chain round her neck, was labelled Victoria de Sett. Always wanted to be a Victoria, she mused. She walked casually around the rows of seats, studying the faces inconspicuously. Each appeared exactly as expected, earnest suited professionals. A handful of women but mostly male.

A tall, grey haired man brushed her as he turned.

"I am most terribly sorry," he said.

"Not at all," Chris responded in her best Victoria accent.

The man wore a tweedy grey check suit and dark blue tie emblazoned with a badge. He raised his thick, tufty eyebrows displaying intelligence and humour in dark grey eyes.

"Are you planning to bid?" he asked.

"Perhaps I might find something," she replied, guessing a cautious reply for competing bidders.

"I don't think we've met, my name is Peter Parker," the man persisted.

He shook her hand.

"Spiderman. Sorry, I couldn't resist."

He laughed nervously.

"Yes, yes, but I'm afraid I apprehend documents rather than criminals"

"I'm Victoria, Victoria de Sett. What sort of documents do you collect?"

"Oh, correspondence, manuscripts, notes, diaries. Just about anything really but nothing of any great value. I do like to read other people's personal letters and diaries. It is more, shall we say, a hobby for me in my old age."

"You must have a large library."

"Ah yes, more like libraries. I think I must have eight rooms for my collection now."

She knew the answer but asked anyway.

"And your wife, is she also a collector?"

"No, no, I never married. Too busy, you see. I had a little managerial position at the Bank of England. Took all my time I'm afraid but I do have four people at home to look after my collection. I live close by at Allmint Hall you know, just 10 minutes away. I'm invited to all the auctions here and must be one of their best customers."

Chris visualised the Hall filled floor-to-ceiling with faded parchment and letters and Peter Parker crouched across a candlelit desk poring over his latest acquisitions.

"You must come and visit, I'm sure you'll find it interesting," he added.

She idly considered a quick seduction and marriage then a few times in bed would surely bring him an early but pleasant demise. Leaving a large country house with a million or two spending money. Then again, she was now a millionaire herself.

"Yes, I'd like that."

He smiled broadly.

"Here is my card. Please just telephone before you come to make sure I'm not out on a buying trip."

"Thank you, I'm sure we'll meet again soon," Chris responded, returning the smile.

"My dear, I'm sure we will."

Both statements were very correct.

They parted and Chris suddenly found Selena next to her.

"New friend?"

"Careful. That could be my future husband and benefactor."

"Three sessions in bed, and then take the money."

"I was thinking two."

Selena smiled.

"It took me three, but that was a woman."

Chris realised she wasn't joking. Selena was full of surprises.

"I've looked round," she offered lamely.

"Find anything?" Selena asked.

"Everyone looks completely as you would expect."

"Checkout the long lost cousin."

Chris followed her gaze to a chunky, florid faced man whose eyes flicked around the room like a cornered koala. He was talking intensely to a woman reporter who had the word "PRESS" on a large badge hanging across her chest. They edged closer to listen in.

"I'm sorry, I am too distressed to talk and I certainly will not give any interviews," he was saying. Accent mid-Atlantic.

"It's hard to know if he is genuine or not," Chris whispered.

Selena's eyes sharpened.

"He's not. A minor utility man for the local gangs in Atlantic City."

"How did we find that out and not the police?"

"We know a lot of things."

Chris felt she didn't know anything, not a situation she preferred.

"So do we expose him?"

"No, we'll see the play. I have a feeling something will happen."

The buyers took their seats in a traditional hierarchy based on buying power. Chris was towards the back with Peter Parker two rows in front of her. He sensed her presence then turned and waved with a schoolboy smile.

The auction began.

"Good morning ladies and gentlemen, I am your auctioneer. The first item is this superb Victorian sideboard..."

The items came and went, most of the major bidders targeting the furniture and paintings. Peter Parker made his initial bid for the first batch of miscellaneous documents, a mixture of old family mementos, personal correspondence and household books. Three others started bidding against him but he was determined and acquired the lot for under 10,000 pounds. Chris sensed his triumph and he turned, waving to her in delight.

She smiled back. There was something rather appealing about his innocent pleasure.

Then she heard a disturbance in the row behind her. One of the buyers, clutching a phone to his ear, left his seat and hurried out of the door. A minute later, it was opened again by a woman dressed in a perfect Darlincia grey trouser suit. Her long black hair and attractive features were unmissable. She took the vacated seat.

Chris turned to speak but Selena nodded.

"I see her," she said with the faintest smile.

More furniture and paintings were displayed and readily sold. The next lot was a further collection of varied documents. Peter saw off the other bidders but then the new arrival stepped in. She outbid him at every raise and eventually he gave up at a totally unreasonable price. As the auction progressed, it was obvious that her only interest was in the lots of documents. Chris scanned the list. Just two more to come and the woman purchased both. The price appeared to be academic as she seemed ready to go to any lengths to obtain them.

At the end of the auction the woman spoke into her phone as she moved to the cashier and two large men entered carrying large suitcases. They joined her and began filling the cases with her purchases.

Chris noticed Selena had left her seat and was standing just behind them. She quickly joined the group, walking around the side where she could best view and memorise the three faces. The woman sensed her and as their eyes met, gave the slightest smile but it was fresh from the freezer. Suitcases packed, the group left, the woman leading.

"She has eyes like scanners," said Chris, surprised to see Selena smiling deliciously.

"Nice figure, beware of stiletto in your back while you're looking."

"What did she want with that stuff?"

"I don't know that yet."

"Where to now?"

"She's seen us so we wait. I've arranged for our man Marcus to tail her."

They left and sat in the car watching the buyers gradually meander from the building.

11

Marcus relaxed as his little Patrina strolled along behind the Caballini. No contact, Selena had warned him, just follow and identify.

He was a wiry, dark, narrow faced man of about 40, the type you check your pockets before and after meeting. Appropriately he had never committed a crime in his life. Pocket checks are really only necessary when meeting an attractive woman, cute faced man or most certainly, innocent looking children.

The Caballini stopped at the Selvira Regal Majestic hotel. The woman emerged, followed by two large men carrying suitcases and they entered the building. Marcus phoned Selena and received the instruction to find names and room number only.

"Remember no contact," she reminded him.

As he left the car, he simulated ignorance of the slim, dark haired woman parked just behind who was struggling to lock the door while holding two loaded Harmads shopping bags. He was well aware she had followed him four cars back for the last eight minutes of the journey. The woman was definitely not the bimbo she pretended, her actions were far too perfectly in character.

He strolled to the hotel, overtly checking his watch and looking down the street as if expecting company, an old trick when danger threatens. He carried no weapons except his cunning but that had kept him alive and in business for over 20 years.

Marcus heard the woman's heels clacking behind him as he entered the foyer. Fortunately, he had visited the hotel many times before. Home advantage. The lounge was off to the right, reception desk in the centre and toilets to the left. The occupants of the Caballini were waiting in front of the elevator near to the desk. He ambled towards the lounge giving an unobtrusive nod to the hotel's chief of security who he knew quite well. He didn't notice the quick glance of the woman in front of the elevator nor her tiny gesture to the one who had followed him in.

Sinking in to a plush leather chair, Marcus displayed no interest in the woman with the bags. However, he had memorised her face and wouldn't forget the snake like eyes. She followed and took a seat behind him. After a few minutes, he checked his watch again and as if looking for his late appointment, rose and walked through the foyer, detouring close to the security chief. His help was needed to identify the new arrivals.

"Toilets," he whispered as he passed.

This is where his plan went badly wrong.

First, he was unaware of the chief's off-duty affinity with men's conveniences, and second, he underestimated the woman. A substantial part of KGB training covers the speed of changing clothes behind a hotel staff-only door in less than 13 seconds. Faster still if you happen to be carrying the garments in a Harmads shopping bag.

Marcus was standing by the washbasins when the chief pushed open the door and approached with a smile. Just at the precise moment he placed a friendly arm round Marcus's wiry shoulders, the smile died as a dart hit his neck. He slumped to the floor.

Marcus barely had time to see the slim, baseball capped figure at the doorway before another dart hit him just behind the ear. Karmen stood over the two bodies. Swiftly removing the darts, she pulled a small syringe from her coat.

"Don't need you. Need you," she whispered to herself.

She spoke quickly into her phone and shortly afterwards the two men from the Caballini entered the toilets, leaving immediately with a third man, who looked a little inebriated, supported between them. Karmen walked behind them. She was satisfied. The complete operation had taken under three minutes.

Selena checked the small electronic box again.

"Something is wrong with our tail."

"How?"

"On this work he sends a signal every five minutes. Just presses a button in a communication box like this."

"Yes, I've used one. How long?"

"18 minutes."

"What now?"

"We'll split. You go to the hotel and I'll wait here."

"Okay, I'll get a taxi."

"No need. I just received a text message. Jerome will be here soon. You go with him."

"Jerome Jones?"

"Yes."

"So we'll meet at last."

A peculiar smile crossed Selena's face.

"You probably won't be disappointed. He's just arrived."

A dark blue Lartis pulled up in front of them and the passenger door was pushed open. Chris switched cars and as soon as she was inside, they shot forward.

"Hello Chris, I'm Jerome Jones," said the driver.

He looked mid 30s, short dark hair, fast brown eyes and aquiline features. She wasn't disappointed.

"Mr Jones, nice to meet you."

Her smile was wasted.

"Call me John on this job."

"Okay John, the plan?"

"Hotel was last location, you know the faces. If our man has been taken, we get him back."

He described in detail the appearance and clothing of Marcus.

"And if he's been killed?"

"I won't be happy."

They slid into a parking space in a side street adjacent to the hotel. Jerome grabbed a small case from the back seat and was out before the engine stopped. He was tall, an inch or two over 6 feet with long powerful strides and Chris caught him up with some effort.

They passed an ambulance outside the hotel.

"Some problem?" Jerome asked when he reached the reception desk.

The small, nervous man behind the counter smiled ingratiatingly.

"I'm afraid that one of our employees, our Head of Security, had a slight heart attack. Nothing serious I believe. How may I help you?"

"I have two rooms booked."

He gave a name and the receptionist checked.

"Ah yes, reserved just a few minutes ago. You're very fortunate to obtain…"

"We've an urgent appointment, need to freshen up."

They quickly completed the formalities.

"Oh just one more thing. One of your guests lost a bracelet. My personal assistant was waiting for me outside and saw her drop it."

Jerome produced a superb solid gold bracelet from his pocket, eliciting a wide-eyed response from the receptionist. It was patently worth a considerable amount.

"Errr, you say the owner is a guest here, do you know this lady?"

Jerome looked at Chris who responded in an archetypal PA voice.

"I can describe her. She was about 25, dark hair and there were two men carrying suitcases with her."

"Ah yes, I know the lady. If you would care to leave the bracelet with me…"

The voice filtered off as his eyes visualised reward.

Jerome was ready.

"Forgive me, I think the owner should know her benefactor."

He paused deliberately to enhance the good news.

"However, we are in a rush and we can leave it with you then call on her later."

The man's eyes moved into neutral as he assessed the possibilities. The decider was the value of the jewellery, no potential criminal would hand that over.

"The lady is in room 614."

Jerome handed him the bracelet.

"Many thanks, we'll ask for her when we get back. Now we just have time to get ready for our conference."

They reached their adjoining rooms on the third floor and Jerome held his door open for Chris to enter. He followed her in and dumped the case on the bed.

"We'll survey. Expect guards."

"Let me go first, I've done this a few times before." responded Chris, anxious to impress.

"I was going to suggest that."

She enjoyed his abrupt manner. He seemed smart and streetwise.

In a research group of 7000 women, 68% were attracted by a man's intelligence, 26% by honesty and diligence, 5% by appearance and 1% by wealth. Another survey showed 97% of women lied to surveys. Yet another survey indicated that 84% of pollsters invented responses rather than stand about on cold streets asking stupid questions.

Chris walked to her room.

"But I really do have to freshen up first," she said.

Jerome was waiting outside her room and they ascended the stairs to the sixth floor. Chris edged open the door to reveal a large, dark suited man strolling up and down at the far end of the corridor. Checking visible room numbers, she confirmed that 614 was in that area and near to the elevator. She reported the layout in a whisper.

"Double-team him face on or become hotel workers?" Jerome asked.

"Either way we need to take him. I can do it but there may be some noise."

He pulled a pen from his pocket.

"Point it and press here. The dart works almost instantly."

The guard looked up at the elevator doors as they opened to reveal a not unattractive, elfin faced blonde girl. She fumbled with her hotel keys and smiled as she walked towards him. As they met she dropped the keys and his eyes looked down just for a moment, quite long enough to receive a dart in his cheek. He fell forward into her and she was buckling under the weight until Jerome silently ran from the stairs and lifted him under the armpits. He carried the unconscious body to the stairway, leaving it sprawled over the top steps.

Chris ran back across the deep carpet to a door marked 'Employees Only', almost opposite Room 614, unlocking it in a couple of seconds with her ever-present set of burglar keys. It was stacked with bed linen, towels and other accessories but there was just enough space for a person to hide. She pulled the door almost shut.

Jerome smoothed his suit, adopted an obsequious face and tapped gently on the door. It was opened by Karmen, her anaconda eyes working over him.

"I am sorry to trouble you madam. I'm from hotel security. I've had a report that one of your party has had an accident."

She stepped forward and briefly glanced along the corridor.

"Here, now!"

She called without moving her eyes from him and two replicas of the first guard appeared behind her.

"Go with this man. He says our colleague has had an accident."

Jerome led them through the stairway door.

Karmen noticed small details. Her life had often depended on it. Doors that were not fully closed represented a possible danger. She produced a silenced automatic from her hip and squeezed an entire clip into the door marked 'Employees Only', spreading the shots high and low. Then, pushing another clip into the gun, she quickly pulled open the door with her free hand. Her reactions were astonishing. She sensed the person behind her and swung round even before the butt of a pistol hit her skull.

Jerome arrived from the stairs to find Chris pushing Karmen into the cupboard.

"Contortionist?" he asked, viewing the bullet holes.

"Old trick. Leave obvious door ajar, hide in guest room next to it."

"You can look after yourself."

"Just need a little sunlight and water."

They entered the room. No one there and just one door. Chris crept to the handle side while Jerome moved to the other, avoiding lining up with the centre. He nodded and Chris flicked the handle, kicked open the door and flattened herself to the floor. Jerome squeezed through the doorway and knelt down, automatic held in both hands.

The scene was definitely not as they expected.

Two naked figures on the bed. Marcus, lying on his back and smiling sweetly while the woman from the auction was kneeling astride him (position 24 for aficionados). She turned her head towards them, eyes half closed in apparent ecstasy.

Jerome's mouth sagged involuntarily, his gun lowered. This was perhaps a small error of judgment as he gained a pretty little hole in his forehead. Not really something to die for, but he did. He knew, too late that Jessica had concealed a pistol behind her thigh. In an instant she had swivelled down on the other side of the bed.

Chris cursed her reactions. She still lay prone holding her gun but brain to finger messaging was numbed by the performance. She knew Jerome was hit badly and now was the time for a cool calculated response.

"You bitch," she yelled, jumping to her feet and squeezing off two shots that narrowly missed Marcus's groin. He half rose, turning towards her with a delighted smile.

"Down," she yelled, but the distraction undid her. Being undid can be nice but is sometimes ungood.

The vase hit just behind her temple (one of the two on her head, she wasn't particularly spiritual) and consciousness switched to negative.

Chris awoke sluggishly on a sofa with Selena standing over her. She shook her head, painful but bearable.

"Sorry, failed. Jerome?"

"Dead."

"It was the woman from the auction. I'm sorry, should have done something."

"It's past. We'll get them."

Chris sat up and her brain made connections in stages.

"How did you get here?"

"Jerome was sending five-minute signals."

"Marcus?"

"Drugged, but he'll recover in a few hours."

Chris painfully recounted the events and Selena shrugged.

"They've all gone including your friend in the cupboard."

"But Jerome Jones has been killed. What happens now?"

"We continue."

Chris agonised. He was dead. She had been there and couldn't stop it. Her headache upgraded and she felt the bruise under her hair.

"I'll kill her." Her voice was steady and certain.

"One of us will. Are you fit to move?"

Chris struggled to her feet. 90% successful.

"Yes I'm ready. Maybe you should tell me what's going on."

"This is what you need to know. I've told you about the attempted burglary at the house of the Countess. She was at dinner with her assistant and one guest. That guest was an employee of Omasor. In addition, we perceived certain aspects of the case that made it different to a normal armed theft. The events since then have confirmed our suspicions."

"That's still not very informative. Those people were looking for something at the auction."

"The woman who shot Jerome was Jessica Crowne."

"You can't mean the beauty millionaire?"

"Yes."

"What? Why on earth would she be shooting people? Is she homicidal?" Chris asked.

"No. A clever woman. That adds to the intrigue."

"She bought all the documents at the auction."

"Except one was sold before she arrived," remarked Selena.

"Yes. Peter Parker."

Chris pulled a card from her side pocket.

"Here's the address. I have an invite."

"Phone now, we need to go quickly. If she reaches him first we're lost."

Chris checked her watch. 6:49 p.m. She phoned.

"Mr Parker's residence."

Surely not a butler?

"Is Mr Parker available? Tell him I'm Victoria de Sett from the auction today."

"One moment please."

Moments vary in length from a microsecond to a helluva long time. This one was 17 seconds.

"Hello, is that Victoria?"

"Peter, yes it's me. I was wondering if I could take up your offer and visit you?"

"Absolutely delighted, perhaps we can arrange a dinner?"

"I was thinking of coming now."

"Now? Well, yes, yes by all means, very welcome."

"Thank you, I'll be there in under 30 minutes."

Chris had a hazy idea of his likely plans for her visit and didn't risk a negative by mentioning Selena.

12

Allmint Hall was exactly as Chris imagined. A large, sprawling Victorian mansion in its own grounds lying back from a side road. A surprisingly modern bell push was mounted at the side of an imposing door made of heavy oak and decorated with ornate ironwork. It was opened by an exquisitely groomed, heavy jowled man, a perfect example of the English butler. Except for the dress. Not a dress as in or on a woman, but the dress. Actually a better word would have been attire or even clothing.

He was attired in the typical clothing of a long retired politician relaxing with a Sunday afternoons gardening. A short-sleeved amber shirt, covered with a button up woolly cardigan atop rather crumpled light blue trousers and what could best be described as a high-class outfitters version of trainers. Not a brushed back grey hair was out of place.

"Good evening, Ms de Sett?"

He looked quizzically at them with eyes barely visible under eyelids as heavy as his jowls.

"I'm Victoria de Sett and this is my friend Annette Smith."

Selena glared at her.

"Annette Virginia Smith," she announced.

"Ah, Ms Smith, I fear we did not expect you."

Chris saw him mentally changing seating plans for dinner.

"If you would follow me please."

He led them through a massive marbled entrance hall, past a curving staircase and knocked gently on a solid wood panelled door.

"Come in, come in."

Chris found her hands gripped by a smiling Peter Parker. He loosened them as he noticed an extra guest but when Selena moved into full view, the smile rose again from the ashes.

"I see you have brought a companion, most welcome."

"Hello Peter, so good of you to allow us to visit at such short notice. This is my friend Annette Virginia Smith."

He beamed.

"Welcome, welcome. It's remarkable that your initials, AVS are exactly the same as the Artistic Vellum Society of which I am a member."

"Really, that is amazing." Selena did her best to simper.

Chris could almost feel her calculating the tactics and as for most men she was trying the groin route first.

"Do you know I had an employee many years ago with several first names, and his initials were a perfect anagram of DEPRAVED. Quite extraordinary and do you know, he lived up to his name, or down should I say."

Silence reigned.

"I wonder if I could freshen up," asked Selena.

"Of course, of course. Dobson, will you show the lady?"

Dobson nodded gravely.

"This way madam."

He led her from the room.

Chris checked her surroundings. A perfect Victorian lounge except for the thick beige carpet. Three deep sofas semicircled an ornate fireplace where flames flickered cosily. A heavy oak table and chairs were behind them and the walls were covered with floor-to-ceiling bookshelves. Documents and books lay everywhere but there seemed to be order within the apparent untidiness.

She chose a sofa and sank into it while Peter politely sat on the adjacent one and almost immediately Dobson returned with coffee. Peter smiled when he noticed she was staring at the butler's attire.

"I insist my staff wear only casual dress. I do hate all that pomp and finery. I lived with it for 25 years and I must say I positively dislike it now."

"You have an impressive historical collection."

"Oh just a part, a small part I'm afraid."

He stopped as Selena returned with an enlarged bosom, or it seemed like it. She held her jacket over her shoulder and the white silk blouse positively bulged. Her navy trousers also appeared two sizes tighter.

Peter stared speechless as she smoothed across the room and sat next to him. Some competitive urge made Chris think 'I saw him first', but it was quickly followed by 'what the hell do I care'.

"Coffee?" offered Peter nervously.

"That would be lovely," Selena said, placing a hand on his arm. Chris noticed admiringly that she had added husk to her voice.

"Now Peter, if I may call you that," she continued.

"Of course, certainly."

"Victoria has been telling me of these wonderful papers you obtained at the auction. You know I am a student of historic documents and I'd really love to see them."

She moved her hand to his knee.

"Well, yes, yes delighted, although I haven't even properly unpacked them yet."

Going well, thought Chris.

Selena pressed a breast against his arm.

"I find that reading them can be so meaningful and well, moving."

His hand began to quiver slightly.

"I see, yes certainly. Perhaps we could dine and look through them afterwards."

"That would be wonderful."

"I'll ask Parkinson to get them ready. I call him my curator you know."

He pressed a bell push concealed at the side of the sofa, an action that was followed shortly by the entry of a tall, thin, bespectacled man uncomfortably dressed in blue jeans and white, open necked shirt.

"Parkinson, these ladies wish to view the papers I purchased at the auction. Perhaps you could set them out in Room Three."

Parkinson had a nervous twitch which jumped the spectacles down his nose every 15 seconds or so. He nudged them back with his forefinger.

"Err, yes, Room Three then, right." Brain and speech appeared to be distant relations.

"We'll be there in about two hours."

"Right, two hours, yes. The documents from the auction you say. Right."

He meandered from the room.

Dinner was elegant and superb, Crepe au Fromage de Chevre, Salade d' Epinards Truite aux Amandes followed by Mousse au Chocolat. Peter was an excellent host, recounting a series of genuinely amusing stories of his career at the Bank and exploits at auction sales. Chris felt an increasing feeling of guilt as Selena continued in seductress mode. It was a shame to tease then leave him hanging.

Tease is a perfect homonym of T's, a letter with a chequered history. It was invented by the Picts as they had become totally disgruntled with being spoken of as if they were the result of some form of selection process.

After coffee, Peter escorted them to Room Three. Better described as a library, it was larger than the lounge with two massive tables in front of rows of back-to-back bookshelves. Piles of documents and volumes filled every shelf. Parkinson emerged from the end aisle, his jeans having gained additional crumples in the last two hours.

"Ah, ladies, Mr Parker, I have placed the papers on the table."

Parker found Selena clinging to his arm and whispering in his ear and Chris noticed his face reddening.

"Thank you, Parkinson, please carry on sorting Room Six."

Parkinson looked grateful for the escape route and disappeared quickly through the door.

Chris moved to the table in front of a small pile of letters, diaries and documents.

"Can I start to look…? "She turned to find Selena and Peter leaving.

"Back soon, you carry on," Selena called over her shoulder.

Chris digitally photographed everything while jotting notes indexed to the picture number. No more than 23 minutes later she had finished, grateful to Selena for giving her the freedom to do the job. She realised how little she knew about the woman she worked for and for some intangible reason, couldn't help wondering how far she would go with Peter.

It was another six minutes before they returned. All women know the look of a man when he's been intimate with a woman. It can't be disguised, even with a clown costume. Peter didn't have the circus outfit, so Chris found it very obvious. Selena looked exactly the same as always, not a hair out of place not a smudge on her makeup.

"We've just been viewing some 15th century parchments," she said to pre-empt any explanation Peter might be contriving.

"Well, I've looked through all this batch."

Selena nodded and her mobile phone rang, probably unconnected events. She answered.

"Hello, Annette here… Charles, how wonderful… yes… oh, now? Yes of course, see you soon."

"Victoria, that was Charles. It's a girl and Eleanor insists we visit her straight away at the hospital to see the new arrival."

"Oh, Eleanor, yes."

Selena turned to Peter.

"I'm so sorry, it's a friend. She's just had a baby girl."

"Of course, I understand, you must go."

He looked a little weary and ready for a nap.

Chris was limited to a handshake but Selena kissed his cheek warmly.

"I hope to come again very soon," she said meaningfully.

As they returned to the car Chris turned to her but Selena spoke first.

"Don't ask," she announced with finality.

13

Bermuda 6:30 in the evening. John Porter drove slowly down the coast road checking the house numbers on a series of vacant white stone villas. All appeared deserted with just security lights visible. He looked across. Mary Duckworth was lying back in the passenger seat with her eyes closed. She wasn't beautiful. Long blonde hair draped loosely round a rather narrow young face. But there was an indefinable and irresistible attraction. The now hidden eyes held a glittering hidden magic that he had never deciphered. They had made love so many times and although he had extensive practice with an unending stream of beach girls enticed by his surfer looks, he'd never experienced such imaginative and wild sessions. Then again, he felt she had never really opened up to him. So many secrets, so many things left unspoken.

Chris Darmant was the only other woman that ever connected with him. Although he had never slept with her, he felt closer to Chris than Mary. A very different relationship to anything before in his life.

"There's something wrong."

Mary spoke without disturbing her eyelids.

He looked at her quizzically.

"Wrong? We're not there yet."

She didn't reply.

He found the house and pulled up. There was something wrong. The windows of the villa were unlit and a handful of security lamps barely illuminated the building and driveway.

Mary opened her eyes.

"Check the building, John. Just to be sure."

He checked. Empty.

"What now?" he asked.

"It happened once before about 80 years ago when they were delayed. We will wait 24 hours for them to arrive or send a message," she replied, settling back in her seat.

Realisation dawned on John. This could be more than serious; it was literally life or death. After all this time the Grim Reaper was standing before him.

The concept of some skull faced man dressed in a long cloak and carrying a scythe is naturally ludicrous. His workload would be impossible, 24/7 and no holidays. When does he find time to eat and go to the toilet? Does he ever wash? And why a man? What's wrong with a woman doing the job?

And this scythe thing, why carry it around? Is it used to finish off any false alarms when he's tight for time? More likely he cleans his nails with it. It's about time humanity united to tell him we're not interested and prefer to wait for his successor, someone smarter, more hygienic and minus any antiquated farm implements.

John checked his watch. 18:58. The night passed slowly and an even longer day followed. Vehicles regularly came into view, raising hopes as they drew near, but none stopped at the house. Evening approached again.

"No one is coming. Time to leave," Mary said.

She noticed the concern on his face.

"Don't worry John, the Octagon will fulfil its destiny. We will not be stopped so close to our purpose."

John wasn't convinced and sat back, buzzing with uncertainty. In more than 20 years since he joined, there had never been a problem with the Renewal. A sudden panic ran through him. He was kept youthful only by the Blessing. What would happen to him if he couldn't get the annual dose? He was well past 50 now and without the elixir, he would quickly age. All those young women wouldn't want him and his physical energy would decline rapidly. No more all night sessions in clubs or bedrooms, no more immunity to illness and even the unlimited wealth could dry up. A bleak future.

"What happens now?" he asked.

"We go to England, Canterbury Cathedral. That's the contingency plan. The Octagon will meet again after more than 350 years."

"Then I'll get to see the other members for the first time."

She looked away.

"Yes but we may need to wait. We don't know if we are the first or last to discover the problem. If we are the last they will all be in Canterbury already, otherwise we'll need to wait for them."

He knew that. The two who kept the supply of the Blessing held the Renewal party for each of the other three pairs at different times each year. They could be the first pair to find the problem and that would mean waiting for maybe up to a year. Of course, he had never met any of the other Octagon members except Mary. No idea of their identity. The only certainty was that they would all be youthful, the Blessing would ensure that.

John pushed back his fears and started the drive towards the airport. Mary had always been right before and he desperately hoped this time would be the same.

14

On the third floor of the Velviva Building in Geneva, Hony Pammican smoothed her white coat and spoke to the man crouching frog-like in front of her.

"Raise your right arm."

He raised it obediently

"Stand up."

He stood with arm still raised.

"Where do you live?"

"Liverpool, England."

The man spoke normally but no emotion showed in his face.

"Put your arm down."

Jessica clapped in mock applause.

"I'm impressed," she said.

"I named the mixture HP47. We discovered it when we tested a psychedelic drug with the nine ingredients."

Hony had read through the research records at the laboratory and was aware that the chemists had found the apparent optimum proportions of the nine known ingredients that now formed the Atlantis Reborn elixir. The unknown tenth ingredient was still missing, the final key needed to complete the formula.

The primary task for the laboratory was to discover this missing ingredient but Jessica had become increasingly frustrated by their failure and had consequently recruited Hony to head the team after very permanently terminating the contract of her chief chemist. She knew that even a massive salary would not attract and had accordingly given her what she wanted. Now Jessica expected results.

Hony was still mystified by the emphasis that her sole priority was to discover an additional constituent that would produce much greater age reduction benefits and without the grey-hair effect. Like all the other chemists, she had been told nothing of the Blessing, the Octagon or of the papers left by Elizabeth Beddowes. Jessica had informed her that she and Martina discovered the nine constituents in their own researches.

Hony didn't believe in a formula for eternal youth. The concept was in the realms of fantasy books and all her working experience at the University had offered nothing to indicate that humanity could ever conquer time. Then again, before joining Velviva she would not have accepted that nine common ingredients, mixed in the correct proportions, could provide a ten-year reduction in age.

Since taking charge of the laboratories, she had attempted the combination of Atlantis Reborn with a series of natural and synthetic elements and compounds. She persevered, despite harbouring definite reservations about the shortcuts being taken as the research was conducted without any of the usual medical structures and safeguards. Jessica provided a seemingly endless supply of volunteers for the experiments although Hony remained suspicious of their voluntary status as each was brought to her already anaesthetised.

Her new life had blinded her to these anomalies. She had changed. In the weeks since taking charge of the project, she had approached the research like an haute cuisine chef on a quest for the perfect taste. For the first time, she felt wanted and at last her work had a meaning, a purpose.

Many believe a purpose is a large fish and are somewhat confused when they are told they need one in life. This is the reason why so many swimming pools are built and subsequently left unused when their purpose is lost. A smaller number are certain of the existence of a small furry creature, the Meaning which journeys to a cliff top and then jumps off to be lost forever.

Hony now felt she had finally achieved something. It was not the formula that Jessica was seeking but the results were remarkable. The 47th chemical she mixed with Atlantis Reborn was Tevandiro 22, a synthetic known for its psychedelic qualities. The result was HP47.

The new experiment scratched his ear.

"You didn't tell him to do that." Jessica said.

"He'll auto run. Wipe his nose, go to the toilet and do all the normal things unless he receives an instruction."

"How do you administer HP47?"

"It can either be ingested as a drink or injected."

"How long is it effective?"

"One dose lasts six to eight hours and we have given this man three consecutive doses."

"Does he obey anyone?"

"Yes, he'll obey. Also he is incapable of lying. Expressed simply, the formula disables the parts of the brain that control deception and rebelliousness. The subject is like a totally obedient small child."

"If I told him to murder, for example?"

"Perhaps, but he would be a lousy killer, he'd stop if anyone told him to."

Jessica was silent for a moment.

"Remove your clothes," she said.

The man dutifully complied, placing the garments in a neat pile beside him.

"Now lick my shoes."

He didn't hesitate, crawling across the floor and lapping her black leather boots with his tongue like a small dog.

"You said he would obey anyone. What if I told him to only obey my voice?"

"The Genie Syndrome," Hony smiled in response.

"What?"

"You get three wishes and your first is for an infinite number of future wishes. No, we tried. It doesn't work for a very complex reason. To explain simply, although he has no willpower over his actions, they must be in some degree rational and to listen to only one voice is not logical. Much as a young child will instinctively listen to several different people and not just one parent."

"Pity. Can I tell him to have sex?"

Hony felt strangely embarrassed.

"I don't know."

Jessica spoke on her phone and a dark haired girl entered.

"You will have sex with this man."

The girl simply nodded and undressed quickly.

Jessica looked down to the man, his tongue now black with polish from her boots.

"Have sex with this woman."

The test was short but successful.

"We could certainly move into porn films," said Hony acidly.

Jessica ignored her. She spoke to the couple.

"Get dressed and leave us."

She turned to Hony.

"You see they both do as I say."

"Yes but you can only trust the man."

Jessica smoothed her hair.

"Send a supply of HP47 with the dosage details to my office and maintain the work on the main objective."

She leant over and kissed Hony on the lips.

"Don't fail me," she whispered.

'Most people will have noticed that, quite astonishingly, the characters HP47 are all included in the American Declaration of Independence. This link is irrefutable and simply cannot be dismissed by sceptics. Having made this connection, it is a simple step to apply HP47 as a keyword to the text of the Declaration using a simple transmorphic code. After removing some of the resulting letters by a method that cryptologists refer to as 'unwanted character disposal', just one sentence remains. It reads simply, 'The moon landings are fake'. Further indisputable evidence of the real truths that lie concealed in so many famous books and documents.'

From the leaflet 'The Independence Code' by Counson Westlo.

15

Jessica's two principal assistants were both ex KGB.

Alec was large in every sense of the word. Tall, heavily built with grey eyes and grizzled grey shortcut hair. He looked a typical KGB assassin but was exactly the opposite. His skills were in his brain and acute business acumen and he had never killed anyone in his life. Fine judgment of people and clarity of thought were his speciality.

The other, Karmen Fidec was completely different. Sharp, tidy looking with strangely snake-like eyes and her lean body belied her strength. She had stopped counting her kills at 31 (31 kills, she was only 28). The first was her husband, found drowned in the river where she had dumped him after an unexpected, for him, immersion in the bath. Many more had expired since. Karmen was currently fermenting with annoyance after Chris had deceived her at the hotel.

The two sat silently in Jessica's small, unpretentious but immaculate office and their boss was unpleased today, very unpleased.

"Karmen, your performance at the hotel was not satisfactory. I was interrogating the man in the bedroom when those Omasor people came. I heard the noises and just had time to strip off and get on the bed before they burst in. Then I had to take care of the couple myself. An unacceptable situation when you are employed to handle such matters."

"I captured the one who was following you," Karmen responded.

"That was simple but you failed with the other two. I had to kill the man and knock out the woman myself."

Karmen pressed her lips together but the snake eyes glittered as Jessica continued.

"The one we captured didn't say anything, even with the drugs. He was either stupid or very well trained. The other two weren't amateurs. They incapacitated three of your men, Karmen. I instructed the two of you to find out the background of these people. Now I want answers."

Karmen remained tight lipped as Alec responded. He carried the smugness of one not targeted by Jessica's wrath.

"We circulated our agents in England with descriptions. Nothing on the man we captured or the one you killed but the woman is known to us. She was a British Intelligence agent."

That surprised Jessica.

"British Intelligence? What would they want with us? You said was with them."

"Our contact in the government provided more background. The woman's name is Chris Darmant. She was a drugs agent of some sort but left just recently. The move was kept secret and our contact doesn't know all the details."

"So she's transferred to another department. Which one?"

"Darmant is no longer employed by the government. She now works for the Omasor Agency."

A sign of concern muscled its way through the anger to appear on Jessica's face.

"What? Omasor can't be interested in a little auction in some backwater of England."

Alec shrugged.

"That's all we know. If their reputation is any guide, they will not be pleased that one of their people was killed."

"That's why I pay you. Just keep them away from me. Our search must not be compromised. Do you understand?"

Alec nodded, head down like a schoolboy but Karmen wasn't the passive sort.

"Your instructions are very clear," she said with a sharp edge to her voice and eyes like black obsidian.

Jessica paused for moment and then picked up a file. She threw it on the desk in front of them

"The lots I bought at the auction were just trivial diaries and letters. Most didn't even belong to the Countess, probably picked up at some damn market stall."

"Are you certain there are no more documents?" Karmen asked innocently.

Jessica stood over her and looked down with frigid eyes.

"Nothing is certain," she responded softly, the palm of her hand caressing the woman's cheek but her voice held a knife behind its back.

Alec interjected quickly.

"Maybe there aren't any. If they exist, they are either still at Carney House or they were taken. Perhaps there was another thief in the gang who managed to escape?"

Jessica shifted her gaze to him.

"Very unlikely but we'll check it anyway. Alec, I want you to look over the house, make sure nothing is hidden there. Karmen will drive me to visit Carl Vistan, the father of the gang leader. We know he arranged the auction and may have retained some papers. I will have the information. Our family have waited 350 years for this opportunity and we must not fail."

"We'll find it. No problem," said Alec. A platitude.

The duck billed platitude is now extinct, natural justice for the gratuitous use of parts of waterfowl in a cliché. However, the primary strain, the suck filled platitude has prospered massively with the advent of daytime talk shows.

Carl Vistan was looking forward to the appointment with Jessica Crowne but remained unsure of her purpose. A company as profitable as Velviva rarely required his involvement. He speculated that she might require capital for some new project but in any case, he was intrigued by this first meeting with her. Initial grief at the killing of his son had faded to a gnawing bitterness and all his energies were now channelled into the expansion of his business interests.

He rose ponderously from his chair to greet her.

"Ms Crowne, you're very welcome. Please take a seat."

She removed her Carlitini cream crimson edged coat to reveal an impeccable Vitrazo red suit with the shortest skirt option and relaxed into a leather chair, crossing her legs.

"Mr Vistan. Jessica, please."

"And you must call me Carl. Now, how may I be of service?"

His sharp eyes scanned the legs and moved upwards, returning to the legs shortly afterwards. She responded with a Hollywood smile.

"Our company is planning a new project based in London, a comprehensive total health complex. It will be an expansion on our existing centres in Switzerland and America. We are encompassing all aspects of health and beauty in one place. A fitness and workout area, pool for aquatic therapy and several other facilities in addition to our usual cosmetic and clinical services."

"You require investment?"

"Not exactly. You own two properties in central London, either of which may be very suitable. I'd like to discuss the feasibility of purchase or lease."

"I think I know the locations you would be interested in. Do you have details of your planned layout?"

She produced a folder of plans, projections and charts, which they discussed in detail for nearly an hour.

"I believe we have an understanding, Carl," she said as they finished.

"Yes, I'll get my legal people to prepare the papers."

He smiled. His financial benefits would be substantial as she had allowed him to negotiate a share of the profits in addition to a rental fee.

"There's just one more thing. Just a small favour I would request," Jessica remarked casually.

"Please ask."

She pouted, raising her knee to slide her skirt higher.

"You might not know that I'm an avid collector of historic documents."

"Really?"

He didn't know and his mind was racing through his collection to identify her possible targets.

"I was at the Countess Pollan auction the other day and I wondered if any lots of old documents were withheld from the sale?"

Ice in his eyes, but he could not prevent his gaze from wandering to the exposed thighs.

"I am also a collector and I did hear about the sale but the items were a little bland for my taste," he replied casually, waving at the expensive pieces of art decorating the office.

The skirt reached new heights of irresistibility.

"Now, Carl, I did hear a little story that you were, shall we say, involved in the auction. That's totally unimportant to me. I simply wish to purchase any documents that perhaps weren't offered for sale, maybe letters or diaries."

He leant forward.

"I think we should terminate this meeting while our relationship remains amicable."

"I can offer a considerable amount, untraceable currency and perhaps also a lady companion."

She mentioned three international movie stars who would do absolutely anything to ensure their continued supply of Atlantis Reborn.

"Ms Crowne, I have more than enough finances and I can have any woman I want. Our conversation is finished."

He stood up.

The thighs disappeared. She rose and slipped on her coat before he could offer assistance. As she reached the door she turned with a panther smile

"You'll be sorry."

She meant it all, except the smile.

Jessica entered the Caballini standing near the entrance. It moved smoothly into the traffic then turned into a side street two blocks away and parked.

"No success?" asked Karmen, reading her expression.

"I didn't really anticipate it. The alternative plan is ready?"

Jessica didn't expect a no.

"Yes, I can action immediately."

"Do it this evening."

Karmen held up a set of papers.

"All his collection, except for the items in his office, is kept in a basement strong room."

"Nothing in his office."

"I couldn't obtain a plan of the strong room layout."

Jessica smiled.

"That doesn't matter, the staff will show you."

The guard on the door of the Vistan building watched with amusement at the girl. She tottered along on high heels, struggling with two shopping bags. Typical dopey blonde he thought, although this one had dark hair.

As she passed, she called up to him.

"I'm trying to find Rejax Street."

He didn't understand the name.

"Sorry love," he responded, pointing to his ear.

She moved up to him with a vacant smile.

"I'm trying to find Rejax Street."

Her left hand holding the bag was pressing against his side and he suddenly felt a sharp prick. Then he felt almost nothing.

Her voice changed tone.

"Ask your colleague to come to answer my question."

He beckoned to the man seated at the reception desk.

"Can you help this lady?"

He walked towards her looking puzzled.

"Yes?"

She moved closer and he also felt the shopping bag against his thigh. HP47 worked almost immediately.

Two minutes later, he was entering the elevator with Karmen and two large men who she had called from a car parked outside. He punched a code number into the keypad and they descended. After a few seconds, the door opened to reveal a small room with two desks manned by guards and behind them was the large metal door of the strong room. The elevator was the only access to the room.

The men looked up but relaxed as they saw the guard strolling over to them while the others stood talking by the elevator.

"These are guests of Mr Vistan. They're here to check our security systems and you're to show them the strong room alarms and monitors."

The men nodded and walked to the new arrivals. Two jabs later they were opening the strong room door. The thick steel lined chamber was about 30 metres square and filled with rows of shelves that contained paintings, sculptures, antiques and antiquities. A collection of manuscripts and first edition books were housed in display cabinets along one wall. The room was humidity and temperature controlled to protect the collection.

Karmen assessed the size of the task.

"Where are the most recent papers?" she asked one of the guards.

He shrugged.

"I don't know. Mr Vistan doesn't allow us inside."

"Has he stored any items in the last two weeks?"

"Yes, he brings packages almost every day."

"We'll just have to search then," Karmen muttered.

She instructed the three guards to help by searching all the shelves and cabinets and extracting all documents or books except those relating to Vistan's business interests. She and her men scoured the resulting finds for any link or reference to the Countess. Forty minutes later they had a finished their search. Nothing.

At that moment the elevator doors opened and Carl Vistan stepped out followed by his assistant and two other men carrying cartons.

The scene froze, a snapshot in time. Why aren't the paparazzi taking pictures at places like this instead of hanging about outside nightclubs? An uninitiated few believe paparazzi is the head of the Razzi family which explains a lot.

"Shoot them," Vistan screamed, eyes bulging. He looked for a hiding place, found none and stepped back into the elevator feverishly jabbing buttons.

Karmen was faster in thought and action. She slid to the floor, her Guutson spitting four shots. The first two hit Vistan in the leg and he collapsed backwards, blocking the elevator doors that vindictively began to repeatedly open and close against his body. Her other two shots found the chest of one of the carton carriers.

Meanwhile Vistan's assistant and remaining man had dived to the floor and were using semi automatic pistols to pin down the group in the strong room. Karmen's two men returned the fire but the drugged guards had simply taken cover in confusion.

Karmen deduced the reason. They would have obeyed Vistan's shouted instruction but 'shoot them' was imprecise.

"Shoot the men near the elevator," she yelled.

One guard had taken cover at the side of a desk. He pulled a gun, popped above the desktop and emptied all his rounds in the general direction of the newcomers. Karmen calculated quickly. Her men and the other two guards had the benefit of shelter just inside the strong room doorway, obediently firing in relay in accord with her orders. She could not afford to wait, as reinforcements would surely arrive soon.

"Rush the men near the elevator," she yelled carefully. The three guards didn't hesitate, sprinting in jagged runs towards the two prone figures. Unfortunately, her two men also obeyed through duty rather than drugs, jumping out from the security of the strong room and following the guards. In a community hall it would have served well as a re-enaction of the Charge of the Light Brigade. Of course, all five were easy targets and fell rapidly, shredded by bullets.

The distraction was long enough for Karmen to take two steps and dive in a graceful gymnastic arc, finishing on top of a paper strewn desk. It was a beautiful, balletic performance although the landing squeezed the breath from her. From this higher angle the targets were fully exposed. She fired twice and couldn't miss.

Several stray shots had found Vistan. He lay coughing as the elevator doors continued their pummelling.

Karmen trapped the door open with her foot and crouched over him.

"Where are the papers from the Carney House auction?"

It was an agonising effort for him to smile but he managed it. One last victory.

"There are no other papers."

His body relaxed in death but the smile remained.

Karmen looked round the room. Lifeless bodies were scattered like a next morning rock group's bedroom.

"Oh shit," she said mildly.

16

Marcus had established an observation post in the trees at the side of Peter Parker's house. He'd fully recovered from the episode at the hotel but still cringed with embarrassment at his own performance. Although he had almost no recollection of events between the needle in his arm and waking in hospital, Selena had described everything in great detail except the presence of Jerome Jones.

It was typical of him to insist on doing this job alone and he was grimly determined not to fail again. The vigil had started two days ago and he had not missed a movement since, even sleeping with a sensor alarm in his ear.

Visitors to the house were infrequent. The staff lived on the premises and there had been just two deliveries of groceries. Parker had left on two occasions, departing mid-morning, presumably to attend an auction as he arrived back each time a few hours later with various cartons and packages.

It was on the afternoon of the third day when he saw her arrive. One memory understandably remained. A beautiful, dark haired naked woman kneeling astride him. Excepting porn movie stars, they had been as physically close as any couple could get without having sex.

Several people, including a Bulgarian man, claim to have been even closer, their accounts usually involving phones and doorbells ringing. Much depends upon a precise definition of the word sex and illustrated dictionaries may be of assistance here.

Now she was walking to the door of the house. He flicked his camera to burst mode, capturing a series of shots using the zoom lens and then he scrambled through the trees to a pre-selected vantage point facing the lounge window at the side of the building. He phoned Selena to report the arrival.

"Take care this time," she said.

He would take care. This was the first occasion he had ever carried a gun although he had no intention of firing it. A movement in the room and Marcus carefully edged forward. Fortunately, a thicket of tall bushes grew alongside the building, allowing him to ease to the side of the lounge window. Now he would use the Twig, an extendable rod disguised perfectly as a small tree branch, even complete with realistic plastic leaves along its length. A microscopic camera and directional microphone were mounted at one end with a small monitor screen and earphones plugged into the other. He carefully moved it in front of the window and checked the screen.

The woman was removing her long white simulated fur coat to reveal a short black dress while her host beamed admiringly, his arm inviting her to the sofa.

As Jessica sat in a cascade of leg and thigh, Peter Parker began to muse uncomplainingly at his apparent sudden attractiveness to young women. Clarification arrived when she began by asking about the auction documents, just like the others. He wondered what could be in these papers to merit such attention. Since the visit of the other girls, he had studied them diligently but found absolutely nothing remarkable. The thought stirred his memory of Annette Virginia Smith who had given him the second most pleasurable experience in his life, exceeded only by that oil share deal he had participated in, all of 24 years ago.

Parkinson brought the papers and this time, Parker was determined to observe closely in the hope of discovering the reason for the search. However, instead of looking at them immediately, Jessica rose, moved to the door and locked it. She returned with a sultry smile and raised one leg, placing a high heel on the arm of his chair. Then she slowly pulled her dress up over her hips.

Most women will have experienced going without pants (aka knickers) for a variety of reasons. These include loss after an adolescent grapple in a field, avoidance of the dreaded panty line and rushed dressing after oversleeping. Claims by Charlene Vesturo that they were blown off on a windy spring day in Denver are certainly apocryphal.

Jessica's underwear deficiency was for the other reason. Parker's eyes widened and cheeks pinkened as he moved towards her beckoning finger. Before his hands reached their target he felt a pad over his mouth and nose. Then darkness fell.

Darkness suffers so many falls you wonder why it doesn't employ a full-time injury compensation lawyer. At the very least it should be on crutches by now.

Without haste, Jessica pulled on her coat, collected the pile of papers, unlocked the door and left the room.

She drove impassively through deserted rural roads towards London. Four minutes before she heard someone speak.

"Stop the car. I have a gun pointed at your brain, the bullet will enter the back of the skull and exit above the right eye leaving rather a mess in between."

She immediately recognised the voice of the man she had captured at the hotel and pulled up on a grass verge.

"Please get out and walk ten metres into the field to our left," he continued.

She opened the door and began to cross into the field. After a few steps her heels stuck in the soft ground and she took off her shoes.

Carefully covering her with the gun, Marcus squeezed from the back of the car and stepped out. The stack of papers was on the passenger seat and he reached for them, grinning. Selena would be pleased with him this time. He later swore that the woman didn't move a muscle but nevertheless two darts bit into his neck like the fangs of a thirsty vampire.

Jessica replaced her shoes without bothering to recharge the dart guns in the heels. She looked down as she passed walked past the unconscious body.

"You're just unlucky," she murmured and drove off into the evening, singing softly to herself.

17

Karmen waited patiently in her office. Waited for Jessica to call. The raid on Vistan's strong room had been a complete failure. It was also inconvenient to lose two of her men. No problem to replace them but training would take time. The killing of Vistan and his people was not a concern, actually quite enjoyable.

No results, that was the problem. If Vistan hadn't kept these papers of the Countess, where would they be? The only hope was that they were in the auction lots bought by that old collector, Parker. Jessica had gone to see him alone and should be back very soon.

Karmen smiled. She found Jessica easy to manipulate. Reasonably intelligent, devious and ruthless but not in her own class. One essential part of KGB agent training was to develop the skill of reading weaknesses in character that could be exploited without the subject being aware. Jessica had several flaws, a major one being her predilection for dominance over others. That could be fed, could be channelled.

Karmen had joined Velviva two years before, as head of security. Not a random job application, Velviva had been investigated by the KGB when she was employed there. At the time, they were interested in military applications for the Atlantis Reborn youth mixture. Velviva's security arrangements hadn't been a problem and Karmen had found out more than she had reported back, particularly the special laboratory dedicated to the discovery of another ingredient that would give eternal life.

Martina and Jessica had told Karmen only that they were seeking a skin ageing treatment named the Blessing that had been discovered by their ancestors in the seventeenth century. It had been stolen by an organisation called the Octagon and Karmen was to recover the formula and return it to the rightful owners.

The blonde Katya had been Karmen's assistant in the KGB. Not the most intelligent person in the world but one who displayed unprecedented skills in a particular aspect of their work. Sex. She had never failed to seduce a targeted man or woman and always found ways to extract vital information from them during the encounter. Consequently, when Karmen joined Velviva, her first task had been to recruit Katya and direct her to a target, Jessica Crowne. Their sessions in bed had been very productive and Katya had discovered and reported every detail of the background. The real story of Elizabeth Beddowes, the Octagon, the Blessing and the search for the tenth ingredient had been revealed by Jessica in understandably less guarded moments.

As a result, Karmen now knew the whole story and could see the opportunity. The chance to acquire unlimited wealth and power when the complete formula was found. She hadn't reached the level of Strategic Planner in the KGB without an acute awareness of tactics. Stupid to act now. She would use the massive finances and power of Velviva to locate the elixir and then dispose of Jessica and the crone who was her mother. She had a plan and it would be shared only with Katya.

The door burst open and Jessica strode into the office.

"Karmen, I am not pleased with you," she snarled.

"For what reason?"

"I again suffered interference from Omasor after I visited Parker. They must have been watching his house. The same man that we captured at the hotel was hiding in the back of my car. He tried to take the papers from me but I tricked him."

Now Karmen looked up, eyes flashing with interest.

"Papers? You found them at Parker's house?"

"Yes, papers and a plaque. I've just left them with Alec. Knowing the Octagon, I expect a hidden or coded message."

"Then all is good. You know that the raid on Vistan was abortive? HP47 worked well but I confirmed there was nothing in the strong room. The good news is that I ensured everyone was dead. One of my men was wounded and I shot him before leaving. No witnesses."

Jessica's anger still burned.

"All is not good. I instructed you to keep the Omasor people away from our search. I do not want to find their agents hiding in my car or interfering in any way."

Karmen lowered her eyes. A calculated gesture to massage the woman's desire for dominance.

"Then I have not performed adequately. Shall I decide what action to take or do you have specific instructions?"

"I shot one of the Omasor agents at the hotel. I think we should warn them off by killing a couple more. That Darmant, for example. She was at the auction and the hotel. I recall how she left you unconscious there and don't expect you to be outmanoeuvred by a girl like that."

Now Karmen was annoyed.

"You knocked her out but wouldn't let me go back and shoot her."

"We had to get away from the hotel quickly. I didn't want to be distracted by a police investigation. Find the girl and kill her now. Also that other woman who was with her at the auction. She looked to be the senior partner. Yes, get rid of both of them."

"I will do as you instruct. Meanwhile I will temporarily allocate two people to act as your bodyguards. My best man will be there in the day and Katya will be with you every night. I trust that is acceptable."

Karmen saw the anger disappearing to be replaced by another emotion.

"Yes, that is an excellent plan," Jessica responded and left the office.

Karmen relaxed in the chair, pleased with herself. She had been smart to use the Omasor threat as a reason to get Katya back into Jessica's bed. Karmen needed to know if the documents contained anything and Katya would find out, no doubt about that.

Now for Omasor. She knew a little about the Agency from her time in the KGB but their paths rarely crossed. They appeared to specialise in more esoteric investigations while the KGB concentrated on practical, usually military matters. How to get the two women? She would select a team and then the trap needed baiting. Karmen began to outline a scheme on the pad in front of her.

Selena activated the large screen on the wall of the office.

"Read it," she said.

Chris leant forward in her chair. Regional newspaper, inside page. The headline was 'Treasure Hunter Strikes Lucky'. A photo showed a beaming man of about 35, holding an ancient rusted metal chest. The story was as expected. Mark Clyson had been spending his usual Sunday afternoon roaming the countryside with a metal detector. A strong signal within a clump of trees and he'd dug down to find the box. He took it home and opened it. A pile of gold coins together with a mass of old documents, all in remarkably fine condition. The gold had been sent away to be valued but he had retained the documents.

Chris shrugged.

"This is relevant?"

"Very. He found the box directly adjacent to Carney House."

"Now I see. So Clyson could have found some Octagon papers?"

"Look at the photo."

Selena zoomed in the screen. The man was holding the chest in one hand and a document in the other. The text was illegible but the symbol at the top was very clear. Two eagles above six swords.

"We'd better get to this man before Jessica's gang sees this."

Selena smiled and passed a note card.

"Here's the address. You're going now."

"You're not coming with me?"

"No. Problem?"

Chris was smiling as Selena accompanied her to the car.

"I think I can just about manage to get the box from him. I'll use the identity of a government official. It won't take long," she remarked, starting the engine.

"Perhaps not. Notice his hands?"

"What?" asked Chris but Selena was already returning to the office.

Clyson lived in a quiet tree-lined avenue amongst a new housing development built around an old village. Chris deliberately drove past, checking a few parked cars. No one inside the vehicles. At the end of the street, she turned into open country and looked back to the houses. They were large by modern standards and one had a large tinted glass conservatory built on the rear. Clyson's house.

She parked at the end of the street and walked back. A delay after she rang the doorbell and a surprise when it opened. A hooded figure greeted her.

"Yes?"

"I'm looking for Mr Clyson."

"Oh, that's me," he responded, pulling back the hood.

Chris flashed an ID card.

"I'm from the government Culture Development Heritage Department. Can I talk to you?"

He opened the door fully to reveal a long blue robe. Like a monks habit but this one was made of some thin material.

"Oh right. You properly think I'm a bit strange. You see, we've just started an earth blessing ceremony. I'm a druid, you know. Come on in."

She followed him through the house and into the conservatory. Larger than it looked from the outside and she noted the glass wasn't just tinted, it was an opaque green. At the far end she could see what must be an altar, covered with a heavy white cloth that was marked with various symbols. No other furnishings but there were seven people, all in identical robes to Clyson and with cowls up. Faces well hidden but she could clearly identify four of them as women under the clinging, thin garments.

Chris suddenly sensed danger as two of the hooded figures moved around behind her but Clyson was still chatting normally.

"So you see, we're all here ready for the ceremony. Just waiting for the chosen one to submit themselves to the Earth gods."

Chris saw his smile fade and immediately twisted round, reaching for her pistol. Something hit her head and she fell.

Chris returned slowly to consciousness. How long had she been out? Not too long, she could sense that. Green glass above her. Lying on something hard, maybe wood. Ankles and wrists tied. The sound of voices to one side. Seemed cooler now. Clothes?

She blinked her eyes open. No clothes and that had a severe effect on her mood.

"She's awake." Clyson's voice.

Chris turned her head round. Just two people. Clyson with a blonde woman.

"You're a very attractive woman, Chris Darmant," she said with a sincere expression.

There was something instantly likeable about her, despite the circumstances.

Clyson was ogling.

"Can I have her first, Katya?"

"No."

"What's the difference? She'll be dead anyway."

The blonde turned to him, still smiling. Then she kneed him in the groin. He screamed in pain, dropping to his knees and then found her pulling his hair back to force him to look up. Katya spoke softly and was still smiling.

"This woman will not be raped. That would not correspond with the plan. Next time you don't obey immediately, I will shoot you."

Chris saw her approaching and squirmed involuntarily. The ropes were tight, biting into her flesh. She twisted her head away as the woman bent close.

"Hello, I'm Katya," she breathed and Chris felt fingers running gently over her chest.

"I don't know what's going on here. I'm a government employee sent to collect papers from Mr Clyson," Chris blustered but found her eyes drawn to the girl who was smiling irresistibly.

"You are Chris Darmant, an Omasor agent and you have walked into a trap. I'm really sorry that we'll have to kill you but your Agency needs to be discouraged from interfering in our business."

Chris put on a mystified look.

"I don't understand any of that. I'm just here to do a job."

Katya ignored her response.

"It's strange but I can sense it. You don't enjoy being naked, do you?"

"No I don't. No woman does."

Chris found she couldn't help responding. An intangible persuasiveness about the blonde that seduced the mind.

"No woman? That just isn't right, you'd be surprised. I think you've only ever slept with two men, at most. It's a shame that you will never enjoy the delights of your body."

"What do you want from me?"

"Just to die nicely. There will be a lot of pain. Omasor have to see you were tortured before you died. That's our message to them. Call the others, Clyson."

The man struggled to his feet and left the conservatory, still clutching the tender area. He was back two minutes later, followed by the other six hooded figures. Katya started to speak and then paused, taking a pistol from her hip.

"Pull back your hoods," she said sharply.

The six faces were exposed and Chris recognised one of them. The man whom she had shot with a dart gun at the hotel. A puzzled look on Katya's face but she shrugged and turned back to Chris.

"This is really going to hurt but it won't take long. When I shoot you, I'll make sure it's instantly lethal," she said and then turned to the others.

"Gag her and cut her up as quickly as you can."

A pair of women came forward, producing scalpel like blades from their robes. Two thudding sounds and they fell to the floor. The group looked at each other, perplexed. More thuds, more bodies falling.

"The door!" screamed Katya, diving for cover behind the altar. Only Clyson standing now and as he scrambled to join Katya, he also collapsed.

"Hello, Katya. Must be 18 months since we were last together."

Selena's voice.

"I don't know you. Please come out so I can see," called Katya with a persuasive tone that took some resisting.

"Then drop your weapon and I won't kill you," responded Selena, still out of sight.

Katya squirmed behind the altar and Chris felt the gun pressed against her forehead.

"Come out or I'll kill this woman."

"Okay, here I am. Nice to meet again."

Chris turned her head to see Selena in the doorway.

"You're the one called Selena Bowman. We've never met."

"Remember Florida, 14 months ago? Your target was that Air Force officer. She agreed you could come to her hotel room."

"That wasn't you."

"Not the one you met in the bar. I was in her bed when you came and she was in the closet, sleeping happily on the pill I gave her."

"That couldn't have been you."

Selena sighed.

"You recall I told you not to switch on the lights. I'd disabled them anyway in case you tried. Then you joined me on the bed and I'll tell you how our conversation started."

Chris felt herself blushing as Selena recounted the exact words.

"That was a very good night," Katya said softly.

"I enjoyed it a lot. Three hours, I guess. I told you to leave while it was still dark," responded Selena.

"But why was Omasor involved with the woman?"

"You wanted military secrets from her but I was trying to recover a voodoo artefact she'd been given by a boyfriend."

Katya smiled and redirected her gun towards Selena.

"I'll think lovingly about you after your death," she said, squeezing the trigger.

Chris screamed, a blur of movement and a noise out of her vision. Then she felt the ropes being cut.

"I suppose lying around naked on an altar is one way to get a man but I've never tried it," Selena remarked.

Chris saw Katya unconscious on the floor. Saw a jagged tear in Selena's jacket. Saw a patch of blood around it.

"She missed from that range?"

Selena grinned.

"I move fast when being shot at."

"Let me check the wound."

"No, forget it. Go as you are or put something on?"

Chris gasped and pressed her hands over various parts of her body.

"I'd forgotten," she cried and ran to the end of the room where her clothes lay in a heap on the floor. She was dressed within seconds and gave sigh of relief.

"They're all alive. You used a dart gun," she remarked as she returned to Selena.

"Quieter, no flashes. Harder to see me."

"You knew it was a trap, didn't you?"

"Told you to check Clyson's hands. No way he'd ever used them to dig for treasure. Fingernails manicured."

"Was that story true about meeting Katya before?"

"Would you like all the details?"

"No thank you."

"Pity. She's so good at what she does. Not too smart here though. Should have left someone on guard outside."

"So what do we do with them?"

"Nothing. We just leave. The purpose of all this was to give Omasor a message and we've decided to return it to the sender. No one threatens us."

Chris was smiling as she followed Selena out of the house.

18

Jim Fischer and Valla Toreus stood near to the main entrance of Canterbury Cathedral closeted in the lower abdomen of England. The historic building, in a place of worship dating back to Roman times, stood serenely in sublime countenance. So many visitors had come to taste its simple tranquillity, to suck memories from its architecture, to consume the power of its atmosphere. Taking, always taking but at some time, one would come. One who would give all in simple piety. Meanwhile, it endured with compassion the daily squalls of humanity.

Jim looked at his watch and spoke impatiently.

"Well, this is the place. Let's hope some of the members are already here, otherwise we'll have to visit every day until they arrive."

Valla shrugged.

"We don't know if we're the first, second or last pair. If we're the first, it will be a long wait."

She saw a blond man and dark haired girl walking towards them and noticed the inquisitive looks in their faces.

"I think these are possibles," she said with relief.

Jim was still cautious and felt for his gun, mounted in a palm release mechanism under his right sleeve.

The couple reached them.

"Octagon?" Jim said distinctly.

The man smiled and nodded.

"I'm John Porter, Secondary."

He looked about 20 with a beach tan and a friendly face.

The woman gave a childish laugh. Dark haired, attractive and even in the cold conditions she wore a tight suit that displayed a large chest. Valla disliked her instinctively, sensing something abnormal about her. An emanation of evil behind a facade of innocence.

"And my name is Catherine Bell. I'm also a Secondary."

Her voice was childlike and peculiar smile played across her full red lips.

"We really are very pleased to see you. Everyone else is here. I guess you're in the car park and if you follow us we can go meet the others," said John with relief.

They returned to their cars and Valla began to tail the Caballini occupied by the couple. After 20 minutes, they arrived at a large suburban house glowing white in the sharp winter sun and set back from the roadway in a quiet avenue. John and Catherine were already walking towards the building and Jim and Valla followed cautiously, footsteps crunching in the chill gravelled frontage. Into an expansive hall and the couple guided them through an open door to the right that led to a large warm room furnished with a conference table, sofas and chairs. Two people stood in front of the table.

The woman stepped forward. She looked under 25 with a narrow face and long blonde hair hanging free over her shoulders.

"You're very welcome. I'm Mary Duckworth, Primary."

The man seemed more reserved. He was below average height with a serious, bespectacled face. An old man in a young man's body.

"My name is Arthur Pierce and I also am a Primary."

Jim smiled while assessing them. An important moment for him. Could he dominate these two and become the accepted leader? First indications were good.

"Jim Fischer, Primary and Valla Toreus, my Secondary. I guess we should sit and talk. Perhaps the Secondaries will excuse us," he said.

Three of them at the table, arguably the most powerful trio in the world and certainly amongst the richest. Mary Duckworth spoke first.

"I see that I am the only original member. I had hoped at least one other would have survived."

"You were there at the beginning?" asked Jim, finding it hard to believe she was over three centuries old.

The wistful look left her and her eyes softened.

"I was there and it was a very different world in the 17th century. I've travelled a long journey, but the end is in sight now. I assure you it has not been an unfettered delight to see so many friends die, to collect the problems and worries of five lifetimes and also to be denied the delight of childbirth for so long."

"Soon you can have all the kids you want," Jim said considerately.

"I have seen so many come into this world and depart. After a time you find yourself withdrawing. All the excitement of seeing or doing something for the first time is lost to me in distant history."

She paused, regaining her composure.

"I believe we should begin. Let us start by introducing our Secondaries and ourselves. I am Mary Duckworth. I was born in 1619 and have been a Primary since the beginning in 1650. My Secondary since 1978 is John Parker who was born in 1950."

"Jim Fischer born 1893, Secondary in 1924 and Primary from 1969. My Secondary, Valla Toreus was appointed by me in 1969 and was born 1950."

The bespectacled man hesitated before he spoke.

"I have guarded our secret for a long time, revelation is not simple for me. My name is, and always has been, Arthur Pierce although I have become my own son several times. I was born in the year 1649 in the county of Devon, England and was appointed to Secondary status in 1672, acceding to Primary in 1804. Catherine Bell has been my Secondary since 1874. She was born in 1861."

He paused sensing their momentary disquiet.

"Yes, I appointed her at the age of 13 as I discerned a certain spirit within her and she has not disappointed me since. I think I must add that in all that time I have had no relationship with her of a sexual nature. In fact, in accordance with our oath, I have not indulged in any sexual activity since I joined the Octagon."

"Our rules don't ban sex, even with a Secondary but we know we can't create offspring. Until the new era that is," Jim observed.

Mary smiled. "For myself, I have had more relationships with my assistants than I can recall and you may agree the current one is somewhat irresistible."

"We must all follow our own path," Arthur sighed.

Jim pondered for a moment.

"It seems like you to have lost a few Secondaries, Mary. How is that?"

Mary continued to smile but her innocent face was like ice.

"I have lost, as you say, seven Secondaries to accidents. I arranged all of them. Men can become very irritating after a time."

"And you, Arthur. Without getting personal, I see you're wearing spectacles. I thought the Blessing gave us perfect bodies."

"No, that is incorrect. It actually keeps us at a peak of our physical and mental powers. It doesn't cure hereditary problems. I was born short sighted but the benefit is that my eyesight will never deteriorate."

"Sure, I guess I was just lucky to be in perfect shape when I first took the Blessing. How did you come to join?"

"I was Secondary to one of the original members, Alice Pergannin," Pierce said.

Mary turned to him.

"We were friends, close friends. How was her ending?"

"She had progressively become more reserved, shutting herself off from the outside world. I believe she was simply bored with her existence or perhaps found the burden of our secret too much to bear. It was 1804 and Alice had lived well over 150 years. That day, she asked me to visit and I found her on the cliff top overlooking the ocean. She handed me a ceremonial sword and knelt down, facing the waters. I waited for perhaps one hour then she simply said, 'For the next world, now' and I sent her head and body to the seas. I had stood by her faithfully for 132 years and I did not fail her at the end."

There was a silence.

"We suffered together," Mary said sadly.

Her gaze moved to the window. She recalled her times with Alice in those distant days when the group feared discovery and execution by the new government. James Smith had required them to confirm that the authorities were unaware of the Octagon and to obtain this information by sleeping with a series of officials. The conversations she and Alice had shared, full of friendship and whispered secrets. All the excitement of a new adventure that seemed so trivial now.

Pierce interrupted her thoughts.

"I suggest that we start our meeting. We have much to discuss and I am unsure how much time we have. The situation is that each of us arrived at the place for our annual Renewal of the Blessing but there was no one there. Something has happened to the Provider, the keeper of our elixir. As the rules say that their Secondary should take over, we must assume that person has also been incapacitated in some way."

Jim concurred.

"As I see it, there are a few problems to resolve. First we must find the supply of the Blessing. That's the most urgent action as it's possible that others are also seeking it. I assume we all brought the envelope?"

James Smith had seemingly allowed for all contingencies when he structured the Octagon. At the first Renewal meeting with each member, the Provider had given them a sealed envelope which contained part of a guide to the location where the Blessing was stored. It could only be found when these were put together. The envelopes were to be opened only in the present situation, the decease of both the Provider and their Secondary. If the hiding place was changed, the Provider gave new guides to the three Primaries at the annual Renewal and they had each received an envelope 12 years ago indicating that the Blessing had been concealed somewhere new at that time.

Jim unsealed his without hesitation, taking out a folded paper and smoothing it flat on the table. Mary and Pierce followed.

"What is this?" Pierce exclaimed.

Each document contained the same short line of printed text.

'YOU ALL POSSESS, BEHIND THE'.

"Behind the what? It makes no sense at all." Jim's voice rose in disappointment.

Mary was thoughtful.

"The phrase needs to be studied carefully. The essential words are 'you all possess'. We must consider any information or item that we all have and importantly, the Provider must have had knowledge of it. So as the hiding place was changed about 12 years ago, it is almost certainly something we received since then."

"I cannot think it would be information. Nothing was imparted to me in the last dozen years that could possibly indicate a hiding place," said Pierce.

Jim nodded agreement.

"So it must be an object we all possess. Logically it should be something that was given to us during the Renewal at the same time as the envelope."

It was common for gifts to be presented after they had received the Blessing, often works of art.

"I recall I received two paintings at that time," said Pierce.

Mary nodded. "I was given three paintings and a sculpture."

Jim had difficulty in remembering. The Renewal meeting 12 years ago was in a palatial villa south of Rome. Then he recalled the three attractive girls with long blonde hair who had performed very personally for him and presented gifts from the Provider just before he left.

Classical scholars will immediately associate a gift with the city of Troy, a reminder for everyone to be on their guard against wooden horses. John Stallion, in his book 'Wood Horse Watch', tells a story of one valiant defence.

'I keep a sharp lookout every day and was recently fortunate to be able to save my neighbour. I saw him arrive back at his house with one of the wooden equine effigies in the back of his car. Of course I rushed out to apprehend the creature and my neighbour, sadly ignorant of the dangers, put up quite a struggle. However, I managed to set fire to the horse before he could call reinforcements. To deceive the unwary, it had a ticket round its neck with the words 'Robin the Rocking Horse' or some such nonsense. His young daughter had become a trifle upset by the proceedings and repeatedly attempted to strike me with a stick whilst accurately aiming kicks at my ankles.

I endeavoured to remind them of the potential menace concealed within the timber quadruped and it is true that in this case, the assassins concealed inside would not have been large in stature but my warnings were dismissed rather painfully, not to mention with a degree of vulgarity.

How quickly the lessons of history are forgotten.'

Jim's face beamed with recollection.

"Now I remember. I received two paintings. One was a view of Venice and the other a picture of a fountain."

Mary smiled.

"The fountain," she said.

Pierce nodded.

Now Jim was in his element. His organisational skills had been a significant factor in amassing the billions of dollars that currently resided in a multitude of bank accounts throughout the world.

"We need to study the picture. I'll ask Valla to get us a copy immediately."

"You can fly it here?" asked Pierce.

"No need, it can be photographed and sent electronically. Valla has the equipment."

Thirty minutes later, the Secondaries had joined them as they gathered round a large colour print of the painting. An ornate garden fountain in the foreground, surrounded by a gravelled area with what appeared to be a typical English country house behind it.

John Porter studied the print with a magnifying glass.

"There are some words, here in the corner."

"The artist's signature?" Mary suggested.

"No. It says 'A cool sea or fallen dew today' followed by our insignia 2/6."

"The phrase is meaningless and I therefore assume it to be some form of cryptogram," commented Pierce.

Jim looked towards Valla. If it could be solved she would do it. It took her less than a minute.

"We are looking for someone or something called Carney. You take the second and sixth letter alternately. Very simple really."

A pause

"Carney? I would surmise that he, she or it would be located somewhere in England," remarked Pierce.

Jim nodded vaguely. His gaze had moved to Catherine. She returned the look with a soft smile, her eyes widening and lips parting slightly. Something about her voluptuous innocence that was irresistible.

"You know, I think I've seen that word somewhere recently," John muttered, brushing a few strands of blond hair from his eyes.

"It seems silly to give us the name and no other clue," Mary complained.

"I'll run an internet check. I guess that should provide a few possibilities," said Valla and left the room with John close behind.

Jim rose from his seat and walked to the window. After a few seconds, he found Catherine standing alongside. Very close. He could feel her chest pressing against him.

"I'd really like to be friends with you," she said softly, big eyes raised to him.

Jim glanced round. Mary and Pierce were engaged in conversation.

"You're an attractive woman, Catherine," he murmured.

She smiled like an infant who just been told she has been a good girl.

"But you can't see me properly here. I can show you lots more in my room."

"We can't go now."

She made a face.

"Don't you want me then?"

"Hell, yes. But we're in the middle of a meeting."

"You don't think I'm nice. It's that horrid Valla girl, isn't it? I don't like her."

She pressed closer and reached her arm around to caress his thigh. Jim fervently hoped their bodies masked the activity.

"So you'll show me around?" he said loudly and turned for the door.

"Catherine's going to give me a quick tour of the house while we're waiting. I think better when I'm on the move," he called to the pair at the table.

Catherine led him up the stairs, her body moving sinuously as she climbed. At the top, she grabbed his arm and guided him into one of the rooms. A large bedroom. She closed the door and turned with a look of excitement.

"You just sit on the bed and watch me," she demanded.

Her voice was lower, lips moist and eyes sparkling. Jim moved to the bed. He had been in many bedrooms with many women but this one was special. She stripped slowly, always keeping her eyes fixed on him. Just her underwear now. Very brief and very pink. And something else. A slim knife was strapped to the top of her right thigh.

Jim's eyes fixed on her massive chest and his body pulsed with the intensity of his attraction to her. Not really attraction. It was the scouring fanaticism of outright lust.

"Do you really like me?" she asked breathily.

"Yes, sure I do. You've got a helluva figure," he responded with difficulty.

"Let me make you very happy. Stand up now."

He rose and she fell to her knees, crawling slowly towards him with her eyes upraised. In front of him now and she unfastened her bra, slinging it to one side.

"Tell me what a good girl I am," she asked in a tiny, appealing voice.

"You're good."

Now her hands were on him.

"And you think I'm the prettiest girl in the world?"

He hesitated slightly. Not as it should be.

"Yes, I do."

She began to giggle.

"You're a lovely boy and I'm such a beautiful girl," she chanted.

Jim's discomfort increased as she continued.

"And now the beautiful young princess wants her subjects to be nice to her."

She got to her feet, stripped off the pants and stood with legs apart. Her expression changed. Something not normal in the eyes and the smile was now somehow twisted.

"Get down before me and look up at your princess," she commanded.

"I won't do that," he responded, passion in decline.

"The princess doesn't like the subjects who don't obey her."

Now the eyes were wild, savage and the knife was in her hand. Jim backed towards the door.

"I'm going now, Catherine," he said abruptly and left the room, almost running down the stairs. How the hell had Pierce made her a Secondary? The girl was an immature psychopath.

He rejoined the other two with some relief.

"Enjoy the tour?" asked Mary.

"Yes, sure," Jim responded quickly but he recognised her expression. Seen it before. She knew why he had left with Catherine but she couldn't realise how unbalanced the girl was.

"Found it!" called John from the doorway.

Valla came in behind him, bearing a sheaf of colour prints. They gathered at the table and she passed the copies round. As he sat, Jim noticed Catherine enter and take the seat furthest from him without looking in his direction.

"Talk us through, Valla," he instructed

She looked down at a page of notes.

"A few weeks ago, Countess Pollan and her personal assistant were having dinner with a woman friend. A gang of three armed men burst in. There seems no doubt that they planned a simple robbery. It's believed they entered the dining room and there was a fight with guns and knives but the details are pure speculation as there were no survivors. The Countess, her assistant, guest, two servants and all three of the gang were all killed. Police medics examined the body of the Countess and reported that she had survived a knife in the back that went right into her and she should have died instantly. She was finally killed by a bullet to the head."

"You think she was the Provider and the PA was her Secondary?" asked Jim.

"Sure of it," Valla responded firmly.

"How does this relate to Carney?" asked Pierce.

"Her residence was Carney House. Check the photos I've given you. In one picture, you can just see the Octagon crest."

"Anything else?"

"One anomaly. A cousin of the Countess suddenly turned up afterwards, apparently from the USA."

"That isn't possible."

"Right. So I sent a picture to every agency we own or use in the States to check him out. Anyway, this cousin took over the property and auctioned the contents. He was also planning to sell off the house but disappeared soon after the contents auction."

"Sold the possessions of the Countess? Hell!" exclaimed Jim.

John raised a palm.

"I think it's okay. I phoned the auctioneers and they say nothing that could be drunk or eaten was there. That wouldn't be allowed by law. Also there were no sealed containers at all."

Jim got to his feet.

"We need to get to this place fast."

Mary and Pierce nodded agreement

Two hours later, Mary's eyes were glistening with sadness as she read the newspaper article again.

"With the passing of the years, it has become harder rather than easier to accept violent death," she murmured.

"Is there anything I can get you?" asked Valla.

"Tea would be nice."

Valla moved to the kitchen, her mind still checking their plan. They had discussed the method of retrieving the Blessing and unanimously agreed it would be too dangerous for all to go. Eventually it had been decided that Jim would take two Secondaries, John Porter and Catherine Bell, leaving Pierce and Mary to wait with her in the house. She knew they were still uncertain of the exact location but Jim firmly believed he would find another clue somewhere in or on the fountain. He hadn't been keen to take Catherine but Pierce had been insistent. Valla recognised that he didn't want to risk his own life but wanted a representative there.

John Porter pulled the car off the road and stopped on the grass verge with a bank of trees between them and the rear of Carney House. Jim was in the back and Catherine sat beside him, dressed in a tight fitting black suit with her hair bunched inside a dark woollen hat. The night was silent and cool and traffic was minimal. Only one vehicle had passed them on the quiet country road. Catherine insisted on making an initial reconnaissance of the area before they attempted to reach the fountain.

"I think I'll be gone for 15 minutes," she said, disappearing into the evening gloom.

Alec was in the house, in accordance with Jessica's instructions. He was thumbing through a pile of books by the lounge window when he noticed a movement outside. Taking cover behind the curtains he scanned the trees with night vision binoculars and saw her immediately. The girl was an amateur. She wore a dark outfit but her face showed pale, almost white in the harsh moonlight.

He gestured to his companion who was searching a cupboard on the other side of the room and the man joined him at the window. Alec handed him the binoculars and whispered a plan.

They left the house by a side door as soundlessly as they had entered. Alec crouched behind a row of bushes and raised his binoculars again. The girl was partly concealed behind a tree and apparently checking the windows for any sign of occupants.

When he saw his man was in position behind her, Alec stepped on to the gravelled area and walked casually past the hiding place. He heard the quick tussle, a faint cry and the noise of a body falling. Turning quickly, he ran towards the sounds only to hit a brick wall. The wall was actually Catherine's heel, launched with such perfect timing that her martial arts tutors would have cracked a few slabs in delight.

Catherine pulled tape and a roll of twine from a pack strapped to her thigh and the two men were quickly trussed with three crossing strips of tape across their mouths.

She held a finger up and began to talk to the unconscious bodies.

"Now you be very good boys and don't move. You've got lots of things I can cut off," she giggled, pulling out a knife. Then she gave a schoolgirl grimace.

"But you're both asleep and it isn't any fun unless you're squealing as I do it."

Jim and John didn't see her return and were startled by the car door opening.

"All clear?" Jim enquired.

"Just two nasty men. They won't trouble us now"

"You don't mean you killed them?"

"No, I didn't. They wouldn't wake up so I could do that," she retorted sharply.

Jim felt increasingly uncomfortable in her presence. He couldn't reconcile her childish ways with the extreme sexuality and apparent capacity for excessive violence. He noticed that John didn't seem to share his concerns, ogling her impressive body like a first year student at the keyhole of the cheerleaders' showers.

The fountain was circular, about ten metres across with an ornate centre shaped like a thick oak tree where the cascading water formed the foliage. They began by searching the outside rim but found only decorative lines and curves.

"I think I can see something written on it," said John.

Without hesitation, all three waded to the centre. The tree was formed with closely fitting stone blocks, each block scored by lines to represent the texture of tree bark. Inscribed around the base of the trunk were the words 'THIS IS THE WATER OF LIFE'.

"Is it under the water?" asked Catherine.

Jim was smiling.

"No, I know where it is."

The word 'THE' was on a separate block. He took a penknife from his pocket and began to scratch around the edge of the stone.

"It's plastic, dammit," he cried, nearly laughing with relief.

Using his knife he quickly cut out the false front to reveal a cluster of small bottles behind. Taking the first one he raised it to his lips and kissed it.

"The Blessing. We've got you. Thank god for that."

The next afternoon, Jim looked up from his papers. He sat at the end of the conference table with Mary and Arthur Pierce each side of him. He had used all his skills to dominate the meeting and now believed he had asserted his position as unelected leader

"I'll summarise our agreement so far. First, we have divided the supply of the Blessing and each of us will have sufficient to last until 2019 at least," he announced.

"Yes, it is not appropriate to appoint a new Provider at this late stage, so close to the event," Pierce remarked.

"Second, we will return to our own residences as quickly as possible and take extra precautions to secure everything related to the Octagon. We will make no attempt to contact each other except in extreme emergency."

"I think that is safer for us all," commented Mary.

"Third, we will obtain a set of mobile telephones. These will be set up in such a way that the location of the caller or receiver is not identifiable. Valla can arrange that."

Pierce seemed satisfied.

"We can then communicate in the case of any other unforeseen occurrence," he observed.

Jim leant forward in his chair.

"I still believe there is no need for so much secrecy now that we've met. I think we should also share details of our locations."

"And I still disagree." Pierce was adamant.

"I support Arthur in this. I believe it is safer if we do not hold this knowledge," Mary declared firmly.

Jim rose from his seat. He wasn't going to risk his assumed leadership by pressing the point.

"Then I guess we're just about finished and we'll come together here again in 2018."

Mary shifted her gaze to the window. A light snow had started to fall.

"I hope it doesn't become necessary to meet before then," she said thoughtfully.

19

Jerome Jones worked silently, feverishly chewing gum as he scribbled. The photographs Chris had taken at Peter Parker's house were clear and sharp. His team had transcribed the words from every item and document shown in the images into his most powerful computer and it had already been scouring the text for six hours. Despite access to sophisticated state-of-the-art cryptology programs, the machine had been unsuccessful so far.

He was sure that a code had been used somewhere in the various scripts and the first task had been to weed out irrelevant documents that clearly did not contain any hidden information.

Jerome had one certainty. A small engraved plaque with the crest of the Octagon at the top and beneath it a Latin motto. 'Fideli Certa Merces'. That translated as 'the faithful are sure to be rewarded'.

Then he found the cookery book. A loose leaf ring binder filled with home printed recipes. Food was definitely not one of his specialities but even he could recognise a clearly nonsensical mixture.

"Clever woman," he whispered and moved again to the keyboard.

Using the pre-programmed pattern analysis, he identified the code. She had used a double helix transposition cipher, which required the correct key phrase to be misaligned and only four computers in the world could unscramble that. Even then it needed human involvement at the pseudo randomisation stage. One of those four computers was housed in the next room and it took just 94 minutes before he had a result. A location.

It was not just for the buzz of beating the machine that he liked to work on the text personally. Some messages could be hidden very easily and be almost impossible for the computer to recognise, particularly if they referred to external sources. The machine could check a phrase 'look in my coat pocket' for a million years and find nothing but a human could solve it in five seconds. Longer if you don't understand English.

He well recalled the Meektown letter, which had included the words 'always keep the church on the right side' and the message had been simply etched behind a bush on the right-hand granite wall of the parish church.

Coincidentally, Meektown was the birthplace of Conrad Swillporter, the 18th-century playwright and poet. His quaint thatched cottage still stands on the outskirts and is regularly visited by swarms of visitors anxious to view the desk where he composed his works. As many will know, he actually wrote on a pad resting on his knee and a cast replica of a knee forms the centrepiece of the display.

Unfortunately, most of his work has been lost including all of his poetry. Of the two remaining plays, the best-known is undoubtedly 'History of the Picts'. This was written entirely in Pict, unfortunately in an unknown dialect and therefore never translated.

His other play 'Bompio And Juliett And Her Friende Sharon' is a classic bawdy romp of the period. Regrettably, in the last 250 years it has suffered severely under the knife of a series of censors. Only three lines now remain.

Bompio: 'Into yon bedde ye maidens.'

Juliett: 'Hither comst I, but ne'er without my friende.'

Bompio: 'Mayhap tis truth that twicer is nicer.'

Finis

Jerome knew there was something else in the cookery book. Another section seemed to require a much longer set of keywords. Why had the Countess set the codes at two levels? He needed time to work on it but meanwhile the investigation would proceed.

Jerome ceased the gum chewing. He picked up the phone and called Selena. She and Chris had a long journey to make. Just seven words were written on the paper in front of him.

'Wang Shu Island' and underneath that, 'What was the Countess planning?'

20

Chris was reading an evening newspaper when her phone rang.

"Hello, it's John."

She always felt a little surge at the sound of his voice. An upheaval in her emotions.

"Hello. How are things on the West Coast?"

"Last I heard they were fine. Chris, I'd really like to talk to you."

She curled her legs under her and relaxed into the sofa.

"Okay, go ahead."

"I thought we might have dinner and chat after."

"Are you flying over soon?"

"I'm standing outside your door."

"What?"

The doorbell rang.

They returned early from a delicious dinner at a nearby Greek restaurant. Chris was glad to involve herself in small talk about the latest Hollywood scandals and avoid any serious discussion. John was a good looker, good talker and good company. Maybe he was right for her. Just maybe. For the first time in her life, love waved from a turret in a distant castle.

She made coffee and joined him on the sofa, smiling as his mouth creased into a grin.

"Now I would like to talk to you."

Chris had a sudden panic. Surely he wasn't planning a marriage proposal?

"A lecture?" she asked.

He laughed beautifully. Hard to find a fault.

"No. There's something I'd like to tell you about my background. I can only reveal a little but I still want you to know."

"Okay."

"Have you noticed that I appear very young? Most people think I'm no more than 20."

"That's not something to be bothered about. We first met a while ago and I suppose you haven't really changed. How old are you now then?"

"I can't tell you that. A man's privilege," he joked.

"Okay. So the point is?"

"I joined a group. Let's call it a society where we all share a secret way to keep young looking."

"Tibetan cabbages or something?"

"No, Chris. Something that really works. Problem is that there can only be a limited number using this secret. I'm wondering if you'd be interested in joining if one of the members leaves?"

"How can I answer that? It's about as vague as you can get."

"I see that but I'm thinking we'd be in it together. You know, long-term."

Chris squirmed mentally. If this was a partnership proposal, it had to be the most convoluted ever.

"John, all I can say is possibly. There's no way I could agree to something without knowing all the details."

He nodded. Possibly was the best answer he could hope for. When she knew about the Blessing, he was sure she'd join him, become his Secondary. Just one obstacle. Mary Duckworth had to die first.

The doorbell rang again.

It's in the nature of doorbells to ring at critical times. They are attracted mostly by the commencement of meals, amorous encounters and showers but often find some affinity with critical moments in conversations. Telephones are their hyperactive offspring.

Chris sighed, checked her gun was in place behind her hip and opened the door to a square, chunky man.

"Hello Chris."

"I don't know you."

Her hand moved to her hip.

"Is your visitor leaving?"

She pulled the pistol out. He lifted his jacket, totally unconcerned.

"Look, no weapons."

"Come inside slowly and face the wall. Hands up and legs apart."

He did exactly that. She kicked the door closed and searched him. No gun.

John appeared from the lounge. His expression merged uncertainty and disappointment.

"I think I'll be going," he said, eyeing the gun.

"Sorry, this is business. Call me tomorrow."

He left, passing the man who showed no apparent interest in him.

Chris stepped backwards.

"Now, who are you?"

"We work for the same company."

"Selena sent you?"

"You might say that."

"Describe her."

He described her in great detail, even including a tiny birthmark on her right calf that Chris hadn't noticed. She relaxed but didn't lower the gun. The man could best not be described as round. Average height with a heavy, muscular body, square jaw and short-cropped hair.

"Sorry to intrude, was that a friend of yours?" he asked.

"An old acquaintance and as we're not sharing names, he's Mr Smith. Look, I don't appreciate uninvited visits. My home is private and not part of the job."

"You want a higher salary?"

"I'm getting irritated."

"Selena will be here soon. You're going on a little trip to Hong Kong."

Like an exceptionally bad dyslexic doctor, Chris was running out of patience.

"Who are you?"

"I'm Jerome Jones."

Chris was hard to surprise but this statement was hard enough.

"You're lying, he's dead."

"There is more than one of that name."

"What? "

"Which part didn't you understand?"

"You're saying it was a double that was killed?"

"Not a double, he didn't look like me."

"Then you could also be an impostor."

"Yes I could."

He spoke as he looked, solid and unshakeable. She noticed his eyes, steel blue and steady.

"Then the real Jerome Jones wasn't killed."

"That is correct."

An idea began to form in her mind but she changed the subject.

"So why the visit?"

"To say you did okay at the hotel."

"I failed. A man was killed."

He ignored that statement.

"We have identified them. You want to know?"

She nodded.

"Not hard to trace. The woman who killed your Jerome is Jessica Crowne, daughter of Martina Crowne."

A big surprise.

"The cosmetics millionaire?"

"Million understates, billion would be more accurate."

"What does she want?"

He smiled at her for a full five seconds. He knows dammit, she thought.

"She is trying to find the members of a secret group. I'm not exactly sure yet who they are or where they live. Countess Pollan was in the group and from the photograph you took at Parker's house, we have now identified the location of another. They're somewhere near Hong Kong."

"What's the reason for our involvement?"

"Jessica and her gang have now killed two Omasor people. I'm not happy about that and intend to stop them. At the same time I also want to find out more about this group. Do you have any ideas?"

"I need time to think it through." She wasn't ready to share, at least for the moment.

"I understand. Selena will arrive in about an hour so you'll need to prepare for the trip."

"Nice to meet you Mr Jones," she lied.

"A pleasure, Ms Darmant."

He gave the smallest bow and left her thinking. He was leaving, she was thinking.

Chris rummaged through the information she now had. The basics were simple. A secret group existed that had some valuable possession. Countess Pollan had been a member and a clue must have been hidden in her papers that apparently pointed to a location near Hong Kong. Jessica Crowne was also following the trail with ruthless determination. What could this group have that she wanted so badly? It was difficult to believe that people with the immense wealth of Martina and Jessica Crowne would be running around killing people for simple financial gain. There must be something else.

The rummaging was interrupted when she noticed an envelope on the hall table. Her first thought was that John had left her a message but then she saw the Omasor name on the top right corner. Handwritten in the centre were the words 'EAT ME' except 'Eat' was crossed out and 'Read' substituted. Underneath this were the initials J. J.

Definitely curiouser.

Inside was a press cutting from that morning's London newspaper. The headline was 'New Sports Stadium'. A council chief was announcing a new multipurpose sports stadium in one of London's poorest areas and 90% of the funding was from a private donation that had already been deposited. Chris felt the tears coming. She cried for fully two minutes, the cutting still clutched in her hand.

Dabbing her eyes she found another slip of paper in the envelope. Just six handwritten lines.

'Why not just go for the Crownes?' asked the thinker.

'Crosswords,' replied the rabbit.

'Only if I'm angry,' said the thinker.

'No, crosswords. Fill in the answers you know and they will lead you to the ones you don't.'

'I'm late, I'm late,' cried the thinker.

'Yes, you need to get ready for Hong Kong. That's six across.'

Chris burnt the paper and prepared for the journey.

21

Alec sat uncomfortably in his office in Zurich. He could still feel the sting of Jessica's anger following his failure at Carney House. It had taken three hours before he recovered consciousness, struggled free from his bonds and released his companion.

Jessica had sent another team to the house the next morning, headed by Karmen and she had reported the exposed and now empty cavity in the fountain. Alec and his companion had been immediately summoned to Jessica's office where they found Karmen waiting with two men. He wouldn't forget the moment. No discussion at all. Karmen had pulled out a pistol and fired two shots. He had fallen to his knees, convinced he was about to die but both bullets had been for the man next to him.

Alec was convinced that his own survival was due only to his long relationship with Jessica. Now he had been directed to unravel the clues buried somewhere in the pile of papers and articles she had taken from Peter Parker. He was very determined not to fail again. There wouldn't be another chance.

He was sure there was something in the plaque. It had evaded all computer analysis using the usual ciphers and he realised that it also needed a set of keywords to unlock, keywords he hadn't yet found.

Forcing himself to relax, Alec started to go through the documents yet again but was now becoming convinced that they were meaningless. A housekeeping ledger, a bunch of invoices, a cookery book. He paused. This was wrong. One pint of salt. Impossible, impossible. He reached for his computer keyboard. A crack had opened and the rest should follow.

At the same moment that Alec was investigating salt, Chris was studying a set of maps and photographs.

"These pictures seem to have come from military satellites," she said without looking up.

"We have unusual resources," Selena responded.

They were travelling in a rented car through the streets of Hong Kong. The car rental clerk had turned to his associate and made a coarse observation about the two women, believing they only spoke English. Selena had responded fluently in Cantonese leaving him looking rather sheepish.

Sheep are not common in Hong Kong due to the lack of grazing areas. One enterprising businessman had experimented with a grass pasture on the top of a 26-storey office block but despite advertising brands such as 'Skywool' and 'Flock From The Top', the high-rise sheep experiment had failed, mainly because the animals kept threatening to jump unless their grass supply was upped.

Twelve minutes later Selena parked outside a pale blue house, large by Hong Kong standards.

"Selena," cried the woman who opened the door. They embraced and exchanged a long kiss, the shorter woman circling Selena's neck with her arms.

Chris wasn't embarrassed and certainly felt no envy. She had no particular attraction to women, nor most men. Love and sex only had walk on parts in her life. She hadn't slept with anyone for over four years and then it was a professor at her University. The physical event had been a failure on both sides and they spent most of the night discussing Socrates. She vaguely wondered what John Porter would be like in bed. Urgent and physical she guessed.

"Hello I'm Ella," the woman greeted her, post clinch.

"Chris Darmant."

Ella was slim, cropped brown hair and maybe mid-thirties.

"Come in and get comfortable, there's food waiting."

Food is an integral part of the cycle of nature. The principle is that what comes out will go in again but thankfully with a few events in between. In a consumer driven society, driving has replaced the cycling and we are left with what is known as 'negative equity'. With the use of inflows and outgoings, economists can run it up the flagpole, outside the box in some sort of ballpark. Doomsday theorists postulate that this will eventuate in a 'revolving door' syndrome, which is apparently the same as nature's cycle except faster.

After a freshening visit to the bathroom and a simple but filling Chinese meal, Chris relaxed in a chair. The room decor was so entirely European, she could have been in a middle-class residence in Germany.

Selena lounged back, eyes half closed as if meditating with Ella sitting at her feet, one arm lying across her thigh.

"We need to reach Wang Shu Island," Selena said.

Ella considered for a moment.

"It's a private island, about one hour's flight from here. Owned by a guy called Arthur Pierce, born in England I think. He's got businesses everywhere, worth billions. He's rarely seen and hardly ever photographed. The few people who've had contact with him say he's young, very polite but utterly ruthless. Visits to the island by invitation only, I believe. I assume you haven't got an invite."

"No."

"You'll need a boat or seaplane."

"Seaplane. We're in a hurry. I have a licence."

"I also understand the place is very well defended."

"We've got a layout." Chris passed her the pack of high-resolution photos. Superb quality, even individual bushes and trees were clearly visible.

The island was tiny, only about one kilometre across and dominated by a large white building at the north end with a small, single storey construction, obviously a guard post, at the southern edge. Next to this was a mini marina where three cruisers were berthed. A group of dark clothed figures stood near the cruisers.

Ella surveyed the pictures.

"A large residence with a separate security building. I guess about six or eight guards and you can see a lot of antennae. I'd assume electronic sensors."

She looked up. "Hey, these photos came from my old company."

Selena glanced at Chris. "Ella was CIA and knows one or two things."

"How did you guys meet?"

Ella grinned.

"She helped me once or twice on missions."

"Three. You forgot Vienna," Selena remarked.

You never forget Vienna. Serene, aloof and all-knowing in a gathering sea of polystyrene and saturated with a '50 years, that's nothing' attitude. A river runs through Vienna and those who know its name call it the Danube. Given that they have exactly the same number of vowels, it's often understandably confused with the Amazon. Fortunately there are a couple of ways to tell the difference, one of which involves crocodiles.

"I was thinking of landing well offshore then a small inflatable at night," said Selena.

"It would be safer to make the final approach underwater. The way it's set up they're sure to have heat and movement sensors."

Humming along at 6000 feet, Chris was poring over plans and photos in the cabin of the Mactor 831 seaplane, a reliable small craft capable of carrying up to six people or cargo. They had added extra fuel tanks for the journey, extending the range to more than 2000 miles as a safety measure.

Selena engaged the auto pilot and joined her.

"Time to get ready?" Chris asked.

Selena nodded and stripped of her tunic. Completely naked underneath and Chris couldn't help assessing her figure. Annoying. Couldn't find a fault. Gleaming dark skin, slim but round hips with a chest maybe a tad larger than average. Then something unexpected. Selena leaned across and kissed her cheek.

"Take care," she said softly.

Chris looked up, perhaps becoming immune to these surprises.

"I messed up at the hotel and don't plan a repeat," she responded positively, watching Selena pull on an insulated black skin suit.

Then she picked up her own suit and changed quickly, retaining her underwear and turning her back.

"I didn't expect modesty with your background," Selena remarked.

Chris fought down a blush. She was right. Like most athletes, she regarded her body as a form of mechanism but she just didn't like to be unclothed. Always been like that, even when young.

"I'm not auditioning as a lap dancer."

"Might need to sometime in your job. The news is that you have a good body. Humanity started naked, humanity decided to clothe themselves. Just another protocol we've created."

Chris glared at her. She sounded like a grandmother but just couldn't be older than mid-twenties, the same age as herself.

"That's like an advert for a nudist society."

Selena smiled radiantly.

"You need to know what we're looking for."

"That would help."

"It may well be a plaque like the one you photographed at Peter Parker's house but we want anything that carries either the crest of two eagles above six swords or the numbers two and six expressed in some way."

Selena returned to the pilot's seat and took manual control, steering a course that would set them down in the sea about five kilometres from the island. She switched off the engines for the last part of the descent. They had no definitive knowledge of the surveillance equipment on the island but traded the risk of detection against proximity.

The Mactor coasted to a halt in calm water. Chris slid open the cabin door and pushed out the inflatable after activating the air pump. This raft had been fitted with special modifications including satellite positioning and auto control that allowed it to be programmed to travel to any geographic point within range and arrive within a set time period. Its accuracy was naturally dependent on sea conditions but still effective within a four minute per hour average variance.

Averages are complex and misleading. For example, to calculate the average age of two people, you can deduct the age of the first from the second, divide this by two and add to the lowest. But what if the second is older? You then have what is known to mathematicians as a 'minus figure' (a minus was a Greek creature which once inhabited underground mazes). Best advice is to always say 'you look the same age' and one of the people will be on your side, particularly if they are mother and daughter.

They manoeuvred the inflatable to 300 metres from the island and fitted oxygen masks. Selena activated the programmed auto control to send the craft out to sea, wait for three hours then return to this exact location. That should give them adequate time to swim to the island, complete the search and return. At least, that was the plan.

Chris surfaced under the wooden pier of the marina after a comfortable swim in the warm, still waters. She jabbed a finger upwards when Selena appeared beside her to indicate the soles of a guard's shoes that were visible through the joints in the boarding. Selena pointed to the left and disappeared underwater with Chris following. No option as they were joined together with a plastic cord. The three boats were tethered together with their sterns against the pier and they came up again on the seaward side of the outer cruiser,

Selena unhooked their connecting rope and scaled a ladder fixed the side of the hull with Chris directly behind. The decks of all three boats were clear with no lights showing but two guards in dark caps and uniforms stood on the pier with their backs to the cruisers. A track led from the pier past the guard building and onwards to the house.

Selena moved quickly to the side of the wheelhouse that concealed them from the shore. They discussed a plan in whispers then opened their waterproof bags. Selena's contained a black tunic style suit and Chris had a similar dark blue outfit and they dressed as quickly as feasible in a semi crouched position. Silently crossing the three boats, Chris followed Selena to the side of the small building and walked round it to the track.

The guards turned at the sound of giggling to see two women walking towards them from the direction of the house.

"They said you'd show us your monitors," Selena said, prompting another outburst of giggles. She put one arm round her first guard's neck while the other stroked his thigh. Chris couldn't manage that but gingerly pressed against the other guard with her hip and put an arm round his waist.

"You must be from the house," murmured Selena's guard, his swarthy countenance revealing a conflict between desire and duty. As usual, desire won and he led them inside the building.

Just one large room with two other doors, both open. Through the first they could see a bathroom and the second led to what was obviously a sleeping area, judging from the sound of snoring that emerged. Chris held a finger to her lips and tiptoed across to close this door while Selena started to unbutton her top. Nature has clearly programmed the eyes of men to stare at naked breasts. The gaze of the guards transmuted to glaze as Chris came behind them and jabbed the needles simultaneously. They went down quickly and silently.

The sleeping quarters housed four slumbering figures and just a few seconds and four injections later, another eight hours had been added to their rest.

Selena checked the monitors that displayed views from all over the island.

"From now we'll just have to play it by ear," she remarked.

"I don't see any other guards. Could be more at the house."

Selena found sets of uniforms in a closet, selected one for size and then changed.

"I'm ready," Chris declared, relaxed but cautious. It had been much too easy so far.

They began a slow march up the pathway with Selena in the rear.

The entrance to the house had been converted to accommodate a cubicle where a guard sat, idly reading a newspaper. Bright fluorescent lighting bleached the area and Selena held back in the semi shadow. He peered at them, shielding his eyes and Chris stepped forward slightly to block his view.

"Look, I was just walking round the island when this man arrested me at gunpoint."

"You are a guest here?"

"Of course I'm a guest."

"Your name please."

"Victoria de Sett."

Secure in the belief that another guard was covering her, he turned to the wall telephone in the cubicle. Chris jabbed a needle into his neck and then arranged his unconscious body on the chair in a dozing posture.

Selena tried the door. Not locked. They entered into a spacious, brightly lit hallway. Then the noise of two wooden clubs striking two skulls and it went dark, very dark.

Chris regained consciousness. Intensive training for these situations ensured she didn't open her eyes immediately. She mentally checked her limbs. Her arms and legs were tied and she couldn't feel the touch of clothing. Her head was still painfully bruised. She raised her eyelids a fraction.

She was on a thick wooden board, tilted at an angle, her wrists and ankles enclosed with steel reinforced leather straps. Both arms were pinned that away from her body so that the hands were at chest level. Her feet were fixed apart with a ledge below the heels to prevent her sliding down. Other straps circled her neck and waist. The tunic had been removed leaving just her underwear.

Twisting her gaze without moving her head, she saw Selena, completely naked and tied to a similar slab to her left.

The glaring lights made it difficult to see clearly and she carefully inched her eyes completely open. A young woman walked into vision. Dark hair, large eyes and dressed in a simple white silk shirt and black trousers. A slim figure but displaying a substantial chest. Her face was all innocence except the eyes. Something in them. Something unpleasant. She spoke into a phone in a voice that was curiously childlike and very Californian.

"They've woken up but I'll wait until you get here, just like you told me."

Then she left. Two minutes later a small, scarred man entered with a syringe and came to Chris first. She felt the jab and then darkness again.

It was impossible to guess how much time had passed when she woke again. The scarred man was holding a steaming bowl in front of her and began to spoon a thick, meaty stew into her mouth. It tasted good and she was hungry. Another man was feeding Selena.

After they left, Chris looked across but Selena gave a tiny shake of the head. Video surveillance was certain.

A further hour passed before the woman returned, this time with a bespectacled, studious looking young man who had to be Arthur Pierce. They were followed by a guard.

"Ladies, you are fully aware what I wish to know," he announced in a very correct English voice, expressing every syllable.

Selena responded calmly.

"We're reporters. We were told to get an interview with the renowned Mr Pierce."

Chris admired the sincerity in her voice. She recognised the strategy and jumped into the conversation in the style of a nervous rookie.

"We know you don't normally give interviews, so we thought up a plan to reach you here. We were just going to knock on your door and ask you to talk to us. We thought you'd say yes after all the effort we made."

He considered for a moment. Words did not seem to come easily to him.

"Interview by the media? Of course that may be plausible. However, I do not believe reporters are in the habit of carrying syringes full of drugs to induce unconsciousness. What do you think Catherine?"

Chris noticed he showed no interest in their bodies. That was strange but reassuring. The woman turned to him. Now her eyes had joined the rest of her face in meek innocence.

"Please let me talk to them alone. Just a little gossip between girls."

She spoke like a young daughter to her father. He paused for a second, eyes fixed on her. Then he nodded.

"I understand. I will not remain."

His face showed that he did understand but didn't want to know. He left but the guard remained by the door. After his departure, Catherine smiled but her expression was changing. Evil back in her eyes. She moved close to Selena, lips nearly touching her ear.

"You'll tell me all about it, won't you?" she asked in her little girl voice.

"Yes of course I will but it's really horrible to be lying here without any clothes on. It would be much better if I was dressed nicely."

Chris realised that Selena was adopting the schoolgirl speak of the woman. Clever. Catherine looked up dreamily, apparently ignoring the response.

"There's a little bracelet on your wrist which sends a message to a dial on the wall. It says you're not telling the truth."

"I'll tell you, I was only hired for this job," Chris called.

The girl moved over to her and she felt a kiss on her cheek. Catherine giggled.

"What's your name?"

"Chris Darmant."

She saw the girl's eyes flicking to the wall behind her.

"It's nice to talk to a woman. I usually have men in here."

Chris didn't want to think about that.

"Look, I'm happy to tell everything. I just want to get out."

"Why have you two girls come here?"

"We were hired by a bank. They wanted us to look into some suspicious transactions by a man named Lin Po and Mr Pierce's name came up in some of the papers. They tried the usual routes and failed so they sent us to talk to him personally. We're from the Adams Agency."

Catherine looked up.

"The little dial says you're lying."

"Then it must be faulty."

"Mmm, really it said you told the truth. Maybe it has gone wrong. It's a silly story and I've never heard of this Lin Po."

Chris thought quickly. In hostage training she had perfected a natural talent for controlling her pulse and perspiration to fool lie detectors, but her fabrication was hanging by a thread.

"Lin Po is maybe better known as Chen Kwang Chai."

She said the first name that came into her mind, one of the most prominent financial powers in the area with an international reputation.

Catherine hesitated.

"I think I must leave you for a little bit."

"I can tell you more about him." Chris didn't want the facts checked before she found a way to free herself.

"You don't need to do that. He works for Mr Pierce."

Chris cursed silently as Catherine continued.

"Anyway, we girls can have some fun together later. You look so nice lying there and I think the guards would really like to come and be friends with you. And I can watch."

She left. Just the guard remained, in the shadows by the door.

Chris pouted as sexily as she could. When strapped out nearly naked with arms and legs apart, there were very few female tricks to use. She was also definitely not an expert in enticement.

"Could you just loosen my arms a little?"

A last try.

She was surprised when the guard moved, walking round behind her, out of sight. Then he was standing over Selena, his back to Chris. She saw him lean forward and whisper to her. Then he pulled a knife from his belt but his body masked his actions. Suddenly he was gone, closing the door silently behind him.

"Nice trick with the lie detector."

Selena was sitting up, slicing her ankle straps with the knife. She quickly cut Chris free.

"Who the hell was that?"

"Don't ask."

"OK, I won't. Now we need clothes."

Selena handed Chris small metal box from a shelf.

"Stand behind the door and use this."

Less than two minutes later two guards entered and three minutes after that they were lying naked and insensible on the floor.

"How did you know they were coming?" asked Chris as she adjusted the uniform to fit as well as possible.

"Our friend said he'd send them."

"I'll be asking later. So how do we get out?"

"We have a job to finish first. Being tied up naked like a bimbo in a bondage peepshow has made me a little annoyed."

Chris pushed back an errant strand of blonde hair. She envied Selena who appeared to have just emerged from a beauty parlour. Then she saw something else. A cold fire burning in her eyes. Perhaps more than a little annoyed.

Selena led the way down the corridor, kicking open the first door to reveal two bespectacled men sitting in front of computers and furiously entering data from piles of invoices stacked beside them. She moved like lightning, hitting their jaws with the edge of her hand. As they slumped unconscious over their desks, Chris began to wonder what she was like when really angry.

The other rooms in the corridor were empty of people but one contained a digital camera, which Selena tossed to Chris.

"Photograph anything with the crest, documents, paintings, ornaments, whatever."

The end door led to the entrance hall they had so briefly seen before. It was also empty but they could hear the sounds of voices coming from closed double doors on the opposite side. Selena was transparently not in a mood to wait. She burst through the doors to reveal Pierce seated at a large desk talking on the phone while Catherine sat on a leather chair beside him. Surprise and fear, a dangerous couple, entered their expressions. Catherine started to reach inside her coat.

Selena was already next to her.

"You've been a naughty girl," she said, twisting the girl's hand and taking the pistol she was holding. Then she swung it quickly, twisting her wrist so the butt cracked the side of the woman's head. Catherine went down limply.

Pierce was frozen, phone still held to his ear.

"I will return your call," he said calmly, replacing the handset.

Selena turned an icy gaze to him.

"Arthur. I'm sure you'll allow me to call you Arthur. You can assume I am a little irritated. We came on a little visit to see your collection and were treated disgracefully. I am very much in the mood to take you and your woman to the comfortable couches you so thoughtfully provided for us and then show you my own hospitality."

"My dear lady, I...."

She levelled her gun to his forehead.

"Do not interrupt me, Arthur. I'm not in the mood. Now you will give us a guided tour of your collection and we will photograph it. If I see the slightest sign of bad manners I will commence to shoot at any part of you I deem superfluous, starting there."

She pointed the gun at his groin. He looked resigned rather than frightened and Chris recognised his character, one she had come across before. Shrewd, calculating with a vein of ruthlessness. Very dangerous, especially in his present passive mode.

"Where do you wish to commence?" he asked.

"In this room. We will follow you."

Chris noticed that Catherine had made an abnormally fast recovery, propping herself unsteadily against the desk. Perhaps Selena hadn't hit her as hard as it looked. She motioned for her to join Pierce and the tour began.

The procession went from paintings to ornaments to books and manuscripts. Fortunately, the digital camera was loaded with an 800 picture capacity card and Chris photographed everything.

As they continued through the house, guards and servants appeared but Pierce waved them away. They returned to their starting point less than an hour later. Many rooms had merited only a cursory look including employees' accommodation, kitchens and bathrooms whilst the contents of the remainder were rapidly photographed.

Now Pierce stood by the fireplace with Catherine beside him. There was an aura about them, an air of assured superiority that remained unshaken by their predicament.

"We haven't seen your safe," Selena observed coldly, mood unchanged

"You examined it in the office."

"Not a safe, the safe."

"I don't have another one."

Selena's sighed, reached out and ripped open the front of Catherine's top. She pulled out a knife and cut through the bra. The huge breasts were amazingly firm and Chris was surprised to see they were natural.

"I showed you mine, now it's your turn," Selena said, holding the knife under the flesh mountains. Catherine's eyes wavered between contempt and hatred and settled on loathing.

"There's nothing of value in it," declared Pierce, still no tension in his voice.

He moved to the fireplace and pressed the nose of a bronze fairy ornamenting the surround. A small panel to the left opened to reveal a safe embedded in the wall. Keying a combination, he opened the door.

Chris moved forward. The top item inside was the engraved plaque with a small crest at the top. Two eagles above six swords. She made no sign and moved her body to conceal her actions.

"Nothing much here, just a couple of documents to photograph."

Every reason to mislead. From behind her, the others saw only the flashes of the camera and after a few minutes, Chris pushed the door closed.

"I think that's it."

She noted the slightest sign of relief on Pierce's face. He believed he had won his gamble but didn't realise the race was fixed.

Selena glanced at her.

"Now we'll go to the plane," she said.

"Shouldn't we borrow a cruiser?" asked Chris.

"No. Mr Pierce has offered us his aircraft, haven't you Arthur?"

She wasn't looking for a reply.

The latest version of the Price-Cutler 42C seaplane floated next to the cruisers. Pierce and Catherine led a procession followed by Selena and Chris with a group of guards and other employees trailing uncertainly about twenty metres behind.

"If we let them go the guards will fire at us," said Chris

"True. We'll take the girl."

"Why not Pierce?"

"She's prettier."

Chris gave her a look but didn't argue and pushed Catherine into the cabin. Just before she closed the door, Selena turned to Pierce who was standing placidly on the wooden pier.

"Expect a visit quite soon from others. Not as friendly." she shouted.

The cabin was sumptuously fitted out. Two pairs of leather seats with computer monitors on tables in front of each pair. Toilets and a kitchen area were to the rear of the plane. Chris hunted through cupboards to find a roll of reinforced plastic tape and used it to bind Catherine's arms and legs.

"You're not my friends now," the girl said sullenly.

"I'll get over it," responded Chris.

Now Catherine's face displayed pure hatred.

"I'll remember how nasty you were to me."

She spat out the words through pouting lips. Chris stuck a strip of tape over her mouth, ignoring the vicious look in her eyes. Then she began to walk forward to the cockpit but Selena held out an arm.

"Wait here and watch her, I'll join you when we land."

She slid through the cockpit door and Chris heard it lock. Then she heard voices. Another subject for later discussion.

Arthur Pierce developed a smile as he saw the plane lift off. They had apparently not been interested in the plaque and there had been no questions about the Octagon. He convinced himself that they were probably customs or tax inspectors looking for anomalies but was confident that his business records were scrupulously maintained. Although angered by the failure of his men, he believed his real secrets were secure.

The head of security ran up to him.

"Do you want us to shoot?"

Pierce shook his head.

"No, let them go. I have decided to relocate. I want the helicopter here in one hour. All my personal collection must be crated immediately and loaded on board. The business records will be collected soon afterwards."

"And Ms Bell?"

"I anticipate their destination is Hong Kong and they will release her there. I will instruct my local people to find her."

"When will you return?"

"I will not be returning. This is a permanent relocation."

In less than 15 minutes, Pierce departed in a helicopter with every item related to the Octagon and his other personal belongings. Four hours after that, a seaplane took off from Wang Shu, loaded with the business records.

Under one hour later, another plane arrived and scattered little canisters all over the island. Then it landed, disgorging 20 men in military dress and wearing gas masks. When the craft took off, it left a small island covered with rubble and incinerated bodies. Arthur Pierce did not tolerate failure.

Toleration is a virtue that everyone should cultivate. It's the stupid, ignorant, intolerant people that cause all the problems.

22

Hong Kong to London. Relaxing in her executive seat, Chris glanced across at Selena who looked as she always did. Perfect. Her hair immaculate, eyes bright and full of vitality.

"We must have a conversation."

"If you like," Selena responded with a slightly amused look.

"I need more information. There's a lot I haven't been told. To start, I'd like to know more about Omasor."

"It's simple. Jerome Jones is the head and I run it."

"You said I wasn't your choice when I got the job."

"Jerome occasionally expresses a preference."

"Tell me about the real Jerome Jones."

Selena paused, her gaze wandering to other pastures.

"No. You may get to know him or maybe not."

She was obviously not open for discussion on that subject.

"What does Omasor stand for?"

"It's not an acronym."

Chris waited for more but Selena simply smiled.

"So who was that guard who released you on the island?"

"You don't need to know."

"That's not helpful. It's difficult to do a job without knowing things like that."

"Tough. Try harder."

Chris pursed her lips.

"Okay. What about you? What's your background?"

"I have been with the company for some time. I was chosen by Jerome."

"Do you have family?"

"I was born in Morocco as you call it. My parents were killed when I was a young child. I married at 17 and had a young son. He was killed in a fire and my husband died trying to save him."

"I'm really sorry."

"Time heals. Eventually I understood that everything that happens, good and bad, is part of something far greater than we will ever know."

"I lost my parents. Car crash when I was 17."

"I know."

"At first I was totally shattered. I kept thinking 'why me?' Then one morning I woke up and found I could live with the situation. I realised that their deaths had been somehow part of a big tapestry, just like you said. I don't know what the big plan is but I lost the fear of death."

"There is a legend of 'He who comes in the night' in Mayan philosophies."

"Like Santa Claus?"

Selena laughed.

"He's not all good and not all bad. Shows you things that cannot be seen in daylight."

"He must have come to me that night."

They sat in silent remembrance for a minute. Not grieving but joyful. Then Chris moved to a new theme.

"Would you mind if I asked how old you are?"

"No."

Chris sighed.

"Okay, how old are you, Selena?"

"That's a stupid question that I won't answer."

"You're not with any man now?"

"No."

"Something you said, I wondered if…"

"You were curious to know if I now preferred women. I have slept with both and they are equally enjoyable with the right person. Different but just as pleasant or unpleasant."

"Sorry. It's not really anything to do with me."

"You're wondering if I will try to seduce you?"

"No. Well, I suppose yes."

"I hadn't considered it. Do you want me to?"

She leant over and kissed Chris long and softly on the lips then shook her head, smiling.

"I prefer to keep business and pleasure separate."

Chris hadn't resisted, it was the first time she had been kissed like that by a woman. Nothing stirred within. Nature had apparently immunised her against all romantic and sexual desires.

"I have a boyfriend, sort of."

"John Porter? You've never slept with him."

"That's private. You can't know anyway."

"Omasor does not employ people without knowing everything about them. Private does not exist. You do not have a job, you have a dedication."

Chris felt anger rising.

"And I can also choose to leave."

"Yes, any time."

Not the response Chris had expected.

"I was sent a contract but didn't read it through. Do I give a months notice?"

"No. You can go immediately if you want."

"Just like that? No repercussions?"

"Absolutely. I will then decide if you need to be killed. It all depends on how much you know."

"What? You can't kill someone for leaving their job."

"Dedication, not job. Your choice."

"I wasn't told this when you interviewed me," Chris said icily, expression rigid.

"No. You should have asked. I see you have a temper. That's interesting and I started it all by mentioning John Porter."

Chris wound down quickly, cursing her stupidity. Selena was manipulating the conversation. It was a character test and she needed to be smarter.

"You're right, I've never slept with John," she said calmly.

"Jerome told me he interrupted you in your flat."

"That Jerome gets me irritated. How many impersonators are there?"

"I honestly don't know."

"Really?"

"Yes, really. Does it matter?"

"No, I suppose not," laughed Chris.

She began to warm to Selena but still felt she was only scratching the surface.

At the moment that Chris laughed, a cell phone rang in one of the luxury offices of a modern complex in California.

Jim Fischer knew it was the Octagon phone and very unlikely to be good news. Now he was aware that other people were attempting to obtain the secrets of the Octagon and that made him nervous. By comparison, business was easy. In over a century of life, he'd learned everything about finance and commerce. Bartering for a lower price, closing deals and understanding financial liabilities. He also had Valla, the best business brain he had ever come across. Sure, he had enemies but also employed a massive number of security people who protected him everywhere. But he couldn't delegate the Octagon's business. That had to be handled personally with only Valla to help.

He clicked the handset.

"Fischer here."

"Arthur Pierce. I'm afraid I have some bad news."

Pierce recounted the events on the island, which only served to increase Jim's consternation level to a new height. He made a big effort to control his voice.

"So these women could well have been government tax people?"

"That is a definite possibility. However, I now cannot be sure of my security arrangements."

Jim paused. He understood Pierce's unspoken request. The man wanted to join him in California. That might not be so bad. Pierce was smart and Jim would have someone to share the responsibility. Then another thought.

"You say you haven't seen Catherine since the women kidnapped her?"

"No. I have a large team scouring Hong Kong as we speak. They have found the aircraft but she wasn't inside."

"You have to consider the possibility that she's dead."

No histrionics, no change in Pierce's tone.

"Of course. I will then select another Secondary. Catherine has been with me for well over a century but I had four other women prior to her appointment."

"Right. Give me five minutes and I'll call you back."

"Very well."

Jim sat back in his chair to think. If he invited Pierce to come over then maybe Catherine would be with him. Good or bad? He just couldn't forget the bedroom in England when she was on her knees, looking up with her innocent eyes. Offering herself. She was as crazy as hell but he wanted her badly. His naturally organised brain began to construct flowcharts. Pierce could come to stay as his guest and subsequently buy up some big property in the area. They would work together. That was something that had to happen anyway in 2019, so why not now? If Pierce came alone, Jim could have some input in the selection of his new Secondary. He'd already picked out a good candidate, a young blonde biology graduate named Della. He'd slept with her many times now and wanted to continue that experience. Jim had considered arranging Valla's death and replacing her with the blonde but her intelligence was irreplaceable, even if her performance in bed left a lot to be desired. After 2019, he could have the best of both of them. Jim's plan clarified. Invite Pierce. If Catherine did turn up, he had to have her, at least once. Then he would get his security people to kill her. Either way, Pierce would be looking for a new assistant.

He picked up the phone and clicked a stored number.

"Pierce speaking."

"Jim again. I just need to run through an idea in my mind. I'm proposing you come over to California. Stay with me initially and then get one or two nice mansions to live here. I can recommend a few."

"That concept has considerable appeal."

"I've got a big security team. You'll have a dozen bodyguards as soon as you step off the plane."

"I think I may avail myself of your offer. I own a fleet of aircraft and will use one of them."

They spent some time discussing travel logistics and Jim became reassured by the imminent new partnership. He felt he could trust and confide in Pierce although he didn't seem like someone a person could ever get close to.

"The security people and the shipping team will meet you at LA airport. Bring all the possessions you want and I'll arrange for you to travel in a limousine behind the vans."

Pierce sounded satisfied.

"That appears to be ideal. I did have one minor consideration. With the current level of danger, would it be safer for Ms Duckworth to join us?"

Jim paused.

"Perhaps. Let me phone her and get back to you."

Jim ended the call and stretched back in his chair again. Mary Duckworth? She wasn't a companion he would choose. More like a sad little hippie from the 1960's. Something distant about her, not in the real world. He guessed she had shut herself away from society, probably living at a mountain retreat in some remote part of the planet. Jim now knew he was the youngest of the three Primaries, born nearly 250 years after Pierce but he felt he could dominate that little guy in spectacles. Not so Mary. She was like a pedantic grandmother. No, Jim would suggest the idea of a move to her but do nothing to encourage it.

He pulled a file of papers from a locked drawer in his desk and pressed the intercom for Valla. She entered within 30 seconds.

"Yes Jim?"

"Take a seat. I want to talk to Octagon business."

He recounted his conversation with Pierce and passed to his notes for her to make all the shipping and security arrangements. Then he pushed his hands behind his head.

"Okay, Valla. Testing your brain again. What other action do you suggest we take?"

He usually phrased it like that. Every time he needed the guidance of her impressive intellect but wasn't going to admit it. He was well aware she knew the strategy but frankly didn't care.

Valla paused before replying.

"Of course I agree that Mr Pierce should come here. These other people have discovered his location and it will be much safer with our security. I suggest it's not good for Ms Duckworth to join us. As far as we know, her residence is still a secret, even to us. Taking a global view, it's too risky for all the members of the Octagon to be in the same place. A natural disaster that could wipe all of us out and there must be at least a couple left to take over in 2019."

"That's my thinking exactly."

It wasn't but he had to say it.

"My suggestion is to set up a team to investigate these intrusions. With all our combined wealth and power, we could employ thousands of people to find out what's happening and why. At the moment, we're in a stupid situation of not even knowing the motivation of these people."

"Right. Go on."

Valla smiled correctly.

"We now have several events to consider. First, the attempted robbery when the Countess and her Secondary were murdered. As you know, I've had teams working on it and everything indicates that the thieves were just a professional gang who knew nothing of the Octagon."

"Sure. That we have already established."

"Subsequently, a man claiming to be the cousin of the Countess turns up and fixes an auction to sell off her house contents. As our people discovered, he was actually a stooge, pulled in from one of the Chicago gangs."

"By the guy called Vistan."

"Right. We made the link. One of the thieves was his son. Soon after the auction, Vistan himself was killed in a gunfight. That's the third event. Media said it was an armed robbery but it couldn't be coincidence."

"So maybe Vistan arranged the auction as compensation for his son's death. But who killed him and why?"

"That's not clear. It could just have been some criminal gang but I think not."

"You're saying it was connected to the Countess?"

"Yes, I'm sure. Then we have the two people that Catherine came across at Carney House."

"I assumed they were just caretakers, guarding the place."

"No. Genuine guards would have turned on the lights, made a ruckus and called the police. From what Catherine said, these two tried to ambush her. I think they were outsiders."

"You mean other people trying to break in? Maybe just common burglars."

"That's not logical. This was well after the auction and they'd have known that everything worthwhile had been sold off."

"The last event would be these two women getting into Pierce's place in Hong Kong?"

"Yes. That's the most overt action to date and confirms to me that there's a link."

"So you're proposing a task force to locate and stop these people?"

"I am. I think I know the sequence of events but need to confirm it. We have to keep the details inside the Octagon so we can use our independent agents but give them only a limited brief. Our security is already under potential threat and we can't risk any of our secrets getting out."

"I see your angle. This is a job for the Secondaries. You can team up with John Porter and maybe Catherine, if she's still with us. Where do we base the team?"

Valla shrugged.

"No question. It has to be in England. The location of Countess Pollan, the auction and also the pair who visited Hong Kong appeared to be from there."

Jim nodded. The woman was smart, irreplaceable. Pity she was so damn frigid.

"Okay, set it up. I'll fix it with Pierce and Duckworth."

He smiled as she left. He'd handled that well. Now for the hippie woman.

Mary Duckworth answered after four rings.

"Hello Jim."

How did she know it wasn't Pierce?

"Hi, Mary. I need to talk through some things with you. Pierce has had a problem."

He went through the story again, embellishing it with Valla's comments and proposals as if they were his own. That was a regular habit.

"So Mary. First off, you have an open invite to come to live in my area but I'm not recommending it."

"I will remain in my present location," she responded firmly and he sensed her resentment at his presumed dominance.

"That's fine. Second, the task force to investigate. I'm pushing for that, makes good sense."

A pause before she replied.

"I find the idea acceptable. You will let me know personally of the headquarters location in England and I will instruct Porter accordingly."

Jim didn't much like the tone and had to massage his esteem by consigning her to the stubborn old lady category. Someone to patronise without them realising.

"That's good, Mary. As I said, Arthur Pierce has already agreed and Catherine will join the team if and when she surfaces."

"That one is not stable. I recommend you do not get further involved with her. She has not come to terms with either her sexuality or adult society."

More irritation. How the hell did she know this stuff?

"I've been around long enough to recognise that. If she's still alive then maybe you and I will sort something out before 2019."

Her tone softened.

"Perhaps we will, Jim. Goodbye."

"I'll be in touch. Talk soon."

She ended the call.

Jim selected Pierce's number again.

Same precise response. Jim filed him firmly as a stiff, correct Englishman. Not much imagination but pretty steady and reliable.

"I recommended to Mary that she doesn't move here and she's agreed."

"You recommended? Why?"

Jim explained, again using Valla's words as his own. Assured now. He was beginning to feel increasingly certain that he would be the unquestioned leader of the planet after 2019.

Mary Duckworth clicked off the phone and looked across at John. She didn't use cosmetics, her fresh young face glowing naturally within the frame of her long blonde hair. The room was air-conditioned but a sheen of perspiration glistened on her forehead.

"That was Jim Fischer. There's been an attack on Arthur Pierce's headquarters."

"What happened?"

"Two women got into his place and held Arthur and Catherine hostage. They forced him to show them his private papers and took photographs. They didn't take anything and Arthur doesn't think they were looking for Octagon items."

"Took nothing? Not just thieves then."

"It is possible they were customs or tax agents."

"But you don't think so?"

"No, John. I am certain there is a major problem. You will be part of a team to investigate these occurrences and you'll be going to England to join Valla and Catherine."

"You said Catherine was missing."

"She is not dead. I feel it. Be very careful of her."

John smiled.

"She's just like a kid, except about 150 years old."

"That is why she is dangerous. After all this time, the Octagon is under threat and we are so close to our purpose."

"Don't worry. All shall be well," said John. He didn't believe it.

23

Karmen relaxed in the big chair and closed her eyes. She still held the gun but that was unnecessary now that the red haired woman was tied to the bed. She felt comfortable, almost amused to see the childish, dark haired girl enjoy herself. Not hard to please.

Karmen had arrived in Hong Kong just as Chris and Selena were leaving to fly back to England. As soon as Alec identified Wang Shu Island as the residence of the Octagon members, she had informed all Jessica's agents in the area. One of them had observed the seaplane returning from the island. They knew the craft belonging to Arthur Pierce who owned Wang Shu and recognised Chris and Selena from identity pictures Jessica had issued. They had been smart enough not to follow them but concentrate on the girl who had been found tied up on the plane. She had been tailed to a small hotel.

Karmen had arrived a few hours later and despite the description she had been given, found the girl's appearance surprising. Beautiful face, exceptional figure with an unusually large chest. Almost the opposite of her own body. But the affinity was instant. Karmen well understood Catherine's childish desires to inflict pain on others. It had been very simple to take the girl to one of Jessica's properties in the area and then procure some new friends for her to play with. Very easy to make this girl happy.

And Catherine had told her everything. About the Octagon, the other members, the Blessing. That information had already been transmitted to Jessica.

Karmen heard a loud giggle. Then a scream of pain. She opened her snake eyes. So gratifying to see a child at play.

Jerome Jones quickly scanned through the photos Chris had taken on Wang Shu Island. He enlarged and printed pictures of the plaque. Just a minute to key into the computer.

The top part appeared to be meaningless.

'Ages Flowed

Far Past The

Storm Over Us

And So By This

I Understand

By Sun And Moon

Abide By Stars

Betraying

Any Goodness

Or Past Regret

The End

Comes Once

Or Not'

On the lower section another Latin motto was engraved. 'Esto Sol Testis', translatable as 'the sun shall be our witness'.

Selena entered his office, shimmering with vitality as usual.

"You wanted me?"

"I have the next location. The place is Asuncion, Paraguay and there's a name, Duckworth," he said.

"I'm ready to go immediately."

"No. Just Chris this time. I'd like you to clear up the Edinburgh case. That shouldn't take more than a day or two."

"Who will be with her?"

"Someone I think she'll like."

"Careful you don't look after her too much. A weakness that could be used against you. I remember that Venezuelan girl you were so friendly with two years ago. I actually had to get photos of her selling the cocaine shipment before you believed me. You've never told me what you did about her."

"When you showed me the prints, I'd just returned from Jamaica. I was with her there."

"Lovers rendezvous?"

He didn't smile.

"I took her for a boat trip. Beautiful sea, clear as blue crystal. I shot her. Tied her body to an old anchor and pushed her over."

"So she was dead when you saw the photos. You were playing with me again, Jerome. You know I don't appreciate that."

"That makes it irresistible. I needed information from her. You'll recall I sent you to Berlin soon afterwards?"

"The perverts who took those kids? That was related?"

"The girl was involved with their financial operation. She told me about it in bed on the cruiser. I killed her the next morning. After her body was pulled under, the sea remained sparkling clear as if nothing had transpired."

Selena smiled without humour.

"I'd like to sleep with you. Just once."

"Who knows what will happen?" remarked Jerome Jones, dismissively.

The lounge of the Grand Diamond Palace Royal hotel in Hong Kong made luxury seem commonplace. An army of waiters hovered, looking for the slightest motion from any of the guests immersed in the deep white leather chairs. Not recommended for the financially challenged.

Arthur Pierce looked across at Catherine with a face that showed no indication of his annoyance. He had expected her to be waiting for him at his Hong Kong residence but the servants there had not seen her. Now, after four days, she had finally appeared at the hotel.

His agents had reported seeing her leave the seaplane. Using some excuse, her two abductors had sent a harbour official to the craft and he had freed her from the tape bonds. Although detained briefly by the police, she had explained the situation as a practical joke and was soon released. Then she had disappeared and this angered him. His agents and contacts had searched throughout the area without success.

Now she was smiling at him with wide, innocent eyes.

"I wasn't sure when you'd come so I hid myself until you arrived."

"You're not being honest, Catherine."

Her eyes lowered.

"No, I must tell the truth. I was ashamed."

"Why would you be ashamed?"

"I wanted to capture those girls to make you happy and I tracked them to a little flat in Tuen Mun district. I tried to surprise them but that dark haired woman tricked me again. They tied me up and did some really horrible things to me. Girl things you know. They went out but left a knife on the bed and I managed to use it to cut the ropes. Then I hid myself until I knew you were here. I try to be a good girl but you're the only one who looks after me."

Her eyes began to moisten.

"What is the address of this flat?"

She gave him the details and he made a telephone call to his main agent in the New Territories, instructing him to check immediately. Then he turned back to her.

"Did you discover anything new from them?"

"No, they didn't talk in front of me. I was tied to the bed all the time. It was really awful. How can I make it up to you?"

Pierce felt no sympathy but took pleasure from her subservience.

"I have had further discussions with the other Primaries and we have formulated our plans. I will move to the USA where I am assured the security is more than adequate and I will remain there at least as long as this danger to us exists. You will return to England to join the other two Secondaries, Mr Porter and Ms Toreus. Your joint task is to investigate these attacks on the Octagon, to discover the identity of our assailants and recommend a course of action."

"John is a lovely boy and Valla, yes, she's nice too."

Catherine's eyes betrayed the last statement as a lie but Pierce didn't see it.

"Report to me each day by telephone."

"Yes I promise. Are you going soon?"

"I have chartered a plane to leave in the morning and you will depart tomorrow evening," he instructed, handing her the flight tickets.

"And your Octagon things, are they safe?"

"They are under guard at our residence here."

"I'll go to watch over them tonight. We mustn't let anyone even look at them now."

"Perhaps you're right. I believe the ladies were released on the island by someone impersonating a guard and I now have no confidence in our security procedures."

"I'll look after your things, I'll be good."

The childish talk never seemed to irritate Pierce, she was like an errant daughter to him. But the year 2019 was approaching and it would be time to lie with her, to procreate. He had no sexual desires for Catherine. In fact he had not experienced sex for well over 200 years, long before he had appointed her. His mission was not to be corrupted by carnal pleasures, the mindless convulsions of the flesh. Perhaps he would replace her with another woman before the time arrived. Someone whose body he could endure to allow his bloodline to populate the new world.

An hour after Catherine left, Pierce received a call from his agent. An armed team had been sent to the flat she had identified. It was empty but they'd found a dishevelled bed with cut ropes still tied to it. Pierce ended the call with some satisfaction. Catherine seemed to have told the truth and he wanted to believe that. He couldn't know that Karmen had invented the story for Catherine to use and set up the flat to support it.

Catherine sat contentedly in the rear seat of a taxi on her way to the Pierce home for her night vigil. Pleased, very pleased with herself. She was convinced she was special, picked out by an angel from everyone in the world to live forever. All the other stupid people would be dead soon and that was good. Just one nasty cloud. She hated the idea that Pierce would still be there in 2019. She knew he didn't like her, didn't want to do nice things with her however much she tried to please him. She also knew he had arranged the killing of every boy she had slept with. He shouldn't have done that.

Her new friends had promised she could choose anyone she wanted to play with and they didn't care if she killed someone she didn't like. They were nice to her. For the first time in over a century, she had a little secret and it was exciting.

24

John and Valla had rented a small unobtrusive house in a commuter village 40 miles west of London as a base of operations. A team of workers had been employed to convert one room into an office with electronic links to agents worldwide. Now the remains of lunch had been cleared and they faced each other across the dining-room table, her teacup sitting alongside his coffee mug.

Valla was all business, intellect and rationale. She had amassed five top degrees with the highest grades in subjects ranging from Business Studies to French History. John found her easy to talk to and rated her an excellent choice for the Octagon.

"I trust you and I'm pleased we're working together. How do you feel about me?" he asked.

She laughed, her nose crinkling in a very attractive way.

"You're okay, for an old man."

"I was born in 1950, older than you?"

It was impossible to tell, she could have just emerged from university.

"Hey, I was born the same year."

"Then you're not bad for an old woman. How did you come to join?"

"I met Jim when I was 19 at a science convention in Ohio. He took me to dinner and, well, it just went from there. What about you?"

"I was 28 and going nowhere. I'd been loafing around the beaches with the surfing crowd for ten years and just didn't know what to do with the rest of my life. I ended up drifting round South America. Then one day I wandered into Mary's bookshop, I still don't know why I went in but you can certainly say it changed my life. I didn't leave the building for a week."

He paused for a second.

"I mean that she gave me a job in the shop."

Valla laughed again.

"That's okay, I understand. You are cute you know. But don't worry, I'm really very happy with Jim."

Not the truth but the right message for this conversation.

"He seems okay. Level headed and knows what he's doing."

Valla knew that was the image Jim projected. She also knew the ruthless streak beneath it. Merciless and unrelenting. She was well aware he employed a secret group of so-called security people. He had never told her about them but she knew. Knew what they did. Knew how he gave them instructions on a dedicated phone. Knew they were employed to murder people. Kill those that caused Jim any problems in business or personal life.

"Yes, he's smart and approachable," she responded.

John looked across at her, blue eyes sharp and clear.

"You sure you're happy with him?"

"Careful John, I see brain gearing to groin. I might be over 50 but I've only ever slept with three men."

He gave a youthful grin.

"Isn't it great? We've got all the knowledge and experience of half a century with the bodies of kids. Immune to illness and almost immortal."

Valla didn't return the smile.

"Do you ever think about 2019? Ever since I joined Jim in the Octagon, I was imagining what the other members would be like. Two already dead, so there are just six of us left, unless the Primaries decide to invite another couple. Now I've met all the founders of our new world."

"Disappointed or impressed?"

"An honest answer?"

"Yes, sure. We're too old to mess around here."

"Okay. Mary seems all right and I like you but don't feel so good about the rest."

"I agree absolutely. You know, we really think the same way. Got a lot in common."

Valla smiled but not inside. That had been a lie. She read it in his eyes. Been here so many times before with so many different men. Unfortunately, he was using the same tactics. Just wanted her body, not her mind, not her as a person.

"I guess we may have similar ideas about some things," she responded, taking the middle road.

The spark in his eyes subsided and he checked his watch.

"I need to get to the airport and collect Catherine," he said.

Valla made a face.

"She is a little unusual, don't you think?"

He shrugged.

"Seems okay to me. We need some strong types in the Octagon now we're under threat."

Valla watched him leave. Disappointing, disappointed.

Delayed flight and it was late when they arrived back at the house. Catherine ignored Valla's chilly greeting and embraced her, kissing her cheeks but then concentrated on John. Her hands were forever touching his arm, her eyes repeatedly flashing towards him. He seemed obsessed with her or more precisely, her chest.

Valla felt uncomfortable. Despite reservations, she didn't dislike John and this woman-child seemed intent on disrupting their relationship. Try to break the enchantment.

"I think we should postpone discussions until the morning. I'm sure Catherine is tired after the journey," she proposed firmly and the others agreed.

Valla lounged uncomfortably in bed, mind still active. The Blessing had reduced the sleep she needed to just three or four hours and many of her nights were spent working through. She turned and found herself facing Catherine. The girl was dressed in something short and flimsy that barely covered her vast chest.

"I'm scared. Can I stay with you tonight?" she asked in her little girl voice.

Without waiting for an answer she slid onto the bed. Valla felt a heavy breast pressed against her and a hand resting on her leg.

Catherine puts her lips close.

"Friends should keep together for safety."

The fingers were moving, caressing softly.

Valla sat up, pushing the hand away.

"No. We're not friends, we're associates. Go back to your bed now."

Catherine pulled the duvet down to reveal her nightdress had fallen open, a view that would have sold tickets in a monastery. The faint light caught the wetness on her lips.

"Don't be nasty to me, I really want to stay with you."

She spread her hands under her breasts pushing them upwards.

Valla got out of the bed.

"Go now, Catherine. We'll talk in the morning"

The girl's expression changed to a venomous pout.

"You're not nice to me. I don't like you now."

She left the bed, walked to the door and turned.

"You'll be sorry," she said with an acid smile.

When Valla reached the kitchen the next morning she found John already brewing coffee. She had decided not to mention the events of the night. The girl was immature and unbalanced, strange for someone of her advanced age. A bad selection for the Octagon, a very dangerous choice.

"Morning," he grinned cheerfully, raising her spirits.

She had just finished a muesli breakfast and was sipping coffee when Catherine entered.

"Good morning Valla, morning John. It's a lovely day."

Dark suit, simple gold necklace and all the cosmetics. She seemed ready for an evening at a five-star restaurant. John rose wide-eyed from his chair.

"You look terrific," he said redundantly.

Then the doorbell rang.

"Don't worry, it's for me," said Catherine quickly.

She left the room and returned waving a courier envelope. Didn't mention that she had given the driver a small package of items she had just taken from John's room or that the driver was a blonde woman who had no connection with any courier company.

"This will help us," she announced.

"Okay, let's get down to it," said John.

Valla burned with frustration. He seemed aware only of Catherine's obvious assets and completely oblivious to her devious character. She sensed resentment building inside. Then analysed and identified it as jealousy. Why? She didn't want to be intimate friends with John. Why the envy? Valla didn't know.

"Let's start by discussing what we each know about the pair who came to Hong Kong," she said firmly.

John thought for a moment.

"All we have is that two women went to Catherine's place and took photos of some of the items there."

"That's about all I know as well."

Catherine smiled and opened the envelope.

"But I'm a clever girl. I've got photos of them."

She handed the prints to Valla. They showed the faces of two women, apparently asleep.

"I don't recognise them. Where was this taken?"

"We did capture the nasty girls and took photos but someone helped them get away. Mr Pierce was very annoyed."

"Then I think we start by asking all our contacts if they can identify them."

"Let me see," asked John.

Valla handed him the photos but didn't anticipate the reaction.

"Oh god," he muttered raising a hand to his forehead.

"You know them?"

"I know the blonde one. Her name is Chris Darmant. She's a sort of government agent, or was until recently."

"Have you told her anything about the Octagon?" Valla asked.

"No. No I haven't."

"Do you know where she lives?"

"Yes but I'm sure she's okay."

"Perhaps she's used you?"

"No, John is much too clever," Catherine interrupted.

She moved behind him, hands on his shoulders.

"She's right, Valla. I might not have your intellect but I can tell if someone is manipulating me. I've never slept with her, if that's what you're thinking."

"Okay, just an idea," she responded, attempting a smile but she was annoyed to have given Catherine the chance to split her from John.

"I've known her for years. She's very honest. It must be a coincidence," he insisted.

"You must admit it's a very unlikely coincidence."

"Maybe you're right, but don't forget I didn't know anything about Hong Kong so she couldn't have found that out from me anyway."

Valla could see that Catherine was now gently massaging his shoulders and a little ice came into her voice.

"Okay, we'll reconstruct the events. First, a gang kills the Provider and their Secondary. The thieves didn't appear to be looking for the Blessing as they made no attempt to keep anyone alive for questioning and we recovered the supply anyway. About three months later, two women go to our Hong Kong location with the objective of photographing the articles and papers of the Octagon. One of them is a detective or agent. I think there's a single logical thread."

"That the Provider had somehow made a record of the Hong Kong location. The women found it and were following up?" asked John.

"Yes. It's hard to believe that anyone in our group would be so incautious but there's no other conclusion, given the timing of the events."

"Why would it take three months?"

"I've been giving that a lot of thought and again there's an obvious answer."

John was silent, reviewing the sequence in his mind.

"The auction?"

"That must be it. All the possessions of the Countess were sold at the auction. Some item or document must have contained the Hong Kong location. Your friend Darmant would have that information. Do you know who she works for now?"

"No, we never really discussed it. She mentioned once that she was employed by the British Government but the last time I phoned, she told me she'd changed jobs. Working in the private sector I think she said. That was a couple of weeks ago."

"Just before she went to Hong Kong."

"Must have been."

Catherine spoke at last.

"You two are really clever. It's all so simple when you explain it."

Valla turned to her.

"Did the women tell you anything when you captured them?"

"No, they told lots of silly stories about being reporters. They didn't say anything about the Octagon at all. Do you think they might know where you and John are living? You're in America, aren't you?"

Valla wasn't going to disclose her location in this conversation and responded with a question.

"I understand you and Mr Pierce are coming to live near us?"

Catherine didn't reply, looking at her malevolently. Then she spoke in John's ear.

"We could all be in horrible danger now. And you John, your Primary could also be a target. I think we should be open and honest and not keep secrets from each other. We need to be good friends together and share everything."

John nodded.

"I think that's right. We have to trust people inside the Octagon."

Catherine's fingers were now caressing his neck while her face exuded innocence and sincerity. Valla was losing and she didn't like it. But an ingredient had been added to the girl's vicious nature. A devious look in her childlike face. She was planning something, Valla could feel it. A strategy formed in her mind.

"I'm going out now to get our agents checking out these photos. Back in about three hours."

She pulled on a coat and left in her hired car.

Catherine watched her departure with a delicious smile.

"I'm glad she's gone. Valla's very grumpy."

"She's okay. Pretty clever, I'd say."

Catherine leant close to his cheek.

"Not as clever as you are. You want to be my friend, don't you?"

He felt her breasts pressing against his arm.

"You're really gorgeous."

"And you won't keep secrets from me, will you?"

"No. Stupid to do that. We're both in this together."

She reached her head round sideways and kissed him, her tongue playing inside his mouth.

"You start then," she whispered.

He told her. About himself, Mary, where they lived, his plans for 2019. Everything. Not possible to resist. As he spoke, she was unbuttoning his shirt, her lips travelling softly over his chest.

He could feel the desire building. On the edge. Just one spark needed to ignite. Walking round to face him, she slowly removed her jacket and then unbuttoned her shirt. The pale pink bra scarcely contained her as she began to softly caress the curves. John's restraint snapped. He reached forward but she stepped back out of reach.

"Not here. Come to my room."

Moistening her lips, she held an arm out towards him and then turned and ran up the stairs with John following like a bull elephant. Catherine reached her bedroom and spread herself on the bed.

"Now take off all your clothes," she instructed, relishing the power.

He ripped them off, eyes glued to her. When he was naked, she rose from the bed and began to undress, very slowly down to her underwear. Then her strange smile widened as she unhurriedly surveyed his aroused body.

"Now lie down like a nice boy."

He lay, totally entranced as she gracefully but teasingly removed her underwear and then slid on top of him. Uncontained, the breasts seemed even larger and her body outclassed any he had seen before. He moved a hand to touch but she pushed his arm flat to the bed.

"No, you stay there and be good. Now close your eyes."

Her lips started to trace down his body and her hands began to tease him gently. It wasn't his style, he usually liked to take charge but this girl stimulated him more than anyone he had been with before.

Catherine reached under the bed for the syringe while her lips continued their rhythmic activity. The injection would be sufficient to keep him out for four hours, long enough for her to get him to Jessica's people. They would test his resistance to pain and had promised she could watch. A spasm of pleasure shuddered through her.

The heel of the gun cracked into the back of Catherine's head. Valla was completely untrained in physical violence and the blow was poorly aimed. The girl turned, stunned momentarily and then her lips curled in a feral scowl. Her fist smashed across Valla's jaw, knocking her backwards. Catherine leapt forward and they grappled, rolling across the floor.

John sat up, uncertain what he should do. He had been suddenly transported from near ecstasy to near bedlam.

"Help me, she's crazy. She's trying to kill us," Catherine shouted.

A combination of her words and natural human sympathy for the naked against the clothed decided him. He was still fully aroused and moved with difficulty but by grabbing Valla's arms he allowed Catherine to swing a fist twice into her face.

Valla lay still. Catherine knelt at her side and grabbed the syringe like a dagger.

"No." John screamed, but it was already too late.

She thrust into Valla's heart. He tried to reach her arm but her free hand struck him in the stomach while she continued to stab like a metronome. He grasped her around the neck, dragging her backwards but she rolled and hit him again near the groin. He couldn't beat her in physical combat and he needed a gun.

Sprinting to his room, he pulled his automatic from the bedside cabinet just as Catherine came through the doorway. Her eyes were wide and she was screeching with fury or madness. Maybe both.

John's shot was wild, hitting the wall above her but she stopped and jumped back out of sight. He crouched naked behind the bed, his gun still aimed at the door. Hands shaking, panic bubbling through him. The memory of his stupidity, the girl's insanity and the viciousness of her attack on Valla.

The sound of a car engine. He cautiously edged to the window to see Catherine driving away. Relief. Panic subsiding. He forced himself to return to the room and look at the body. Valla lay very still, very dead. The Blessing couldn't help her now.

Oblivious to his nakedness, he began to think. What to do? How would he explain this to Mary Duckworth? Police involvement was unthinkable, much too risky. He needed a guardian angel to take all the problems away.

"I can help," a voice said.

He turned. This blonde angel had no wings.

25

Jessica Crowne lay on a sun lounger sipping chilled orange juice from a tall glass. She was in the large underground chamber beneath the Velviva centre that housed a large pool and tanning room. Scattered around the side of the pool was an assortment of chairs and sunbeds. The floor had a padded non-slip synthetic finish and ceiling mounted tanning lamps covered one corner area where clients could relax. A bar-kitchen supplied drinks and refreshments in conditions similar to an Acapulco 5 star hotel.

The chamber was vacant in the evenings and Jessica frequently took advantage of the facilities, usually completely alone. Today she was wearing a black bikini and sunglasses. She finished her drink and lay back, soaking up the warmth from the overhead tubes. Hony entered, also in a bikini, deep burgundy. Moving quietly across the room, she bent over the top of the lounger and kissed Jessica warmly. A one-way kiss.

"I'm thinking," Jessica said.

"I finished the blood sample analysis. It looks very normal, perfect really. Not a sign of any additives, nothing out of the ordinary. Maybe too perfect. Do you want the detailed report?"

"No. I didn't really expect you to find anything. It's from someone who is taking the complete formula, including the tenth constituent."

Honey was more than surprised.

"Are you sure? Who is this person?"

"A new member of our organisation, a woman."

"Doesn't she know the formula?"

"She has no idea of the chemical structure. Just takes it every year."

"Look Jessica, all you've told me is that the Atlantis Reborn mixture needs one more constituent. How do you know that? If someone's already using it, there must be a record somewhere. You should be able to get this information."

"You don't need to know any more than I've told you. There is one missing ingredient and your job is to find it. At the same time, I'm doing everything I can to locate the original. I don't care who gets there first as long as I have the answer."

Her voice carried the warmth of an Arctic breeze.

"Sorry. I'll go back to the laboratory if you prefer."

"No, wait here. I'm expecting someone."

"The woman whose blood I tested?"

"Yes."

Hony didn't want to recognise the coldness. She had to believe her affection was returned despite all the evidence. There wasn't room for any more disappointments in her life.

The door opened and the girl entered. Young, very beautiful with long dark hair. She wore only the bottom half of a bikini, exposing an extraordinarily large chest in relation to the rest of her figure.

"Hony, this is Catherine. She has just joined us."

The girl looked at Hony, her eyes full of arrogant dismissal. Walking directly past, she embraced Jessica.

"I killed one of them, that nasty Valla but John Porter got away. I took his stuff though."

Hony was appalled.

"Look, I don't want to be mixed up in murder."

The girl turned.

"Not murder you silly woman. It's killing."

"I am a scientist and I think you need psychiatric help."

Catherine pouted.

"You're horrid and you're old. You've got lines all over your face and your body is all saggy but I'm young and beautiful and I'll still be like that when you're dead."

She giggled and ran her hands over her own curves.

Children have an instinct for a weak point. Catherine was a woman, a very old woman but her childlike words still exactly hit the target. Hony felt the tears welling up but forced a frigid smile.

"I doubt if you'll live longer than me, you infantile witch."

Jessica had been watching with faint amusement.

"Catherine, what were these items you took from John?"

The girl turned to her, deliberately switching on a smile and started to count on her fingers.

"First there was a sort of diary, then some typed out letters, a cell phone, some keys and a funny little pipe you can play tunes on."

"What did you do with them?"

"I gave them to Karmen."

"You're a very good girl."

"I didn't stick that needle in John but he told me where he lives. It's a place that sells books in Paraguay."

Jessica sat up. "Did you tell Karmen the exact address?"

"Yes I did. Are you pleased?"

"I am very pleased with you. Come and sit next to me."

Hony was horrified. Catherine was obviously seriously unbalanced and worse than that, Jessica seemed not to care. The girl had killed someone but both of them appeared totally unmoved by the act of murder.

"Hony, I think we may be getting very close now," said Jessica with a smile.

"That's great." Hony tried to sound pleased but was wondering what her future would be when her main task was achieved, particularly by someone else.

"Now I think we deserve to relax. Would you like to play, Catherine?"

The girl nodded with enthusiasm.

"You're very nice to me and I like you."

Hony suddenly felt very alone and isolated.

"I'll leave you if you want to talk," she said quietly.

"You can join us if you like. That would be interesting, wouldn't it Catherine?"

The girl turned to face Hony and the baleful stare told everything. Hony backed away.

"No, I'd better go back to the laboratory. Lots of work to catch up on."

Jessica waved a hand dismissively and then put her arm around Catherine's shoulders.

10.39, the next morning. Karmen entered Jessica's office and displayed no surprise to see her behind the desk, dressed only in a pale blue silk robe. Also no surprise to see Catherine playing with dolls on the carpet. The girl nearly wore an identical robe but it had lost the battle to confine her chest and now hung open. She held the figures of a man and woman and was walking them together on the carpet.

"You called me," Karmen said dourly.

"Catherine has given me an idea," announced Jessica.

"Yes?"

"To use her words, why don't we capture the king rather than his subjects?"

Karmen shrugged. It was difficult to believe that the woman was now taking advice from an immature girl.

"Who is this king?"

"The leader of Omasor, Jerome Jones. As far as I can see, he controls the whole organisation. Why bother with the branches when we could cut the roots?"

"It may not be easy."

Jessica rose from the desk and stood over Catherine, idly caressing her hair.

"I do not pay you for easy work. It was a very clever idea, wasn't it darling," she said, looking down with a smile.

Catherine looked up, beaming with pleasure.

"You're very good to me and give me lots of lovely things to play with," she giggled.

"That's because you're very pretty and such a sweet girl."

Catherine smile grew wider and she returned to her toys.

"I think it would be easier to kill Bowman and Darmant," muttered Karmen.

"You can do that later. First you will carry out my instructions."

"Very well. I do understand the benefits of capturing Jones but it will mean diverting some people."

"Our resources are unlimited. Do it immediately," instructed Jessica, her eyes drawn down again to the girl at her feet.

Catherine gave an appealing look.

"I want something."

"Yes darling? What would you like?"

"A man, a real one. This silly thing is useless."

She waved what had been a complete male figure. Now its arms, legs and head had been ripped off.

"Of course you can have one, Catherine. You're such a beautiful girl and you do everything I want you to. Arrange it, Karmen."

The dark haired woman nodded and left the room as Jessica joined Catherine on the carpet.

Karmen returned to her office, deep in thought. In one way, Jessica was correct. If they could capture Jerome Jones then the Omasor investigation could be stopped immediately. Torture him first and get his people to comply with Velviva's instructions. Those bitches, Bowman and Darmant would be forced to obey and could easily be induced into a trap. Karmen visualised the two of them strapped out on tables. A sharp knife. The blood and screams of agony. The begging for it to stop. That would be nice.

The big problem was the first stage. Find Jerome Jones. She knew that many had tried to locate him and none have succeeded. No one had even come close to discovering his appearance. The first task was to get a starting place. Any sort of lead.

She picked up the phone and contacted one of her old KGB associates. No, they had nothing. Jones had never been a target for them. She made another call and issued instructions. A message to all her security team and their contracted agencies throughout the world. Instructions to ask questions, report any reference, any link to Jerome Jones. An hour passed before her telephone rang. She picked it up.

"Fidec here."

"Hello, Karmen. It's Jerome Jones. You wanted me?"

She was rarely shocked but this was rarely. The call was on her private, encrypted line, known only to her security team.

"Is this a hoax?" she asked coldly.

"If you don't want me, I'll go away."

"Wait. I just want to talk to you. A proposal."

"Certainly. Where and when?"

As he spoke, Karmen was clicking keys on her computer. All calls to this phone were automatically traced and she waited for the screen to refresh.

"I can come to you. Anywhere in the world. Where are you?"

"I wouldn't ask a lady to make a long journey just to meet me. We can rendezvous at the Cassarata cafe tomorrow morning at ten. It's just 15 minutes from you in Geneva. Incidentally, I'm calling from England to save you waiting for your trace."

"Tomorrow?"

"See you then. Goodbye."

Karmen was on the intercom in a flash. How had the call got through? The line needed a unique code that only a handful of her people knew. Now the screen refreshed confirming the call was from London, England.

Her phone rang again.

"Yes?" she snapped

"Hello Karmen. Jerome Jones here. You wanted to see me?"

Not the same voice. This one has an American accent. For once in her life she was confused and that made her angry.

"How did you get this number?" she shouted.

"See you tomorrow at ten."

The call finished.

Check the trace screen. It refreshed. The call came from Florida, USA. Karmen slammed a fist on the desk. What had happened to the security? A number of her team would suffer for this. Suffer by death. A flicker caught her eye. The screen had updated again. Just three words in a large font. 'See you tomorrow'.

09.50, the following morning.

Karmen sat in the car with dark windows that was parked opposite the Cassarata cafe. She had 26 people at the scene. Ten of them as customers, six at outside tables, four inside. Three cars, in addition to her own, with two agents in each. The other ten were all round the building, covering every exit.

The cafe wasn't large but very exclusive, very expensive. Karmen looked at the screen that was mounted to one side of the steering wheel. A video camera on all four cars. The screen clicked through the pictures from each. Eight customers in the cafe apart from her people. A party of four, comprising an elderly man and woman with a pair of teenage girls. Then two average looking couples. Middle-aged and appearing very normal.

Karmen clicked her communicator.

"Go." she instructed.

Katya had been looking in a nearby shop and now she walked quickly to the cafe. A waiter approached.

"My name is Karmen. I'm meeting a Mr Jerome Jones here. Has he arrived yet?" she asked loudly.

He shook his head and she moved to an empty table outside.

9.58 am

A grey-haired man strolled to the cafe and summoned a waiter.

"My name is Jerome Jones. Is anyone waiting for me?" he asked.

Karmen spoke quickly to all her people on the communicator as Katya moved towards the new arrival.

"Mr Jones? I'm Karmen," she said invitingly.

He smiled.

"Ah yes. Delightful. You look most attractive today. May I join you?"

They moved to the table and Karmen triggered a series of still photographs.

"Take him when he leaves," she instructed on the open line.

9.59 am

A mini coach pulled up in front of Karmen's car and six track suited figures emerged. She scanned them. No sign of any weapons. They looked like a sports team ready for a training session. Surprising that they all crossed the road to the cafe. Then she saw it. A name on the back of each tracksuit. Jerome Jones. All six of them.

The group moved to Katya's table.

"Hello, I'm Jerome Jones," said the first.

"So am I," added the second.

All six the same. And more came. Young men, old men. Business suits and leisure outfits. Now the cafe was full.

Karmen clicked on the microphone again.

"Katya stay in the cafe. Everyone else get out and wait at the perimeter line," she instructed.

The plan was to contain the area. It was possible that one of the men really was Jones. Perhaps take all of them but that would be difficult. She estimated there were about 14 of them in the cafe now.

For a few minutes, she monitored the melee around Katya and then a knock on the side window of the car. Policeman. She wound down the window, smiling.

"Yes, officer? Is there a problem parking here?"

"Not at all but you have a problem with your rear lights. Please take a look."

She emerged from the car and moved to the back.

Yes, there was a problem. No rear lights visible, something was covering them. A strip that ran across, just above the bumper. A strip that displayed a brightly lit, scrolling message.

'Hello Karmen. Just you and Katya left now. All the other 26 are happily unconscious in a coach that is heading out of town.'

She looked around quickly. None of her team in sight. Then she turned to the policeman, feeling for the pistol in her jacket pocket.

"Okay, Mr Jerome Jones. That was clever but I do have you," she said with a grim smile

He looked mystified.

"Sorry madam? I'd just like your assurance that this display will be removed before you leave. It is distracting for other drivers and masks the rear lights. That is against the law."

"Yes, of course," she responded and he walked away, shaking his head.

Now Karmen hesitated. She had been certain but the policeman was transparently genuine. She looked across at Katya who is now surrounded by a group of talking, laughing men. Still more were coming. One brushed past her as she opened the car door.

"Nice to meet you, Karmen," said the man in the passenger seat.

Young, student face. Tousled brown hair. Brown rimmed spectacles.

"I felt him take the pistol," she responded as she climbed in beside him.

"Didn't want you to shoot me on our first date."

"Then I will do it next time. No warnings, just shoot. Maybe a rifle. Long-distance laser sights."

"That's not very encouraging for a man to hear from his new girlfriend."

"I don't go out with men," she replied with a half smile.

"Nor women, so I hear but Katya does both jobs for you."

"Where are you taking my people?"

"They'll be left at an empty house and should return when they wake."

"What do you want?"

"You ordered a lot of people to find me. I thought it would save time if we met."

Now Karmen was more at ease, despite the circumstances.

"I have a proposal. If we joined our forces, everything would be much simpler and we would share the benefits between us. Why not?"

"I can't think of a logical reason," Jerome replied.

Not the response Karmen expected and she fumbled for words.

"Then we just need to agree the details. A simple division of the proceeds or would you prefer a fixed amount? That would be easier. As soon as the formula is located, I can transfer two million US dollars to you. Then I retain all the future rights."

Jerome turned to her, adjusting his spectacles. The boyish face showed surprise.

"Two million? That's a lot for a simple skin treatment."

Karmen hid her relief. He didn't know the real secret of the Blessing.

"You'd be surprised how much a woman will pay to make her skin look younger. Velviva are the world leaders in the field and you wouldn't get the same offer anywhere else."

"I think that's true."

"You are reputedly a very wealthy man, Mr Jones and but I guess that the money would buy another nice house, somewhere in the sun."

His eyes drifted away from her to look towards the cafe. Katya was still the centre of attention although only four men were around her now.

"I suppose I may have reached the point where money isn't a great incentive. That is a very attractive lady," he remarked wistfully.

Karmen sensed the obvious.

"She's a lovely girl and I'm sure she would give anything to meet you."

"Then it settled. I'll have a night with Katya. If she agrees, of course."

"She will certainly agree and I think we have finalised a deal, Mr Jones," Karmen said with a smile.

He got out of the car and then bent down to respond.

"No, of course we do not have a deal. All this is simply a message not to try to find me. Expect Katya back tomorrow."

He grinned and closed the door. A car stopped next to the cafe and the driver emerged. Jerome took the keys, calling to Katya and she moved quickly to enter the car without looking towards Karmen. Within seconds they had driven off, followed by the coach with the track suited men. The whole area was suddenly clear again.

Karmen couldn't prevent a feeling of admiration for the efficiency of the operation. She wouldn't forget her meeting with Jerome Jones. There were also good points. She had identified two weaknesses in him. The first was women. That was good. His lust could be used in many ways. Second was his lack of ruthlessness. Everything about the event was designed to avoid killing or even injuring. In his position, she would certainly have executed her captured people. In addition, Katya was sure to get information from him that night. Her report would be very interesting indeed.

The next morning. 11.07 a.m.

"What?" Karmen shouted.

Now she was angry and Katya cringed.

"We just went to his house and straight to the bedroom. The blinds were drawn and the lights were off. That was it."

"That was it? Your job was to get him to talk. He must have said something."

"Just a few words."

Katya repeated them and in the bright morning light, they seemed distinctly incongruous.

"I do not mean that sort of talk. You've never failed to get men to reveal things to you. Listen, you left about this time yesterday. You can't have just spent the whole day having sex. What else happened?"

"I think I must have eaten two meals yesterday and breakfast today."

"Then there had to be conversation."

"After arriving, we were in bed for three hours and then he left. I checked the door but it was locked. Then a woman brought a meal for me. The room was lovely and large I dined on a sort of balcony. Then I slept for two hours and had a shower. Soon after, the woman returned with another meal. I was just having coffee when Jerome Jones came back. After that, we went to bed again. When I woke up this morning, he'd gone. I had another shower and the woman brought me breakfast. Then I waited for a while but no one came so I tried the door and found it open. The house was completely empty but next to the front door was a lovely bunch of roses with my car keys in them."

"Your car? How did they get that?"

"I don't know. It was parked outside the house and I drove back here."

"So you were alone in bed with Jones for hours."

Katya averted her eyes from Karmen's steely gaze.

"Well, yes. If it's any help, he was very, very good. Exceptional really. I didn't need to fake anything."

"That is no help whatsoever. A miserable failure. Remember, Katya, you are not immune to my ultimate discipline."

"Perhaps I would get something if I did it with him again?"

"Get out of the office!" Karmen yelled.

26

There are beautiful places in the universe - where else would they be? Paraguay is one of them. Magic oozes within multicoloured oases of humanity consorting playfully with the verdant trees of nature.

Three things you didn't know about Paraguay. The two sides of the National Flag are different and there are two official languages, Spanish and Guarani, the indigenous speech. And something else that slips the brain for a moment. Then again you may already know these things, especially if you are Paraguayan. How would I know what you don't know? If that's how you feel, I'm not telling you the third thing.

The clarity of the air flushed like a cold shower or if in the Arctic, a warm shower. A day of irresistible imperfection.

Chris was contentedly relaxed in accord with the atmosphere, sipping a hot coffee. She had already been on a refreshing early-morning run and was now waiting for her contact. A cafe table in front of her then more tables, a perimeter of natural rocks and beyond them, a sweeping panorama of lush green valley. It was 32° centigrade, the coffee was hotter.

She had arrived in Asuncion the previous evening via Buenos Aires. Selena had told her that the clue to the next location had been solved and she needed to grab the first plane to Paraguay. Chris would be going alone this time as Selena claimed other business to resolve. Someone would contact her at the hotel and her objective was clear. To find another Octagon plaque together with any relevant items or documents.

Chris was pleased to be going alone this time. She was more comfortable making her own decisions than operating as an assistant and hopefully her contact would be amenable to her taking the lead. There was also the possibility of meeting Jessica Crowne again, an encounter she was relishing.

A chattering scattering of tourists and locals adorned the tables. A nerdy couple bespectacled, bejeaned and seemingly bemused giggled together. Two local businessmen argued in friendly fashion. A guide was plying his trade to a group of German women, enticing with promises of trips to the local must-be-seen whilst assessing their financial and sexual potential.

The waiter approached, placed a fresh coffee in front of her.

Hello, I'm Jerome Jones," he murmured.

Her thoughts returned from the daydream.

"Number three I think, but I'm losing count."

This one was tall and lean. Mid to late 20s, the youngest version yet. Short black curly hair with eyes very dark and very deep-set. The sort of face that transparently demonstrated he had travelled to many places and a good few taught him something.

"Maybe I'm the real article. Your room in 30 minutes."

"Thank you," she replied loudly for the benefit of spectators.

Back in her room she tuned into the sound outside her door. Chris had always possessed a special talent for targeting her hearing, cutting out all the background noises and talk. Memories abounded of the times she spent by the river at her parent's farm in eastern England, wandering by herself near the riverbank while finding harmony with the sounds of the small creatures and wildlife. Chris had refined it to the point where she could distinguish the special quick noises of the beautiful otter, scuttering in the grasses by the water. Now she was applying the skill to more serious work.

There was the softest shuffle in the corridor outside and she opened the door.

"Your abilities were well reported," he said.

"Tea is on the table," she responded with a smile.

Two minutes later he was sipping from his cup and speaking in a deep, gravel voice.

"Welcome to Paraguay. It will be necessary to achieve our objective with some alacrity as I am sure the opposition are close, if not already in the country."

"Opposition meaning Jessica Crowne and her friends?"

"Yes."

"I'm told we're here to find another plaque and more documents?"

"Right. From the photographs you took of the plaque in Hong Kong we were able to decode the name of a person and a place. The person is called Duckworth and the place is here. That's all we know."

"How are these people connected?"

"You met Arthur Pierce and Catherine Bell in Hong Kong. They are two members of a society called the Octagon. We're here to find another member."

"Okay, this Octagon. What else do we know about it?"

"Simple logic indicates that it originally comprised eight members. The two in England were killed, the Countess and her associate. You met Pierce and his assistant in Hong Kong. They work in pairs so two couples left to find. One is here and we need to track them down before your friend Jessica and her people get to them."

"Why are the plaques so important?"

"They carry the insignia of the Octagon, two eagles above six vertical swords. More importantly, each plaque contains keywords that allow us to decode the location of one of the members."

"The Crownes are massively rich. Why would they want to run round the world after little coded messages? What has this Octagon got that's so precious?"

"I believe the trail will eventually lead to something of great value."

"Do you know what?"

"I'm not certain."

"You may not be certain but I think you know more than you're telling me."

He shrugged. "Your thoughts are your privilege."

Chris abandoned the question. She was used to working without the whole picture.

"I met Jessica in London. She killed your namesake and I couldn't stop her. I'm looking forward to seeing her again."

"Her death is certain. Just a matter of how and when."

"So where are we going?"

"I've already sifted it down to two possibilities, both here in this city. One is a businessman with interests in finance and the motor trade and the other is a bookshop owner. We'll take one each and you have the bookshop. The proprietor is a woman named Mary Duckworth."

"How do we keep in touch?"

He handed her a satellite phone.

"I'll be there quickly if you call me."

A stony look crossed her face.

"Jerome, or whatever your real name is, you seem more of a thinker than a fighter. You call me if you need help."

"I will," he said, nearly smiling.

Chris got out of the taxi in a street adjacent to the bookshop. She wore a denim jacket and jeans with her hair bunched under a cap and would hopefully pass for a student, probably a poor one. The sun beamed bright and friendly on a multitude of exotic scenes. People worked, bought, sold and laughed. Houses and shops were decorated in a thousand hues, the inhabitants decorated with a thousand smiles.

The bookshop was almost concealed in a row of run-down retail stores and old houses. Its facade had probably been a rich dark brown but the covering of dust and grime made it pure speculation. A few decrepit paperbacks dotted a bookshelf in the window and it was impossible to see into the gloomy interior.

Chris pushed the door and an aged bell clanked somewhere. The shop was a warren of dusty, old wooden shelves untidily loaded with scuffed and fading books. Shelves versus books to decide which would decay and fall apart first.

She sensed something was not right. This couldn't be a commercial venture. It must be owned by some venerable, studious old lady as a final time-passing activity.

Chris didn't hear footsteps but a curtain parted at the back of the shop to reveal a young, dark haired woman. Totally out of context with her surroundings, she wore tiny blue shorts and a tight white shirt.

"Can I help you?"

Her accent was unmistakably from the Akinor Valley, East Ukraine. An indication that she could be part of Jessica's team.

"Thanks, just looking around. Where is the history section?"

It was obvious that the woman didn't know.

"Sorry, I'm only looking after the shop for my friend."

"Okay, I'll just browse."

"I close now. You would like to visit again tomorrow perhaps?"

"Well, can I just buy this one?"

Chris randomly selected a book from the shelf and brought it to the counter whilst fumbling in her handbag. The girl turned to the antiquated till and had just begun to press a key when Chris hit her exactly at the vital area where the jawbone meets the neck. It was perfectly aimed, perfectly timed and the woman collapsed, unconscious.

Chris pulled her out of sight behind the counter and cautiously opened the back curtain to display absolutely nothing. More accurately it revealed a brick lined cubicle, just large enough for two people. She searched every millimetre for a door, lever, button or catch. Nothing. The woman must have been standing in the small space, but there had to be purpose for it. Far too small to use as a storage area.

"Think, dammit," she murmured, faced with the prospect of getting the girl conscious to reveal the secret.

Just then the bell rang as a man entered the shop and strolled to the counter.

Jerome.

"I have a confession to make. This was the only possible. I followed you and was watching from outside."

She should have been angry but found herself pleased to see him.

"Any good at locked room mysteries, Jerome?" she asked, opening the curtain.

He moved fast and lively as a cat, his hands exploring the alcove like an inquisitive spider and then he nodded like a water buffalo.

"Do you have the key?" he asked.

"Don't even have a lock."

He knelt down, searching the girls clothing and then pulled a pipe from her pocket. A musical pipe, not one of the other varieties.

"This is it. Microphone in top of doorway."

Chris cursed herself for missing it.

He held up the instrument. Made of brass with eight holes and a crest was engraved on one side, a crest she had seen before.

"Know what to do?" he asked.

"Yes."

They crammed into the alcove and Chris played the second and sixth notes. The floor immediately began to descend slowly and silently, walls changing from brick to smooth steel as they went down. Crouching as low as possible in the confined space, she pulled out a gun.

"Jerome, don't get killed on me this time. Someone could be waiting."

He gazed at her, his dark eyes barely visible in the gaunt face.

"Who knows what will happen?" he said softly.

Chris guessed they had descended about 20 metres before a space began to appear at the bottom of the wall and exhaled thankfully when she saw the room was deserted. They would have been an easy target for anyone waiting there. Before the platform stopped, Jerome jumped out and she followed instantly.

The room was circular, about twelve metres across with concrete floor and walls and completely bare of any furniture or ornamentation. In front of them were three closed steel doors devoid of keyholes, buttons or signs.

The silence was broken by a humming noise and they turned to find the elevator ascending again.

"Must be automatic. No one up there to call it," Chris remarked.

Jerome quickly explored the doors.

"Well?" he asked.

"If I was using this as a hiding place I'd have one or two false doors to confuse burglars."

"With certain death behind them?"

"Could be."

"So you think we first need to choose the right entrance?"

"I'll find it."

Chris dropped to her knees, carefully examining the floor in front of each door. She pointed at the one on the left.

"You found more wear on the floor."

"And scuffs from shoes."

"Nice work, detective. How do we open it?"

She checked the door and pointed at three almost microscopic holes at face level in the flat steel surface.

"Another sound lock maybe?" she asked, taking out the pipe again.

His expression didn't change. She had an irritating feeling he'd already worked it all out before asking her.

"Don't humour me, Jerome."

"I don't think I have a sense of humour. Not the pipe, not two locks with one key."

"Perhaps it needs a pin to push into the holes?"

"No, there would be scratch marks around the edges. If it was some type of voice lock there would be a slight discoloration around the holes from the moisture and compounds in the breath. But there is a very faint mark around them, too small for a breathing area."

"But large enough for a fingertip?"

"Yes," he replied firmly.

"Two and six again?"

"I think so. The hole on the left is more marked, that would be the six."

She covered the right hand hole with her finger, pulled back and covered it again. Then she repeated the process six times for the other hole. The door slid silently open.

Chris couldn't resist a gasp of surprise. Twenty metres underground and she was looking at the interior of a delightful villa from a previous era. Posters on the walls displayed the earth goddess, green man and children of peace. Bright coloured, striped drapes adorned the gaps between and framed pictures acted as simulated windows. It was furnished with natural wood chairs piled with deep, comfortable cushions. Three doors, all closed. Everything immaculately clean and the whole area brightly lit with daylight fluorescents. It was barely believable that such a structure could have been constructed and maintained under a tawdry bookshop.

Jerome walked casually to a chair and nestled comfortably in the large cushions. He pointed at the centre door.

"What?" Chris said.

Then the door opened.

The woman was dressed in a blue top and billowing dress composed of multicoloured fabric squares. Her long blonde hair hung loose over her shoulders. A perfect hippie minus a straw hat and the word peace printed on her shirt. However the flower child image was somewhat incompatible with the Yazoto submachine gun she carried.

"Good day, madam. I am Jerome Jones and this is my associate Christine Darmant." said Jerome, rising from his chair and giving a little bow.

The thought of a curtsy never crossed Chris's mind but she did manage to nod amicably.

"You have good manners, young man," remarked the woman.

"A gentleman always stands when a lady enters."

"Sadly, I'm afraid I have no alternative but to shoot you."

"If you will permit, I would offer an alternative for your consideration."

Chris was transfixed by this English Victorian drawing room conversation. Then she noticed that the Yazoto's safety catch was on and began to assess the feasibility of getting her own gun before the woman fired. She was just reaching for her hip when Jerome spoke.

"As a gesture of good faith, I would bring to your attention that your weapon still has the safety on."

Chris glared at him.

"Thank you Mr Jones," the woman responded, releasing the catch.

"May we sit? I'm afraid we do not have the honour of formal introduction."

Chris sensed she was relaxing. A good sign.

"I am Mary Duckworth. It is a pleasure to meet you and your friend Christine. You were about to offer an alternative to death, Mr Jones."

"As I perceive the options, you can either justifiably shoot us as we have entered your residence uninvited or you can allow us to save your life."

"You were in Hong Kong?"

"Christine was there."

"Arthur Pierce was rather upset."

"Ms Duckworth, we are not your antagonists. Your enemy will come here, perhaps very soon and will not hesitate to kill to achieve their objective."

"Who is the enemy?"

"People determined to obtain knowledge of your secrets."

"Then who are you?"

"Omasor Agency. You can regard us as detectives. Two of our people have been killed by the mutual opponent."

Her eyes widened with recollection.

"You are the Jerome Jones, the faceless billionaire? I have read about you."

"My face has never been my fortune but it is displayed before you."

"Too modest Mr Jones, you are not unattractive."

Chris interrupted.

"I'm sorry to implant a sense of urgency but they could attack this place at any second."

She was impatient but also strangely irritated by the woman complimenting Jerome's appearance.

"It is in your hands," said Jerome, looking calmly at Mary.

She paused and then her wristwatch began to bleep.

"Someone has entered the elevator in the shop. What do we do?" she appealed, a tinge of fear creeping into her voice.

Jerome was on his feet immediately.

"Any other exits?" he asked.

"No."

"What is in these rooms?"

"My bedroom, kitchen and a storeroom."

Chris took out her gun.

"The elevator only holds two at most and if they do come then we could take them."

Jerome shook his head.

"No, I'd expect a number of opponents. If two arrive, the remainder will still be up in the shop. Better to wait. I presume the other doors in the circular room are trapped in some way?"

"You were lucky to choose this one," Mary replied.

The thought struck Chris.

"Hold on, they can't use the elevator without the pipe and we have that."

Mary was thoughtful.

"There are three pipes. I have one, another was held by Pablo, my manager."

"I took it from a girl in the shop."

"I don't employ a girl."

"Who has the third pipe?"

Mary's eyes drifted to a photo on the bookcase. Chris could only see the edge of the frame and moved round for a better angle. Then wished she hadn't.

"No, this is a joke. That's John Porter," she exclaimed.

A pause and shocked surprise on Mary's face.

"You know him?"

"I thought I did."

"He has the third pipe."

Jerome studied the photo.
"Either it was taken from him or he is one of the enemy."
"He's not one of the enemy," said the two women spoke simultaneously.

Karmen played the notes on the pipe and then crouched low alongside one of her men as the elevator descended. She had delegated Katya to secure the place until she arrived from Switzerland. Instead of waiting for her, Katya had led three of her team to capture the shop manager and take him to their base, a rented house on the outskirts of the city. Finding no one else in the shop, the woman had been left there while Katya questioned the captive after injecting with HP47.

Karmen had arrived at the shop with Katya and five men to find the unconscious girl and that hadn't improved her mood, particularly as repeated heavy slaps to the girl's face had failed to bring her round. Fortunately, she had brought the pipe that Catherine had taken from John Porter. The manager had revealed details of the musical elevator lock and now Karmen was descending with one of her men. As they reached the bottom she pushed him to the right while jumping off to the left, keeping as low as possible. Three doors. She spoke quickly into her phone and the response came a minute later.

"The manager doesn't know where the doors lead. He was only allowed to leave items in the lower room for someone to collect."

Karmen made round trips to bring down two more of her team. Then she began to check the doors meticulously, finding the tiny holes in each of them. After whispering instructions to the men, she took a prone position near the elevator with her gun ready. Her instincts were always to be trusted and they were currently screaming danger.

One man pushed pieces of wire into the holes in the centre door and it slid open, as did the one on the right. The two entrances led to the same room, small and faintly lit but bright enough to see the stack of gold bullion bars piled against the far wall. Hundreds of gleaming blocks.

The gold drew the men into the room like a magnet and Karmen was just about to join them when she saw the flash and the holes. The three figures were stationary for a second, randomly perforated like high number dice. Then they collapsed to the floor.

She saw the lasers go to standby and then switch off. Pulling off a shoe she threw it through the doorway and waited. Nothing. It was a one-shot arrangement. She retrieved the shoe and it was only when she was in touching distance that she realised the gold bars were a hologram. Karmen pondered for a second. She had two men with Katya in the shop above and reached for her phone to call them.

As she did, a gun touched the nape of her neck.

"Drop the weapon and don't move a muscle," Chris said.

Karmen knew when to fight and this was not the time. She dropped her pistol.

Karmen's lean body looked insignificant, buried in one of the deep chairs. No fear, just sullen compliance. Chris kept her gun firmly aimed. She recognised KGB training in the woman's every action. Mary stared at the captive with an expression of contempt while Jerome wandered round the back of the chamber, seemingly disinterested in the proceedings. Chris noticed him checking Mary's bedroom and the kitchen before entering the storeroom that appeared to be full of crates and cartons.

Mary was showing another aspect of her character. No longer the hippie. Now her face was hard, her eyes bitter, her voice like a razor.

"Who are you?" she almost screamed.

Karmen didn't reply, didn't look at her. Yet she seemed instantly set to spring, like a feral canary.

"I'll get a knife. She will talk," Mary shouted.

Jerome spoke almost casually.

"I wonder what this does."

He held up a syringe from the small pile of items taken from the captive's pockets. Karmen's eyes displayed momentary disquiet. She wasn't going to reveal the HP47 secret.

"It's a poison, deadly. Kill me if you like."

"Yes, we might I suppose," he responded vaguely, replacing the syringe.

Jerome's offhand attitude puzzled Chris. They needed a quick plan of escape and he wasn't contributing.

"I can take her up as hostage in one journey. Then you two can follow me," she proposed.

He shook his head.

"That's a possibility although we can't be sure if she's valued enough by our opponents to make an effective hostage. Now I'd like Mary to join me in the bedroom."

She followed him meekly and he closed the door behind them.

Karmen looked up, a smile on her lean face.

"You can't succeed, we're too powerful. Unlimited resources," she said softly.

"Maybe I should join you?" asked Chris.

"Why not? You can have a million pounds and a residence anywhere in the world. The Omasor Agency just can't compete with us. You know that. Just let me go and I'll guarantee the other two won't be hurt. We'll just take the items we need and leave. No bloodshed, no fighting."

"It sounds very attractive but I'm going to say no," Chris responded.

"Then I'll have to kill you," Karmen said mildly but her eyes glinted with intent.

"You're welcome to try but wishes don't always come true."

Two minutes before Jerome and Mary emerged.

"We have formulated a plan. Need to go through it with you," he said.

Mary produced a pistol from a drawer and they moved to the bedroom, leaving her guarding Karmen.

"So what did you two talk about in here?" Chris enquired.

"I asked where the other exit was."

"She said there wasn't one."

"The design and material of this underground area indicates it was constructed no more than seven years ago. There is furniture here, not to mention a stove, crates and other items that could not have come down in the small elevator. Even if they were disassembled, some parts would still have been too large. They are all of more recent manufacture than the structure so it could not have been built around them."

"So there is another way out?"

"Yes, she's revealed that to me. It will take a while to move her collection so we need to buy some time. We will start clearing the store while you delay them as long as possible. As soon as we're clear, I'll come back for you."

"No problem."

He still didn't smile but there was the slightest crinkle around the eyes as he outlined the strategy.

Chris confirmed that Karmen was tightly bound around the arms and ankles and then taped her mouth firmly. She nodded to Mary who pushed a button on a remote control to call the elevator. When it arrived, Chris squeezed into an awkward position to keep Karmen in front of her. As they reached the top she bent lower to ensure her captive was the first person in view. Two men waiting, guns ready and she recognised the blonde Katya standing just behind them. Chris noted with satisfaction that the dark haired girl was still lying unconscious.

"Don't move or she's dead. Now drop your guns," she shouted. A line right out of a gangster movie.

The weapons fell to the floor and she kicked them to one side. Chris could sense that Karmen was making signals with her eyes but didn't notice Katya squeezing a button on a tiny transceiver concealed in her palm.

"What now?" enquired one of the men.

"Sit on the floor."

She pushed Karmen to join them and the four sat in a semicircle in front of her.

"How long do we have to wait here?" Katya asked.

"Not long," Chris responded.

She was tempted to instruct the blonde and Karmen to strip as recompense for their last encounter but decided against.

Not long seemed like hours to her. Jerome had estimated that he needed about 12 minutes. After nine minutes the bell rang as the shop door opened. Not Jerome. The police. Four of them, uniformed, with guns in hand.

Chris now had a problem. If they were real police, she needed to explain why she was holding a gun over four captives. If they were impostors, she was faced with eight assailants, four of them armed.

She grabbed the nearest person, Katya and held the gun to her head.

"This woman stole my husband," she shouted in Spanish.

The response was immediate. The police, or pseudo police, dodged for what cover they could find behind the bookshelves and the two men took advantage of the distraction to join them. This left Karmen frantically squirming on the floor. She wriggled towards the shelves, shouting as loudly as is possible with her mouth still taped. Not very loud and extremely indistinct.

Finally, one of the uniformed men dragged her behind cover and started to pull the bonds from her legs, which just resulted in louder noises. Then he fumbled with the ropes holding her wrists and eventually her hands were free. She grabbed the gun from him with one hand while the other ripped the tape from her face.

"Shoot, you idiots! Shoot through the girl!"

Katya gave a loud squeal, broke free and dived for the floor and Chris scrambled behind the curtain just as Karmen's first shot hit the wall. She was trapped. Didn't even have the pipe to start the elevator and anyway there wasn't time to use it.

Then, as if in miraculous response to her unspoken wish, she felt the floor descend and joyfully emptied her gun into the fast disappearing space in front of her.

Mary Duckworth was waiting at the bottom.

"This wasn't the plan," Chris gasped.

"Jerome called me to start the elevator. Come, we must hurry," Mary responded, holding up her phone

Chris ran after her into the now empty storeroom. Mary pressed her fingers against two screw heads that secured a small shelf and part of the apparently solid concrete rear wall opened up.

They dashed through, the door closing behind them and entered a dimly lit tunnel. Straight with no doors or turnings and it finished at another solid wall but this one had a large black button that Mary hit with the palm of her hand. A panel slid back and Chris emerged, blinking in the bright lights of a small warehouse where three men were loading the last crate in to a white van.

"Where's Jerome?" Chris yelled. She didn't want to lose this one.

Mary didn't need to reply. He sprinted into view from a side door.

"Ready?" he shouted.

The men waved, the last box was on.

"You two get in the back."

He jumped into the cab and the van was already moving when the two women scrambled inside and pulled the door shut. Mary brushed the long blonde hair back from her face

"I must say it's been an interesting day," she said calmly in the darkness.

27

During the journey Mary recounted the events while Chris had been in the shop. As soon as the elevator ascended, she and Jerome had hurried to the warehouse where he made a telephone call. Three men had arrived almost immediately in a van and she suspected that he had already arranged for them to wait in the area. They brought trolleys and the crates had been moved more quickly than planned. When they were nearly finished, Jerome had left to collect Chris from the shop, arriving on the scene just as the police were entering. Then he phoned Mary to start the elevator.

"The police, were they real?" asked Chris.

Mary shook her head.

"Jerome said no. The uniforms were copies."

After 20 minutes, Chris felt the van stop and Jerome opened the rear door. The women emerged squinting in the evening sunlight.

"There's a hotel just round the corner. You two sleep there and I'll stay with the van. Collect you here at nine tomorrow morning," he instructed.

"I wish to tell you that I have now decided to leave this country," Mary announced.

"Where are you going?" Chris asked.

"I will not reveal that. I'll arrange everything tonight. There will be an aircraft and some of my people waiting when we get to the airport."

Jerome checked his watch.

"I need to move now to get to the hiding place I have in mind for tonight."

"You'll definitely come tomorrow?" asked Mary dubiously.

"I said I will be here at nine in the morning. This will happen."

Mary firmly closed the rear door of the van and then waited, looking at Jerome. He sighed and pointed at a small ironmongers shop across the street.

"Go to that shop and buy the best padlock they have. You lock the van and keep the keys."

A few minutes later, Chris and Mary were walking to the hotel. Jerome had driven off, a new lock on the rear doors.

He arrived exactly at nine the next morning and the short journey to the airport was uneventful. Waiting near the entrance was a team of six men with a Fulwhite 439 small passenger jet on the runway. Mary looked relieved.

"I feel safe now with my plane and my men here. I must thank you for all your help and regret that I am unable to divulge more."

As Jerome made no effort to respond, Chris smiled and hugged her.

Then Mary put her arms on Jerome's shoulders and kissed him on the lips.

"Goodbye, Mr Jones" she murmured.

"Au revoir, perhaps," he said.

The kiss had been longer than Chris expected and she felt another curious annoyance.

They left Mary organising the shipment and took a taxi. As they sat in the rear, Chris started to ask a question but Jerome held a finger to his lips. A journey of 10 minutes and they emerged from the taxi next to an office car park. Just a few seconds before a smart, pink suited girl approached. She brushed past Jerome and clacked away on high heels. When she had gone he held up a set of car keys and pointed at a new Cussler Avarria in the row of cars.

"How did you do that?" asked Chris as he started the engine.

"I turned the ignition key."

"No, I mean how did you foresee needing the men and the transport?"

"Perhaps you could call it anticipation. There's no magic if I reveal everything."

"I'm sure you got inside the van."

"Why would you think that?" he asked.

"Because I can read your mind."

Chris knew it wasn't as simple as that. She felt strangely close to him, as if sharing his feelings as well as his thoughts. A new experience for her. New and pleasant.

"That's worrying. If my brain is exposed, I'll have to keep my secrets on a little notepad."

"Avoidance of question, Jerome."

"I spent last night unpacking and repacking crates and photographing."

"I knew it. There was another door from the cab."

"No other doors. Mary would have found them when they offloaded at the airport."

"But the lock was still in place and she had the only key."

"A friend of mine runs the ironmongers shop."

Chris grinned.

"You told him that a woman would come asking for his best padlock and to let you have another key."

"Something like that."

"Jerome Jones, you're sometimes a little devious but I enjoy working with you."

Chris didn't know why she was elated with the truth of that statement. These emotions were becoming unmanageable.

"So I've convinced you I'm the real one."

She shook her head, still smiling.

"No, I've worked that out. There is no Jerome Jones. Selena runs everything using a series of men with that name."

His expression didn't change. Perhaps he never smiled.

"Disappointing if I'm only one of many. I'd hoped that I might be a little unique," he remarked, stopping the car.

Chris desperately wanted to respond to that but knew this wasn't the time.

"Okay, what now?" she asked but found herself buzzing inside.

"You're going back to England. You need a holiday."

"I'm fine. I want to see it through."

"You need a break. I think I can almost guarantee that this job will not be finished without you."

"I hope we're going to meet again."

"We will definitely see more of each other. Here's your hotel. Goodbye."

He handed her an air ticket for London.

She leant over and kissed his cheek.

"Au revoir, perhaps," she said.

The real Jerome Jones was working in his office in the centre of England. He had received the electronic copies of the photos from Paraguay. Another set of apparently meaningless words were inscribed at the top of the small plaque.

'Spell Magic For

All Mages

Ebbed And Flowed

I Bring You

Few Mixtures

Abide Eternally

Open Amid Our

Flying Ocean's Deep

Abyss'

Five minutes before he decoded the answer. A famous location in England.

The Latin motto was 'In Pretium Persevero'. Very appropriate, thought Jerome. 'I will persevere for my reward'. He set the computer to apply the text of the motto as keywords to the next lunch recipe in the cookery book and this time the laser print took under a minute. Jim Fischer, Cragbutt, California.

28

After returning from Paraguay earlier in the day, Chris had immediately donned a tracksuit for a seven-kilometre run. Now she was jogging to the entrance of her flat in Pickham, London. Suddenly, she crouched and turned in one movement, pistol in hand. It wasn't easy to miss the footsteps behind her.

"And hello to you," said John Porter smiling comprehensively.

"John, what the hell are you doing here?"

"Heard the surf was up in Pickham. The last time I called we were interrupted."

She put the gun away.

"I didn't know you were in England and I remember I asked you to phone me."

"Sorry, lots of business to do. To make up, I'm inviting you to dinner."

"I just got back, I'm really tired."

He produced two shopping bags.

"You rest, I'll cook."

Chris didn't want to mention right away that she had seen his photograph in Paraguay. It could wait until later. She dozed on the sofa for 30 minutes and woke to find him kneeling by her side.

"Dinner is served," he announced.

Refreshed by the sleep she attacked the meal with enthusiasm and then John brought coffee, joining her on the sofa with a mischievous grin.

"The book says now's the time to put an arm round you."

"Revised in the second edition. It now reads 'woman kisses man's cheek'. I'll have to do that then."

As she pulled away, he turned his face, held her chin gently and kissed her lips.

"Okay, I jumped 2 pages," he murmured, eyes sparkling.

"If you stay, you'll have the sofa."

"Fine, that's in chapter 2."

"Then you're welcome and I'm off to sleep. One more thing."

"Yes?"

"Don't read books in bed."

Chris woke at her usual 6 a.m., showered, dressed and went to the kitchen to brew coffee. John was still asleep when she dumped the steaming mugs on the low table and opened the curtains on a bright crisp autumnal morning. She picked up her mug and then sat watching him.

It's said that seeing a man wake up tells you a great deal about him. For example how much his beard grows in the night and if his lovely eyes blink as they open. Actually it reveals very little except whether you are attracted to him. He blinked, rubbed a hand over his chin and sat up.

"Coffee's still warm," she said.

"Guess I was also a little tired."

He didn't mention he had been awake thinking until three hours ago. That was all the sleep he needed.

"Chris, I need to talk to you."

"Secret wife, prison record or part-time porn film star?"

He laughed, looking down into his mug.

"You discovered some things about me. First, will you tell me the details of your involvement with this business? We found out that you work for the Omasor Agency but don't know who's employing you people."

"Yes, I work for Omasor and no one is employing us. It started as part of a routine investigation into the murder of one of our people. Soon after, another one was killed and I was there but couldn't prevent it. The murderers are looking for something and we've been trying to stop them finding it whilst attempting to terminate their organisation."

"So your involvement was based purely on the killings at Countess Pollan's house."

"That's how it began. I met your friend Mary Duckworth in Paraguay. I think she likes you."

He looked faintly embarrassed.

"I've known her for a long time."

"Now what were you going to talk to me about?"

"I want to formally ask you to join the Octagon."

"Is that the Pentagon on a bigger budget?"

"I'd like to tell you a long story and I think I can trust you now."

She nodded and he continued.

"It begins in the 16th century when a man called Dr John Dee was the chief scientist in Queen Elizabeth's court. He was a genius, covering a vast range of subjects and even reputedly having an influence in the defeat the Spanish Armada."

"I've never heard of Dee."

"He was before his time in many ways. These days he's best known for his attempts to communicate with the spirit world. He worked with several assistants, psychics if you like and the best-known was a man named Edward Kelly. Kelly demonstrated an aptitude as a medium, usually using a scrying stone during the experiments. He passed on messages from the spiritual domain, often in a completely new language."

"What's a scrying stone?"

"It's almost any object, usually translucent, which helps the medium concentrate. Kelly used a piece of natural obsidian that's now in the British Museum."

"This is not a film script?"

"It's not fiction. The messages gave the names and hierarchy of the angels in great detail. However there were two negatives that most people quote to dismiss the researches. First that Kelly had a previous record of fraud and second that one message from the angels dictated by Kelly required the two men to swap wives for a period."

"16th-century debauchery. Sounds conclusive to me."

"Yes, superficially I'd agree and I felt exactly the same when I was first told. Most people would look no further but if you study the texts, the size, scope and sheer complexity is amazing. It's almost impossible to believe Kelly could have concocted it. Of course, he may well have added the wife swap for his own purposes but that doesn't invalidate the substance of the work."

"So I'll keep an open mind. Why is this relevant?"

"I'm coming to it. Everything I tell you from now is outside the public domain. It was apparently recorded by the founder of the Octagon and has been passed down since then through the members. In 1585 Dee became close friends with a man called James Smith who was also a keen student of the spirit world but very much a sceptic. Eventually Smith convinced Dee to allow him to borrow Kelly for his own experiment. This was conducted under the most stringent of conditions that wouldn't have disgraced a modern research laboratory. At first, Kelly was unable to produce anything but on the third day he suddenly began quoting text as if in a trance, speaking so quickly that Smith was barely able to transcribe his words. After 20 minutes Kelly collapsed and didn't recover for two days. He had no recollection at all of the session and was completely unable to perform for Smith again, returning to Dr Dee a day later."

"Now I'm intrigued. What was the message?"

John paused, considering his words.

"Essentially there were three revelations. The first was a warning of a future event, the second was the Blessing and the third was the location of the Lifeblood."

"Well that means nothing to me. What was the future event?"

"I don't know the details. I've only been told that it will occur on the 20th of March 2019 and result in the death of every person on this planet except those who are taking the Blessing."

Chris grinned in disbelief.

"I've heard a few of these stories before. Not many years to go so maybe you need to build an ark and start collecting pairs of animals."

A cloud breezed over his face.

"Yes, perhaps."

"So what is this life saving Blessing?"

"It's a mixture that we usually take in liquid form although I'm not sure if that's its natural state."

"And it will stop you dying along with everyone else in 2019?"

He hesitated.

"Not just that. It also gives eternal youth."

Chris laughed harshly.

"John, I really thought you were intelligent. This is complete rubbish, some old weirdos coming up with a Shangri-La story. It might fool a few desperate old women I suppose."

"I expected that response and felt just the same way when I was told"

"So you are now going to tell me you're a hundred years old."

"I was born in 1950 and I guess I should be retired now. I could show you a birth certificate or other documents, but you'd suspect they were forgeries. There just isn't a conclusive way to prove it unless you take the Blessing yourself."

Her disbelief secure, Chris poured another coffee.

"And the last revelation, the place to find this Lifeblood?"

"The Lifeblood is the vital, tenth constituent. Its hiding place was revealed through Kelly. Let me finish the story, it might help you to understand."

He sipped from his mug and continued.

"The message also contained specific instructions regarding the number who could share the gift of eternal youth. It was limited to no more than four men and four women at any time."

"So just eight of you would populate the world after 2019?"

"That's what the spirit said. As you can imagine, James Smith was stunned by all this information but he determined to at least test the formula. After locating the Lifeblood, he created a supply of the Blessing. With some reservations he decided to try it on himself, taking just a couple of drops of liquid. Within 24 hours he was astonished at the change. He felt stronger and fitter and his appearance was more youthful. That gave him a problem as he realised that people who knew him would be amazed to see the transformation. Amazed and suspicious. He would almost certainly have been accused of consorting with the devil and executed. So he left his house immediately and obtained a property in a remote part of Devon where no one knew him. At first, he was too cautious to divulge the secret to anyone but he finally decided to confide in his friend Christopher Marlowe."

"The Marlowe who wrote plays?"

"That's the one. Smith gave Marlowe a dose of the Blessing, mainly to confirm if it worked on others. It did but Marlowe then had the same problem of people noticing how young he'd become. With his knowledge of the theatre, he used various devices to conceal his youthful appearance but it soon became impossible to keep doing that. Eventually he faked his own death in 1593 before anyone became too suspicious."

"As I recall, he knew Shakespeare."

John laughed.

"He was Shakespeare. The Stratford guy was a close friend and they agreed initially that Marlowe could use his name for some of his works. Then, from 1593, Marlowe used the name for everything as it would have been a bit strange for a dead man to be writing plays. The impersonation ended with Shakespeare dying in 1616 and then Marlowe needed a new identity so he became Greville Benville."

"You're rewriting English history. Go on."

"James Smith and Marlowe-Benville kept the secret to themselves for 40 years, revelling in their continued youth. By the 1640s they were both over 80 years old with the bodies of men in their late teens or early twenties. They were close companions and reputedly each of them bedded more women each year than Casanova did in a lifetime. That's another effect of the Blessing. It gives you an increased sex drive."

"I'll take that as read, no need to expand."

"Then, in 1642 the English Civil War properly began. Marlowe-Benville became a staunch Royalist but Smith didn't take a side."

"I know a bit about it from college. It wasn't really a Civil War at all as the vast majority of people were neutral."

In his book 'Who's Fooling Who? History's Hidden Truths', Counson Westlo includes a relevant section.

'The so-called English Civil War split the country between Royalists headed by a 'King' and so called 'Roundheads' who they say supported parliament. These armies supposedly fought a series of battles at places no-one has ever heard of like 'Adwalton Moor', 'Naseby' and, laughingly, 'Winceby'. All I can say is that if you believe Winceby, you'll believe anything. Despite claims that 'thousands of men' were involved, not one of them is alive today and my researches have revealed that even the horses are dead.

Coincidence? I think not. This charade makes the grassy knoll seem like a small green hill.'

John nodded.

"Everything changed when Marlowe-Benville was killed in battle in 1649."

"How could he die if he was taking this Blessing?"

"It's for eternal youth, not eternal life. Whatever age you start taking it, within a few days your body reaches its optimum physical condition. That's usually somewhere between the ages of 18 and 25. Providing you have the Renewal, your body will remain at that age."

"Renewal?"

"The name for the annual event where we take the Blessing. It's now developed into a sort of party for the recipients."

"So you can die?"

"We're not susceptible to any illness ranging from the common cold to cancer. Cuts and wounds heal almost immediately. However we can die from anything instantly lethal, a shot in the head or heart, a car crash or similar. Benville was killed by a sword to the heart."

"This is a good story."

"James Smith was completely shattered by the death of his companion. Remember that they'd known each other for over half a century. He decided to select four of his closest friends to share the Blessing and in 1650 he held a meeting, known as the Resolution, to decide the future. They agreed that the group should split up, moving to new locations and preferably to different countries to reduce the risk of detection. Each of the four, known as Primaries, was to select another person to share the Blessing. These assistants were to be known as Secondaries and I'm one of them. Smith named the group the Octagon."

"My addition makes a total of nine which breaks your commandment."

"No it was eight. Smith had decided to die. Perhaps he was afraid of imprisonment because of his association with a Royalist, maybe he was distraught at the loss of his friend or it could be that he just got tired of life. He was the only one who knew the constituents of the Blessing and the location of the Lifeblood. He also held all the transcriptions of the spirit's revelations. Smith announced he would conceal everything in new hiding places and then take poison."

"So how could they continue without the youth drug?"

"They had it. Smith made a supply of the Blessing, sufficient to last to the year 2019. This was to be held by one of the Primaries, to be known as the Provider. Once every year, that person and their Secondary would arrange to give a dosage to each of the other three pairs. This event, the Renewal, was to be held at a different place and time for each pair."

Chris nodded.

"Okay, assuming that the Provider and their sidekick took their dose when they wanted, there would be three of these Renewals every year, one for each of the other three pairs. But if the members were in secret locations, how did this Provider communicate the venue and date?"

"Very simply. At every Renewal, the Provider secretly advised the recipients the details of where and when they would meet in one year's time. Remember that each of the four pairs was unaware of the location of the others. It could be anywhere in the world. As extra security, the Provider and their Secondary were not to attend the Renewal personally. They were to delegate another person to act as the host who was to unknowingly give the recipients the dose of the Blessing and also the details of the next year's Renewal in a sealed envelope."

"Is this Blessing like a potion?"

"It's taken as a liquid and usually presented in a wine bottle. The Provider gives it to the host with instructions to serve only to the recipients."

"But something went wrong this year."

"Yes. Each of us turned up at the appointed place but there was no one there."

"Meaning your supplier had a problem?"

"More than that. If the Provider had suffered an accident then their Secondary would have arranged the Renewal and told us. We all suspected that both were dead but didn't even know who they were and certainly not where they lived."

"So what did you do?"

"Smith had specified a location, Canterbury Cathedral, where all the Octagon would finally get together in 2018 on the 20th of March, exactly one year before the event. This was also the place where members should meet in case of an emergency and so we all went there when our Renewal didn't happen."

"How did that help if you didn't know where the Blessing was?"

"Our founder was a remarkable man. He had even allowed for this situation and one duty of the Provider was to give each of the other three pairs a sealed envelope that contained a guide to the location of the Blessing. The place was only revealed if all three guides were put together."

"What if this Provider changed the hiding place?"

"They gave a new sealed envelope to the others at the next Renewal. Our three Primaries all received one twelve years ago which indicated the location had been changed at that time. We got the three clues and found the Blessing. This time we've split the supply between us so we each have enough to last until 2019."

"All these procedures seem a bit convoluted."

"Sure, that's what I said when I was told. As Mary Duckworth, my Primary explained, you need to remember that all this was organised by James Smith way back in 1650 when the country was in turmoil after the Civil War. Lots of suspicion and treachery at that time. He also had to base the system on the communication methods available at that time. No electronic stuff then."

"But there's something else, isn't there? The other thing that Smith concealed. This Lifeblood, the tenth component of the Blessing."

John nodded.

"The critical ingredient. It's something very special but I don't know what."

"So your group got together recently and found the ready mixed Blessing stock but nothing else."

"That's right. The formula and the Lifeblood are really much more valuable than the Blessing itself and Smith had concealed both of them in another place. That is revealed in something possessed by the three Primaries but even they don't know what."

"That doesn't make sense. How could they have the information and not know?"

"It was another failsafe that Smith instituted. All I've been told is that each Primary, including the Provider, were given something at the first meeting, the Resolution. Each of these items contains part of a clue to the location of the Lifeblood and formula but none of the members knew what the item was."

"With your man Smith's usual obsession with secrecy, I presume that you need all four things to find this place?"

"That's my understanding."

"So why didn't you do that during your recent get-together?"

"I don't know the exact answer. Only the Primaries know for sure. I can guess, though."

"Go ahead."

"Okay. First problem is that we didn't recover the possessions of the Countess, so one of the four components was missing. Second, there isn't a desperate need to find the stuff as we've all now got a stock of the Blessing to last until 2019."

"I'll try for a third. The three remaining Primaries don't trust each other enough to share the secret?"

John grinned.

"You're reading my mind. That's worrying."

Chris smiled.

"What other little secrets does your Octagon have?"

"In the original messages, the spirit applied one other limitation. When you take the Blessing it is not possible to conceive children. Until 2019, that is. Men are effectively infertile and women cannot become pregnant."

"So you've given up the naughty stuff until then?"

He laughed.

"No. As I mentioned, it actually increases the sex drive. It's just that conception is impossible. Don't ask me the how and why, that's just the way it is."

This was starting to seem too complex and practical to be pure invention but Chris remained sceptical, particularly about the everlasting youth part.

"That seems ridiculous but I won't push it," she remarked

"There's one more thing. From the fact that you and our enemy were both able to find Mr Pierce, it's obvious that the Provider must have been keeping some information about the location of the Primaries. That was against the rules of the Octagon and we still don't know how this information was recorded."

"I can't tell you much about it. Somehow the details are linked to an engraved plaque. The Countess had one, there was another on Wang Shu Island and I guess one in Paraguay as well. These must have contained a something that helped to provide the location of another member."

He nodded.

"Mary has never shown me a plaque but we thought it was something on those lines."

"I think I understand your structure now. There were two people, a Primary and a Secondary, in each of four places. The Provider, as you call her, was Countess Pollan who was killed along with her Secondary. Then Arthur Pierce with Catherine in Hong Kong and Mary Duckworth and you in Paraguay. That leaves one more pair."

John's expression darkened.

"There was a pair but the Secondary was killed. The Primary is based in the USA, California to be exact. I guess you found information in Paraguay to confirm that and you'll be heading there next?"

Chris needed time to think.

"I wasn't invited. I think Selena may have gone."

"Do you think she wishes to harm us?"

"I'm sure she won't, unless you cause her problems. Her main target, and mine, is our mutual enemy."

"Then we're on the same side."

"Let's say we have an opponent in common."

He paused and looked directly into her eyes.

"Okay, I've told you the background. Will you join the Octagon?"

"Of all people in the world, why pick me?"

The odds of being one of eight people selected from the whole population of the world are very large. You can calculate them exactly by very simple arithmetic. Mathematicians, using Torkman's Theory call the result 'extremely unlikely'. The average person (see definition) knows it as 'no chance'.

"The Octagon members have discussed it and believe you have all the qualifications. You're intelligent, naturally fit, trustworthy and you already know much of the background."

"Also you're all scared now and need my firepower. I've decided to tell you who the real opposition is. You've heard of Martina Crowne's beauty empire?"

"Even men know about that."

"Your enemies are Martina and her daughter Jessica, an evil bitch if ever there was. They employ a team of killers, headed by a vicious woman called Karmen. Unlimited funding, I believe and they're determined to get what they want."

"You're joking. Women from a beauty salon heading a gang?"

"No joke. I saw Jessica murder a man."

"And they're after the Blessing?"

"Must be. I still don't know if it's real but they must believe it is. The Octagon is in big trouble and you're in danger, John."

He gave a rueful look.

"I was nearly killed a few days ago."

"What?"

"It was Catherine, the girl you met on Wang Shu Island. She's definitely unbalanced. She tried to seduce and then murder me. The USA Secondary, Valla Toreus, tried to stop her but got killed."

"How did you escape?"

"I fought her off and then she disappeared."

"Why did she do it?"

"I don't know. Maybe she just went completely mad or perhaps the Crowne gang got to her. Anyway you're right that we all feel threatened and need help to defend ourselves. But it's not the only reason for the invite. We do like a lot of things about you."

Chris reached an arm around his neck and pulled him into her kiss.

29

Arthur Pierce settled on the wooden chair. Yes, much better. He had grown up before padded seats and never found modern office furniture comfortable. The desk in front of him was a simple design, again in wood. Pierce had always been a frugal man and wasn't going to change after 350 years.

He sat in the largest of a four-office suite at Jim Fischer's operations centre in Cragbutt, California. A massive complex of buildings with more than enough space to accommodate Pierce and the two business managers he had brought with him. They occupied another of the offices. The third held four people, all provided by Fischer. Two secretaries and two advisers, both experts in a wide number of languages.

The last office, the one next to Pierce, was for Della, another person supplied by Fischer. She was his personal assistant who arranged everything. Although he was no stranger to American business, he needed someone with local knowledge to smooth out problems and open doors. Pierce found her very acceptable. A smart and intelligent young blonde lady. He was oblivious to her overt, even overwhelming sexuality and she masked it as much as possible with ordinary business suits and lack of cosmetics.

Pierce was satisfied. His team had already set up all the necessary links to his worldwide business empire. Just one concern. John Porter had made a video call to advise the three Primaries that Valla had been killed. It had happened while he was out of the house and he had found the body when he returned. But Catherine had disappeared. John reported that he believed Omasor were responsible and that they had taken Catherine away for questioning.

It wasn't a major concern. Pierce cared little if she was alive or dead. This latest absence had sealed her fate and he had already issued orders to his agents to kill her as soon as she was found. His new assistant could take her place. Fischer had strongly recommended that. Yes, Catherine would be executed. Just another in a massive list of dead that Pierce was responsible for.

Mary Duckworth had arrived 48 hours ago and set herself up in another part of the complex. She appeared to prefer a separate existence and Pierce had seen little of her. That suited him well as he wasn't a socialising person.

In the adjoining office, Della settled back in her chair. She was very content with her appointment and felt it was a justified reward for all the hard work she had put in, nearly all of it in bed with Fischer. He'd given her a huge salary, house and car and she believed there were good prospects of replacing his previous partner, that proper and passionless Valla.

Her phone rang and she conversed for a few seconds before connecting to Pierce.

"Yes?" he responded sharply.

"A woman is calling. She claims she is Catherine Bell, your Secondary."

"Trace the call while I speak with her."

"Yes sir. Putting her through now."

A pause.

"Catherine?"

"Yes, it's me. I'm so glad I could get through, I've been trying to find you for ages."

Definitely her voice and she seemed nervous, breathy.

"You obviously know where I am. Come here as quickly as possible."

"I really want to but I can't because they might get away."

"You are not making sense. Tell me clearly what the situation is."

"I've found the horrid people who keep trying to take our secret things."

"What? Who are they?"

Now Catherine was whispering.

"I can't tell you on the phone, they're in the next room. I went to their place and pretended to join them. They don't know who I really am. You must come quickly to meet me and I'll tell you everything."

"I'll send an armed team."

"No, just you. Lots of people will make them run away. Meet me at 47 Jackson Street in an hour."

The call finished and Pierce paused for thought. The girl's message could be plausible but he had never taken a risk his life and this was to be no exception. He was a man of many intellectual qualities but found interpersonal relationships difficult, particularly with women. Subconsciously, they frightened him. Pierce regarded the female gender like porcelain figures on a shelf and never recognised their emotions, passions and deceit.

He summoned Della who entered primly, well briefed by Fischer to correspond with Pierce's image of a perfect woman.

"Yes sir?"

He looked at her with approval. Dark suit with below knee skirt. Tidy hair, light cosmetics. Yes, she was very acceptable. He would have been less impressed by the crimson basque she was wearing in Fischer's bedroom the previous night.

"Catherine requests that I meet her alone in one hour."

He gave her a copy of the address.

"You can't go by yourself. I suggest you contact Mr Fischer to arrange suitable security. All the indications are that this girl is not trustworthy."

She had been working hard to split Catherine from him, knowing it was another chance to step in as replacement in case she didn't get Valla's position. Della found this dour man positively obnoxious. She had also grown increasingly repulsed by the attentions of Jim Fischer. His massive wealth had initially attracted her, more than enough to use her body effectively but now his overbearing attitude and shallowness disgusted her. But she had been told about the ultimate reward of the Blessing and that was worth any sacrifice to both men.

"I accept your viewpoint," Pierce responded and picked up the direct line to Fischer.

After hearing the outline of the situation, Fischer responded positively.

"The story doesn't sound right. I'm going to send a security team to the address and clean it out. The problem is that Catherine may not survive the attack."

"I am also unconvinced of her account and feel that my interests will be best served by Catherine's death."

A pause.

"You're right. Leave all that to me. Della will drive you down there and I'll have two cars following. By the time you arrive, I'll also have a squad staked around the area. My people will have ultimate force instructions."

Within 15 minutes, Jim Fischer had completed his arrangements. 15 armed agents were already on their way to surround the property with another four in two cars to tail Pierce. His instructions were clear. Kill everyone they found except Catherine. She must be restrained and brought to him. He had to have her once, by force if necessary and she could be disposed of afterwards.

Della pulled up outside 47 Jackson Street, one in a row of old tenement buildings in a rundown area on the outskirts of LA. The fading afternoon light exposed a few groups of shabbily dressed people loitering aimlessly. Not a place to be in after sunset.

She wore jeans and leather jacket and had bunched her hair under a woollen hat. An attempt to look as unfemale is possible. She knew about this neighbourhood and was taking extra care. Arthur Pierce was not at all comfortable here. He retained his usual dark suit and tie of the sort unknown in these parts.

"Are you sure that I am protected?" he asked quietly.

"Yes, sir. Two of the groups of people on the street are our agents. Plus that man sitting on the steps of number 47."

Pierce emerged from the car and looked around nervously. Then he opened the door again.

"You will accompany me."

A flash of uncertainty in her eyes.

"Mr Fischer said I should wait here."

"This is instruction. Disobey and your employment is terminated."

His eyes indicated that the words employment and life were interchangeable here and Della briefly balanced the risks against the rewards to come. She got out of the car and Pierce kept behind her as they mounted the steps. An apparently drunken man there. He looked up blearily and held out a palm.

"A few dollars, Mister?"

Pierce ignored that but was reassured by the man's subtle wink. Yes, Fischer would ensure he was safe here but he still wanted Della to be the one to enter the house first. She pushed at the door and it swung open. Large hallway with several doors and old wooden stairs. Pierce jumped as the door clunked shut behind them.

"It's okay. Just spring-loaded," whispered Della.

Pierce leant close to speak in her ear.

"I see no sign of Catherine and certainly do not propose to visit every apartment in the structure."

Then a figure appeared at the top of the stairs. Catherine, dressed in a skin tight black outfit. She put her finger to her lips, beckoning urgently with the other hand.

"I'll wait here," whispered Della.

"No. You will ascend in front of me," replied Pierce, pushing her to the staircase.

Creaky stairs and darker as they climbed up. No windows and the dimmest lighting. Catherine had disappeared. Turning at the top, they ascended another flight to reach the next floor. The girl was at the top of the stairs again.

"Come here!" hissed Pierce but she continued upwards, still beckoning.

When they reached the next floor, she was standing beside an open door. The finger on her lips again but now her expression was pleading.

At that moment 20 men, divided into two equal groups, had gathered outside number 47. The drunk had suddenly come to life and was giving orders.

"You ten come with me, we're going right to the top and work downwards. The others start with the ground floor and work up. Kill anyone suspicious."

"What's the definition of that?" asked one man.

"Everyone is suspicious except Pierce and Della. Is that clear?"

The group nodded, some with grins. Then the sound of an engine as a large street cleaning lorry pulled into the street, hoses on the near side spraying the sidewalk.

"Not normal. They come early morning and he's driving too fast. Get ready," instructed the ex drunk. The men were still scurrying for position as the vehicle passed. The water spray had been switched off the liquid now spurted from another set of tubes, cascading out in a torrent. Screams as it struck the scattered men. Screams of agony. The liquid sizzled on the skin, burning into the flesh. Acid.

Suddenly, another vehicle screeched into the street, disgorging a number of figures with automatic weapons. Thudding noises from the silenced guns as a barrage of bullets hammered into Fischer's men.

Inside number 47, the sounds were dull and barely recognisable.

"What's that?" asked Pierce as he approached Catherine.

"Just silly cars in the street. Come in, quickly," she whispered with a smile.

Pierce pushed Della in front of him as they entered the apartment. He looked around quickly. A large room with a bed at one end, sofa and tables at the other. Kitchen alcove set back and one door that must lead to a bathroom.

Catherine closed the door and moved close to him.

"Who is she?" she hissed.

He disliked her close proximity and edged back slightly.

"This is Della, my assistant. Now you will tell me immediately what this is about. I am very displeased with your disappearance."

"But I'm your assistant. She looks like a horrible girl."

His voice changed, as near as he ever got to anger.

"Catherine! You will answer my question."

The girl didn't reply, looking up at him with a sullen expression.

"Is she on drugs or something?" asked Della.

Now sullen changed to fiery anger as Catherine spun round.

"I am a beautiful princess and you're a nasty little girl who lets old men do things for money. I hate you."

Della's eyes widened at the ferocity in her voice but she wasn't ready for the physical attack. Catherine jumped forward to rake her nails over the blonde's cheek. Della screamed and then gasped as a fist sank into her stomach. She fell to the floor and Catherine began to kick her.

Pierce had no intention of getting involved. No intention of continuing to question Catherine. Only one thought in his mind. Get out of here. He moved quickly to open the door. A woman outside, holding a gun. Slim with dark hair and snake eyes.

"Please come with me, Mr Pierce," Karmen instructed.

Now he was frightened and walked obediently in front of the woman to another room on the same floor. A blur of events after entering. Clothes stripped from him, manacles on wrists, the flash of cameras.

Two hours later, Jim Fischer was looking at prints of a photograph and the accompanying email. The request was very simple. Bring all the Octagon plaques to a specific location and Pierce would be exchanged for them.

"What's your opinion?" he asked.

Mary sat opposite him, looking at a duplicate set. The photo showed Arthur Pierce looking directly at the camera, handcuffed and naked.

"Why did they take his clothes?" she asked.

"Mainly to prove the picture wasn't rigged. I'm certain they got him and that the crazy bitch Catherine loaded the trap. They also got Della but no mention of her in the note."

Mary's expression was totally dispassionate. She recognised that he was more concerned about the woman than Pierce.

"They will not be given the plaques. That is the fundamental of any strategy we institute."

Jim nodded. He still had no affinity with her but shared that opinion.

"I agree totally. Don't think I'm happy about this. I sent a large armed team to protect Pierce but they were decimated in some sort of acid attack. I'm already recruiting double the number to replace them but what's done is done."

Jim was floundering and desperately hoping that Mary would have an idea. He looked at her expectantly.

"In my opinion, we should agree to the request but provide duplicates of the plaques with meaningless text. There is therefore no limit to any activity by your people."

"That's my thinking. We use the blackmail to get rid of a few of them while my men take any necessary action to find this gang."

"After talking to Darmant, John has identified the leaders. Martina and Jessica Crowne. We have no idea how they discovered their existence but it's very obvious that they know about the Blessing."

"I've even thought of sending a hit team to their place in Switzerland."

Mary shrugged.

"Do as you like. The critical aspect is that time is on our side. We just need to last out until 2019 when the Crownes and all their people will disappear forever. Our only duty is to ensure they do not locate the Lifeblood and the formula."

"Right. No worries, we'll be fine."

An out-of-town crossroads. No habitations in sight. No traffic on the road this early in the morning. Two cars came into view, travelling smoothly down the highway. They pulled off at the crossroads and the driver of the second transferred to the other vehicle. It drove off rapidly.

A mile away, on the other road, two other cars were parked. Karmen was in the back of the first, studying a large laptop monitor that displayed an ultra-clear view of the crossroads from the high-resolution camera she had positioned there.

"I still don't trust them," she muttered.

Catherine squirmed in the seat beside her.

"Not fair. I thought you were my friend," she grumbled, lips down turned.

Karmen looked up.

"Stop this now. You can not kill Pierce. He is needed for this trade-off."

"Just for a few silly plaques? We should kill all the nasty Octagon people, they were horrible to me."

Karmen sighed. She hadn't wanted Catherine on this mission but the girl had begged Jessica and she had agreed.

"Listen. I am going to instruct my people now. I want you to sit here quietly like a good girl."

"I know! Let me cut off his things before he goes."

The girl was wide-eyed now, appealing.

"No. We will give you other men to do that with. Now be quiet."

Karmen spoke quickly on her communicator and the other car pulled away. She monitored the screen for its arrival. Six minutes before the picture showed it pulling up at the crossroads and she switched on the speaker.

"What now?" asked a voice.

"You remain where you are. The other one to take Pierce to the car."

She saw her man emerge, pushing the captive in front of him. Pierce was now back in his dark suit but still handcuffed. The pair walked to the parked car.

"Wait there. What do you see?" she asked.

"There's a package on the back seat, wrapped in brown paper."

"Anything not right? Look carefully but do not touch the car."

Two minutes before he responded.

"It seems okay to me."

"Tell Pierce to get the package. Take off his handcuffs."

She stared at the screen. Handcuffs removed. Pierce opened the car door and picked up the package. He carried it to her man who was waiting, pistol in hand.

"You want us to grab it and go?" he asked.

"No. Do not touch the package. Tell him to unwrap it first. Then wait."

She saw Pierce kneeling down and unwrapping the brown paper.

"What do you see?"

"A set of plaques. I'll check the first one."

She saw him reach down.

"Wait!" she yelled.

Screen white. Screen black.

"Get there fast," Karmen shouted at the driver.

"Your little camera isn't working now," observed Catherine.

"I told you to be quiet."

The girl made a face.

"That's a horrid thing to say. You know I'm very special and you shouldn't talk to me like that."

"Yes. I'm really very sorry, Catherine. Please forgive me," Karmen responded, calculating brain overriding emotions as usual.

They reached the crossroads in three minutes. Nothing much to see. Not a small bomb. A saucer shaped crater that extended well beyond the remains of the two cars. A few body parts scattered around amongst the scraps of metal.

Catherine leant forward to look.

"Look! There's a leg and most of a head just near to it," she shouted with excitement.

"Go now. Fast," Karmen called to the driver.

30

The first shafts of dawn skimmed across Hawaii, its pale tendrils stimulating a faint shimmer of foreboding over the island. A lone Alsatian dog awoke on a porch then howled with strange certainty at the rising sun. Something evil filled the atmosphere with a malevolent vigour that chilled the heart and bones.

Meanwhile, in sunny California, the town of Cragbutt was warm and optimistic, a twelve house town dominated by the Fischer complex on a hill to the north.

Jessica racked her eyes from semi closed to wide open to appraise Karmen who was above her, lying prone just below the brow of the hill. The lean woman was holding high-powered zoom binoculars for a close-up inspection of the Fischer home. Karmen had never attracted her. She was not the most tempting woman in the world and maybe they were too similar. But then Jessica had never been attracted to a person, only to domination over them. Usually she could buy this control as she did with Karmen but others, like Hony and Catherine, needed another incentive. When she had the secrets of the Octagon, she wouldn't require any of them and they would disappear from her life rapidly and very permanently.

Jessica had traced the Fischer location from credit cards and papers Catherine had snatched from Valla's body. Now she was certain that all the remaining members of the Octagon were here, in this building and their possessions must be with them. The quest her family had pursued for so long was almost fulfilled. Almost but not quite. All she needed were the plaques. Karmen had failed to get the one in Paraguay but Jessica knew it had been moved here. It must be in the complex, together with the one owned by Jim Fischer.

Karmen slid down from the crest of the hill and Jessica studied her face. The ruthless snake eyes betrayed no emotion but something was there. Something she couldn't control, something she didn't like.

"What do you see?" she asked.

"The building is protected by three concentric electrified fences with probable infrared, movement and heat sensors in between them. There are guard posts at the outer and inner fences, just an automatic gate in the centre one. Video cameras everywhere. I can't see a simple way for us to get in."

Jessica didn't like negatives but respected the woman's combat knowledge.

"Underground routes?"

"No, I checked the surveys."

"We could walk up to the gate and seduce the guards."

"I saw those 25 films. Never works in reality."

"How then?"

Karmen gestured to the three cars parked off-road below them.

"We have eight men with us. I can have another 40 ready for tomorrow."

"You said we couldn't get through the fences."

"We cannot go through or under so we go over."

"I think I see."

"But we'll need a diversion and also people on the inside to secure these plaques you are seeking."

"Right. If fighting starts, I can't risk them being destroyed."

"We don't know where they are kept so perhaps two of us have to be in there to locate the plaques during the attack."

"And the diversion?"

"I am thinking of the Busser brothers."

Jessica grimaced. "Surely not them."

"They are very expendable."

After 30 minutes, the plan had been formulated.

"This is going to be one helluva battle," said Jessica.

Karmen's eyes sparkled.

"Yes, I expect so."

At two minutes before eight the next morning a van drove up to the outer gate and stopped at the checkpoint. Klaus Busser wound down the window and spoke to the guard in a broad, mid-European dialect.

"Food supplies we have to deliver."

He shifted his large bulk in the seat and glanced nervously at Vini. Klaus was over 19 stone of blubber with not an ounce of muscle on him while his brother was small and wiry with quick little nervous eyes.

The guard looked at the delivery note, hand written on a sheet of lined paper.

"You're not the regular delivery people."

"It is illness they have. We come because." Klaus smiled but beads of sweat appeared on his brow.

"Do you have ID?"

"No, just potatoes and carrots."

"Identification papers."

"Ah, yes have."

He pulled two cards from his pocket and passed them to the guard. They looked like inkjet photos and recently printed by the signs of the smudge marks. The names were of two male movie stars.

"Wait here."

He returned to the building and showed the IDs to the chief officer, seated at the desk.

"Can you believe these guys?" he asked, leaning over to zoom in the video camera and up the microphone volume.

"I think we fooled them, Vini," Klaus was saying.

The chief reached for the phone. A two-minute call.

"We let them in," he said.

"You're joking."

"Orders. I guess they want to question them."

The guard walked back, arriving just as a voice came from the back of the van.

"Damn hot it is inside box."

"Quiet, Morno, they will hear," whispered Klaus, very audibly.

He turned quickly to the guard.

"Van make noises. Cold weather is cause for that."

He brushed more sweat from his brow. The fierce morning sun could have fried eggs on the van roof.

"Okay, go ahead. You'll get full instructions at the next checkpoint," said the guard, handing back the flimsy ID cards.

They drove through the outer and middle fences, remote-controlled gates opening and closing behind them.

"We're through and all is great," called Vini, mainly for the benefit of the boxed Morno.

A reception was ready at the inner checkpoint. Klaus counted 12 armour-suited guards with Callioni semi automatic rifles levelled at the van. No one approached but a speaker boomed.

'Turn to your right and enter the area marked Vehicles.'

Klaus turned the wheel and saw the sign mounted on a massive reinforced steel door. It slid open and they entered what was effectively an open topped box, five times the size of the van with massive concrete slab walls on three sides and the now closed steel door behind them. No people or exits visible.

'Stand in front of the van and leave the vehicle open,' the loudspeaker instructed.

As soon as Klaus and Vini complied, a concealed entrance opened in the steel door and three dogs leapt forward, followed by a massive, smiling woman.

"I'm Tara, I run security here," she said.

The dogs had just started searching the van when one of the cartons burst open and a red-faced, sweating Morno leapt out, waving a pistol.

"We get them now, brothers."

Before he had moved two paces, he dropped the gun, primarily as a result of Tara's bullet hitting his arm. The leaping stopped when another hit his leg.

Klaus shook his head

"Not good, maybe."

He looked at the skies for redemption. The heavens came good this time.

The distant throbbing sound rapidly increased in volume. Two Switzenberg Blue Fire helicopters suddenly appeared and all hell broke loose. The first came towards the gate entrance launching rockets at both the outer and inner guard posts.

The chief officer had already left the outer post and was sprinting for the inner when they hit. The explosions threw him to the ground but he was up and running again a second later.

The second Blue Fire came low and slow from the opposite direction, spouting a curtain of machine-gun bullets. The guards began returning fire and saw two figures dropping from the craft. They didn't notice the bodies were dressed in replicas of their own uniform or that they were very much alive.

The battle continued for six minutes with the helicopters now circling the complex. They continued to launch rockets, grenades and bullets, rocking the whole area with explosions.

Suddenly, as if a whistle had blown, the defensive fire ceased completely except for one central two-storey building. Both helicopters dropped to a metre from the ground and armed figures jumped out, running for cover. They began to form a decreasing circle around the central building, satisfied they had cornered the defending force. Jessica surveyed the scene from the first helicopter and shouted into her handset.

"We can't wait, hit them hard and get in there."

The Blue Fire lifted to 50 metres. She could see that the bombardment of the central building was increasingly effective. Rockets and explosive bullets had torn great gouges out of the walls. The roof was half destroyed and grenades were being lobbed through the shattered windows. Still the defenders maintained a continuous stream of bullets.

Her handset beeped. Karmen.

"A trick. No one there."

"That's crazy, we're getting blasted."

"Robot weapons."

"What?"

"Guards…tunnel."

The speaker crackled and went dead.

Jessica ordered her mystified forces to return to the helicopters and as they were scrambling on board she noticed two men struggling towards them, supporting another limping figure

"Woman banged Morno with gun," shouted Kurt.

"Don't you ever die?" Jessica responded.

"Too clever us we are, too clever."

She gave the order to lift off, ignoring the shouts of the stranded brothers.

Karmen and Catherine had jumped from their helicopter already dressed in an adequate reproduction of the guard uniforms copied from photographs. The plan was to mingle with the defenders in the confusion of the attack and then locate the storerooms. Karmen was satisfied they had not been noticed but waited undercover for a few seconds before joining the action. Two guards appeared in a doorway to the right and she started firing at the helicopters, careful to aim well above them. Then they ran across to join the men.

"Another 30 seconds and then we go," yelled one above the tumult.

Karmen nodded, wondering what he meant. After the half-minute, the men backed into the room, opened a steel door and sprinted down a long corridor with the two women close behind. The first guard unlocked another door at the end and rushed them through. They descended a long flight of steps with a third door at the bottom. Muscling past them, the man opened it and they found themselves in a tunnel large enough for a car to drive through. The men waited, looking down the tunnel to their right. About 20 seconds later they saw lights approaching. It was a sort of buggy train, electric powered and no sound. Rolling behind the lead vehicle were six open carriages almost full of uniformed guards. Karmen and Catherine jumped on as the train slowed briefly and it continued down the seemingly endless tunnel.

Karmen guessed they travelled 2 kilometres before reaching a floodlit area that bustled with activity. A commander was instructing the guards to form into their units.

"Follow me," she whispered to Catherine and they moved unobtrusively through the nearest door.

"What do we do now?" Catherine asked.

They had entered a short walkway with one door each side and steps leading up at the end.

"Check the rooms," instructed Karmen. She opened the left-hand door. Just an empty storeroom with neatly stacked cabinets of uniforms and weapons. Nothing useful here.

Catherine opened the opposite door to find a huge black woman seated at a desk. Tara.

"Who the hell are you?" she shouted, reaching for an automatic lying in front of her.

Catherine blazed off a shot that went well wide then slammed the door and sprinted along the walkway. Karmen was a better athlete and passed her before they reached the steps. She heard gunshots and saw Catherine stumble momentarily. Then they were through the door at the top and swung it closed behind them, ramming a chair under the handle. Catherine had a bloody deep groove across her neck and another on her thigh. To Karmen's astonishment, they began to heal in front of her eyes, flesh and skin repairing itself in seconds when it should have taken days or weeks.

"I get better quickly," said Catherine sweetly.

Karmen pulled out her phone and made the call to Jessica while Catherine surveyed the room. It was windowless and empty apart from a chair and a couple of packing boxes. The sound of raised voices came from behind a white painted door in the far wall and they could hear Tara beating upon the door behind them followed by a thud as she hit it with her huge shoulder.

"Let's go," said Karmen and they rushed through the white door, almost falling into an armed guard standing on the other side.

He'd chosen a bad place to be at that moment and didn't say another word. Ever. Speech is tricky when a bullet has entered the forehead. Catherine began to fire again and again at the prone body and Karmen grabbed her arm, conscious of the unnatural lust in the girl's eyes.

"You've already killed him."

"We'll kill everyone," the girl shouted, slamming another clip into her gun.

They were outside in a small Mexican style courtyard. Karmen sensed potential danger from the overlooking windows and pulled Catherine away from the body as she heard Tara finally demolish the inner door with a mighty crash. She dived into an archway on her left, just in time to avoid a burst of bullets fizzing past. Not Catherine. She was standing in the centre of the courtyard with a childlike smile on her face. Tara slammed another clip into her submachine gun.

"Drop your weapon and lie flat on the ground," she yelled.

Catherine gave a girlish giggle and shook her head. She began to sing.

"Humpty Dumpty sat on a wall, Humpty Dumpty had a great fall."

Then she walked towards Tara firing her pistol in time with the song. The huge woman was so surprised she didn't react. The first shots hit her in the head and then continued down her body. She crashed to the ground while Catherine continued walking until she stood over the body.

Then she started laughing. She didn't stop when Selena came through the doorway. Didn't stop as she turned to face her. She stopped when Selena blew her head off with a Cattanat shotgun.

Karmen cursed the girl for her stupidity but was relieved by her death. Catherine was completely insane. She looked through the archway. An open tarmac area with a group of guards standing about 50 metres away. No cover there and she was sure Selena would be coming from the other direction very soon. A door next to her. No choice. She dived inside an empty room, locked the door and phoned Jessica again.

"Catherine's dead. They are at a building about 2 kilometres north east. Use helicopters. They leave soon, hurry."

"Worked that out. We're nearly there," Jessica replied, apparently untroubled by the news of Catherine's death.

Karmen looked around for escape routes. Only one. A flight of stairs leading up. Shouting as the remaining guards, ran past the door of her hiding place. She sprinted up the stairway to reach a small landing with a single door. Crouching low, she opened the door and rolled inside, gun ready.

Jim Fischer turned quickly. He was alone.

"Don't shoot, I'm the boss," he screamed.

She remembered she was still in guard's uniform.

"I was sent to protect you, they will be here soon."

A movement through the window as she spoke. The two helicopters had now arrived and the first explosions shook the building. Karmen briefly considered capturing or killing Fischer. No point. He was unimportant, she only wanted the set of plaques and knew he wouldn't leave without them. The best plan was to keep with him.

Fischer grabbed papers from his desk and finished filling a briefcase.

"Okay, let's go," he shouted.

Darting eyes and rolling sweat betrayed his fear. He had built an impregnable fortress and it was being impregnated.

Karmen followed him through a door at the back and down another stairway into a loading bay. Two lorries with engines running were ready to leave with at least 20 guards milling around.

Jim screamed at them.

"You men open the doors, we're going now."

Seconds later the shutter doors lifted revealing three of Jessica's men. They were as exposed as naked pandas and the guards quickly mowed them down. As Jim hurried to reach the cab of the first lorry, Karmen ran along the rear of the vehicles, her hand slapping under the trailer bodies. The lorries raced off and Karmen sprinted back through the door to wait on the stairs. A successful operation. Now all they wanted was on two exposed vehicles.

Selena had arrived at the Fischer complex just after the attack started. It was obvious that the defences were superficial and the personnel poorly organised. She had driven up to the outer fence just as the guards were disappearing from sight underground. Following them through, she had then jogged along the tunnel out of sight of the train. At the terminus she slipped through the same door Karmen and Catherine had used earlier, arriving in the courtyard just too late to save Tara but soon enough to take care of the crazy Catherine.

Now she was running for a row of cars parked outside the shutter doors. She had watched the two lorries leaving and deduced their contents. At the same time, concurrently, just at that moment, a helicopter thundered into view and she saw the slim figure of Karmen run towards it then leap on board. The Switzenberg rose and veered away in the direction taken by the lorries.

Selena again cursed the stupidity of the defenders. They had obviously grossly overestimated the time it would take to discover the tunnel. Much safer to make a defence within the complex instead of taking their chances on an open road.

John Porter was happy and relaxed as he cruised from the airport towards the Fischer residence. He'd enjoyed being with Chris on the flight from England. Her elfin smile, her intelligence and something else intangible made the journey memorable. He felt content and secure in her company and drove slowly to maximise their time together.

"Not far now," he said.

She smiled.

"When this is over, maybe we could holiday somewhere?"

"I'd like that," he understated.

"What is this place like?"

"Valla said it's very quiet here. The complex is pretty isolated with almost no traffic."

He pointed at the empty road ahead.

As if this was a signal, three police cars and an ambulance burned up behind them with klaxons blaring at full volume. They swept past and disappeared round a hilly bend.

"Speed up, John."

"You think there's trouble?"

"Certain of it."

The road followed a twisting course through a hilly area and then they emerged suddenly into the aftermath of World War Three. A panorama of wrecked buildings and blazing fires with pillars of smoke everywhere. Bodies littered the ground like pins on a magnet. They could see small but increasing groups of police and fire fighters attempting to bring order to the scene.

Chris barely heard her phone ring in the mayhem.

"Are you here yet?" Selena's voice.

"I'm in California."

"Yes. Are you at the Fischer place?"

How the hell did she know?

"Yes, just arrived. What's happened here?"

"Jessica attacked. Octagon escaped in lorries, helicopters chasing. Go to Grace Highway, Mitchell crossroads. Jerome waiting. Fast."

"I'm with a friend."

"Yes. Tell him to move now if he wants to save his people."

Chris was surprised at that but quickly gave directions to John.

Jerome was waiting, waving his arms. The chunky version from her flat. Before they stopped, he was beckoning them and running towards a black Lustas

Repique, just about the most powerful car on the planet. The one known as Earth, for alien visitors.

Chris pushed John in the back and jumped in beside Jerome just as the car rolled forward.

"Strap in guys. I may need to hurry just a little."

A little goes a long way. While this statement can be evidenced by the dropped five cent coin or the vital little screw, the expression 'little things mean a lot' is patiently erroneous. Most women would never agree with it and etymologists believe it is a corruption of 'little kings lean a lot', which makes perfect sense.

Chris had never travelled so fast on land, the view from the side windows like a fast forward nature program. Jerome seemed completely relaxed and she could hear him humming in the amazingly quiet interior of the car.

"What are we doing?" she asked.

"About 150, I'd say. Never bother to check." The speedo showed he underestimated.

"You are irritating. I mean who are we after?"

"It's a chase straight out of the films. There are two lorries full of valuable stuff with bad guys in two helicopters chasing them and we're after both. Hold on."

He pointed at his headset. Someone was calling.

"Okay, we're on our way," he said after a few seconds.

"Selena?" Asked Chris

"Yes, she's ahead of us."

31

"I think we lost them," called Jim Fischer.

He was in the large cab of the first lorry with Mary Duckworth in the second, each of them with three of his best men. They hadn't heard the helicopters since they started and he saw only two cars on the road some way behind them.

The engines of the vehicles had been specially upgraded, enabling a top speed to match almost any works car, even when fully loaded. Jim's plan was to reach one of his other residences, Los Kalamo, about one hour's drive away. He had 12 men based there and had left instructions with the guards who had survived the attack on the main complex to join them as quickly as possible. Los Kalamo was built on the side of a hill, very compact with six secure underground rooms. Safety, he believed. If they could just reach it.

Jerome screamed round a curve.

"We'll try to get ahead of them," he muttered.

"Can you tell us what happened in the attack?" asked John.

"All I know is about 20 guards and eight attackers bit the dust. Selena told me she shot a woman called Catherine. Apparently the girl had killed her boss, Arthur Pierce plus Fischer's security chief."

"Is she really dead? You know we can recover quickly from wounds," asked John with concern.

"Yeah but not with your head blown off."

"Catherine murdered Valla and tried to kill me. I think she'd joined Jessica's gang. She just wasn't normal."

Chris grimaced.

"Pity Selena got to her before me. So Jerome, how did you know I was here?"

"Omasor knows many things."

"Yes and it's starting to annoy me."

"Fortune cookie say annoyance like North wind. Only comes one way, feel it less when go in other direction."

"But we're heading north."

"That's right, so you'll just have to live with it."

"Have I told you that you're very irritating?"

"Not in the last 30 seconds."

He was hitting the edge of the speedo and Chris stopped the questions.

Jim was the first to see the helicopter as they crested the top of a ridge. It was standing across the road next to a gas station with a rocky outcrop rising up the other side. The route was completely blocked, no way to go round.

"Stop, stop now," he shouted.

The heavy vehicle ground to a halt 150 metres from the roadblock.

"What now, boss?" asked the driver.

"I don't know yet. Wait a minute."

Jim was starting to panic. No Valla to ask. A man ran up from the second lorry.

"I see the roadblock, what do we do?" he asked.

"What do you suggest?"

"All I know is that we'd be sitting targets if we go forward."

"Then we'll turn and get out of here," Jim said decisively.

He remembered as he spoke. There were two helicopters.

Right on cue the second Blue Fire appeared behind them and the man began to run back to his lorry. He looked up and saw the dark haired woman seated in the open cabin door with a machine gun mounted on a tripod in front of her. Jessica pressed the fire button, perforating the running figure with a stream of bullets. He fell, then was up and moving again. She held the button until the feed of bullets was gone. He fell again, his body shredded like a cat's evening newspaper.

Jessica couldn't risk an all-out attack on the vehicles without the possibility of destroying the contents. She grabbed a microphone and her voice blared out through the speakers.

"Leave the lorries, drop your weapons and start walking towards the gas station."

To reinforce the instruction, Karmen emerged from behind the grounded helicopter followed by a group of ten armed figures. Jessica smiled grimly. They were trapped at last.

Then she felt the thud of a projectile followed by a loud blast. The helicopter slowly tipped forward then fell like Newton's apple. Just before it hit, she jumped out and sprinted for a group of large boulders. The crew were not so lucky. An explosion reverberated, shooting a huge ball of fire upwards. Once a

Blue Fire, now just a wreck remained. The apple, being hypothetical in this context, never reached the ground.

Karmen had watched Selena pull up her car beneath the helicopter and then fire the Soxvin armour piercing missile. She swore as the craft exploded and then turned to see her men scampering back to the gas station.

This was not going as planned. It got worse. Jerome and Chris came round the side of the parked helicopter holding machine guns. Chris sprayed a round of bullets in front of her men and they stopped uncertainly, trapped in the open. Meanwhile the occupants of the vehicles were emerging and approaching Karmen from the opposite direction.

She ran for the rocky area to her right with just enough time to dive for cover in a narrow gully as bullets pinged around her. Running around the curve of the ditch she crashed into Jessica. Karmen saw the vacant expression of one who has just been denied the prize of a lifetime. She didn't hesitate, slapping Jessica's face twice and hard. Then, grabbing her shoulders, she pushed her face close.

"We can still succeed but now we go quickly."

Karmen had her own plans but still needed Jessica for the present. Dragging her by the arm, she continued around the edge of a large boulder and emerged at the top of a slope. Down below, a car was parked by the side of a long straight road. A massively fat man stood in the centre of the highway, waving at passing vehicles that totally ignored him. Kurt Busser.

"Come on," she shouted and towing Jessica behind her, stuttered down the slope.

Kurt approached as they reached the bottom.

"Hello, lost we seem. Where we are? Help please."

Then his eyes widened as recognition burst in to his brain.

"Not good, I think," he murmured, a microsecond before Jessica rammed her foot into his huge stomach and then a neat fist to his jaw as he fell. The ground trembled with the impact of a mass of blubber.

"I feel better now," remarked Jessica

High-pitched squeals indicated the other brothers were in the car.

"Out," she called, jumping into the driver's seat. Vini helped a dismal Morno from the back seat.

"He hurts," said Vini in a pleading voice.

"So do I," replied Karmen crashing the heel of her hand into his face. She jumped in the car and they raced off to the east.

"We will not fail next time," said Jessica, the fires burning anew.

Karmen gave an anaconda smile.

"Yes, there is always another chance."

32

Mary and John sat at the large oval table in one of the upper conference rooms of Los Kalamo. They looked more than concerned, their eyes fixed on the man opposite. Jim Fischer was transparently shaken by events and his previous reliance on Valla had now become very obvious. After the attack, the helicopter had been dragged to one side and the lorries driven through. They had continued the journey without further problems arriving earlier that day and now John had filled in details of his appearance on the scene.

Chris had arrived at Los Kalamo after John. She'd not seen Jerome and Selena since the attack on the road but expected they were in the vicinity.

"Pierce, Valla and Catherine are dead. Just three of us left," said Mary unhelpfully.

Jim ran nervous hands through his hair.

"I don't know what to do."

"I can tell you," called Chris from the doorway.

She entered the room and joined them at the table before continuing.

"I still don't believe this everlasting life and spirit stuff but it's obvious that others do. It's really very simple. You have something hidden and other people want it so badly they'll go to any lengths. You either need to destroy this thing or get ready for a battle."

Mary looked at her.

"Destroying the Blessing is out of the question."

"Then you'll have to beat Jessica's army but it won't be easy. If I understand your scriptures, you three will be the ones to start a new civilisation in 2019. If I may say so, there hasn't been much sign that you're capable of running anything."

It was a statement carefully calculated to unsettle their arrogance and establish her status.

"John, you told her about 2019? We didn't agree that," Jim snapped angrily.

"I told her all I know, which isn't a lot. Why don't you give us the details of what's going to happen then?"

"No. Secondaries are not permitted."

"Listen. Five of our original eight are dead and we're only here thanks to Chris and her people. At this rate, we'll be lucky to survive until 2019 so let's forget the stupid rules."

Mary held up both hands and spoke calmly.

"Gentlemen, John is correct in that we need to adapt to the new situation. The main objective is to ensure our survival. First I will answer John's question and then I have a proposal."

She possessed an indefinable authority, perhaps to be expected from probably the oldest woman on earth.

"The truth is we do not know exactly what will occur in 2019. I was at the original meeting, the Resolution and we were told only that there would be a dreadful calamity. It would be something that will mark the end of humanity, except for those who were receiving the Blessing. The spirit had appeared in order to offer assistance and guidance to the people chosen for the continuance of life after the event."

"Maybe a meteorite crashing into the planet?" John asked.

Mary shook her head. "I have had a few hundred years to think about it. I believe it is most unlikely to be a physical, violent occurrence. That would be as dangerous for us as for the rest of the population."

"So what do you think the event will be?" asked Chris.

"I honestly don't know. As the Blessing appears to protect us from illnesses, I think it's likely to be some form of bacterial plague."

John nodded.

"That sounds logical but I'm surprised you don't know for sure. So what is the proposal you mentioned?"

"In our current circumstances there is safety in numbers. We need to replace our fallen members as quickly as possible."

Jim gulped coffee with shaking hands.

The Corporate Coffee Confederation Consumers Committee, or CORCOFCONCONCOM as they are much better known, have requested that it should be made abundantly clear that they (hereinafter known as the 'first party') have demonstrated irrefutably that the consumption of coffee (the 'product'), even if mixed with water or milk ('other parts') by any person or persons (the 'second party') does not cause hands to shake and that such 'shaking' is therefore entirely due other causes ('third parts or parties').

The first party imparts this, partly to second parts or parties partial to product parts with other parts, providing these parts or parties do not partially depart the first party parts apart from third parts or parties specified herein.

Our gratitude to CORCOFCONCONCOM for this succinct clarification.

"Anyone special in mind, Mary?" asked Jim, calmed by the golden beverage.

"We have already agreed to invite Christine here. I propose we also extend an invitation to her lady colleague."

"Selena." Chris interrupted.

"And to Mr Jerome Jones."

Chris's laughter filled the room.

"What is so humorous? My experiences with Mr Jones in Paraguay lead me to believe he is very suitable."

Chris decided not to reveal that he didn't exist.

"I'm sorry. I think it's a great idea."

"Then you will join us?"

"I'm still thinking. I need to be sure of what I'm signing up for. It seems I'm wanted mainly as a sort of breeding mare for post 2019."

"It's your choice whether you have children," said John.

"Maybe, maybe not. What's the effect of starting to take this Blessing and then stopping? For example, if I were to join and later leave."

Mary responded firmly.

"No one has ever chosen to leave. I have appointed several Secondaries who used the Blessing once and then stopped. There is no harmful effect."

She didn't mention that they had all subsequently found a permanent resting place on her orders.

"Very simply, after the initial consumption, your body attains its youth at the optimum physical age somewhere between 18 and 25. If the Blessing is taken each year this situation is maintained. If you do not renew, you will begin to grow old normally from the new youthful point," she continued.

"So if a 70-year-old took this stuff just once they will become about 25. If they didn't renew they would begin to age normally from then, 25, 26, 27?"

"That is correct. In nearly 400 years, I have never experienced or seen any adverse reaction."

"I'll think about it and decide soon."

Mary appeared somewhat displeased by her prevarication but didn't pursue it.

"It is also very clear we must undertake another task. In addition to preserving the supply of the Blessing, we have to recover the formula and the Lifeblood, the missing ingredient before our enemies take them. We know the hiding place is disclosed within our possessions."

"And you need to do it quickly. Jessica could be here any time," Chris observed.

All eyes turned to Jim. His face was a mask of uncertainty and he desperately missed Valla's guidance. With a sigh, he rose from his chair.

"I told my people to transfer all the stuff from the lorries into the strong room here. They should have finished by now."

Mary, John and Chris followed Jim down concrete steps two levels below ground and entered a tiny square room where a pair of guards stood by an open, reinforced door.

"Have they finished offloading?" Jim asked the first man.

"Just finished, Mr Fischer. They brought the last crate 30 minutes ago. But if I may say so, I don't think they sorted the contents very well."

"Sorted? What do you mean?"

"They opened the boxes and just left things strewn around."

"I didn't give instructions to unpack."

"See for yourself."

They entered the strong room. Empty crates, paintings, sculptures and documents were scattered everywhere. As he walked through, Jim saw a large envelope pinned to one of the crates. It was labelled 'Mr Fischer, please read this'. He ripped it open and Chris looked over his shoulder at the paper inside. The message was short.

'Mr Fischer, my apologies for the untidiness, we were in a hurry. Sound advice is to follow routes 36 and four. Hope to see you in England. Jerome Jones.'

Chris could see the fury in Jim's face as he turned back to the guard.

"Who did this?"

"Your shipping people. They had ID. A thickset guy was in charge. He had a woman with him."

Jerome and Selena thought Chris.

Jim turned to her. "So your people are our enemies as well then?"

She found her temper stretched by his attitude.

"Listen to me. Whatever Omasor is doing, never forget we saved your lives more than once. You wanted me to help with my knowledge in these situations. Now I'll tell you what you should do. This store contains the collections of yourself, Mary and Pierce so the location must be hidden here somewhere. I believe the clue is in the plaques so we'll photograph them. Then three of us will

226

fly to England immediately while one remains here to guard this place. We'll try to decode the clues on the flight. That was the message from Jerome. He's trying to help."

"I don't react to instructions Ms Darmant. This Jones man does not convince me. How do we know the Lifeblood is in England? This may just be a diversion."

Chris wanted to squash his self-importance but settled for advice.

The word advice is from the Latin, not meaning in favour of debauchery. Ad always means in favour of except admire that can't indicate a liking for boggy ground. And admonish. What is a monish anyway? Not to mention adultery. Strange how this ultery stuff attracts so many.

"You need to trust someone who knows more than you," she announced with jaw set.

"I'm with Chris," said John.

Jim sighed.

"What can we lose? I'll have a plane ready at L.A. in two hours. But I'm not leaving here."

Chris saw his panic bubbling like methane in a mudpool. She was pleased he was staying. A nervous companion would just have been a hindrance.

"Are you coming, Mary?" Chris asked.

"I'm very tempted to go back to South America. I can disappear there until 2019. However for the sake of the Octagon, I'll go with you. If I find that it's a false trail I will leave."

"It's not a false trail."

33

Two hours into the flight before Chris completed her analysis of the plaque photos. She sat facing Mary and John in the luxurious cabin of the Trisken Wellbringer jet chartered by Jim Fischer, heading for Birmingham in the centre of England.

Chris placed three prints in front of them.

"I'm certain these contain the location of the missing ingredient and formula. Jerome's letter referred to routes 36 and four and also mentioned this was sound advice. Roots with a double o sounds like routes and the square roots of the numbers are six and two, symbolising the two eagles above six swords on the Octagon crest. Each plaque has two parts. The upper section is fairly meaningless and obviously some sort of coded message while the lower part is a Latin motto."

"Taking the motto part first, my guess is that it was used as an identifying name for each Primary member of the group. I still don't fully understand the how and why but somehow it enabled Jerome Jones and the Crownes to find out where you were. Logically the Hong Kong location must have been on the plaque of Countess Pollan, Hong Kong contained the clue to Paraguay and the one there pointed to California. That's why Jerome had to see the plaques before he knew the next destination."

"How did our residences become known? The rules of the Octagon forbid it," Mary enquired.

"I don't know that. Maybe Selena does."

"Sorry, please continue."

Chris leant forward in her seat. She was enjoying her new leadership role.

"So the location of this Lifeblood of yours is somehow held in the upper parts of the plaques. The first one from Hong Kong is very simple. You just read the second and sixth letters in each row. That gives you 'Glastonbury Abbey, North Door'."

"The second plaque, that's yours Mary, is a little more complicated. You still take the second and sixth letters but you then jump two and six letters respectively. The second letter in the text is P, jump two and this becomes S. The sixth letter is M, jump six and this is T. You tail round the alphabet so, for example, if Z was the second letter it would become C. This plaque gives the location 'Stonehenge Heel Stone'."

"The other plaque, from California took the longest to decode but it's really not too complex. It uses the same system of jumps as Mary's but this time you have to keep adding two's and sixes to the jumps. So the first jumps are two and six, the second four and 12, the third six and 18 and so on. The result is the main entrance of the parish church in this place."

She pointed at an unusually named little village on a detailed map of south west England.

"Didn't the Countess also have a plaque to give us a fourth location?" John asked.

"Yes, she had a similar plaque, I've seen it. On that one the lower part had another motto but the top section was simply the crest of the Octagon with no text. I don't think it can be part of the clue to the location."

Mary looked downcast.

"I must admit that I'm impressed with your analysis. But we now have three places in a large area. We'll need to visit each one to check for any signs or messages. Another chase round."

A brief pause before Chris shook her head.

"I don't think so, I've given it some thought and that doesn't feel right. Put yourself in James Smith's shoes. At the beginning, he has three Primaries going to different parts of the world. Would he then give each of them a clue to a place in England just to find three more hidden clues? That just doesn't seem sensible. The other thing is that two of the places, Stonehenge and Glastonbury Abbey, are very popular destinations for visitors and have been, I think, since Smith's time. I certainly wouldn't choose to conceal a clue in an area where lots of people were constantly milling about. Too great a risk it would be discovered, moved or even destroyed. But there's another factor. Why select two very famous places and then an ordinary church in a virtually unknown town?"

"So what is the purpose of these locations?" asked Mary.

"Since we took off, I've made contact with the caretaker of the parish church. He told me that, in 1650, a person gave a huge sum of money to be held in a trust fund. These finances were to make certain the building was maintained in its original condition for the next 500 years. The amount was actually enough to pay for twice that time. The name of the person, of course, was James Smith."

"But why would he do that?" asked John.

"Why? Just to ensure it was there. If you're forming a triangle, the first two corner points can be almost anywhere within reason. The third point is the critical one. I think these three locations are markers."

Mary and John looked up quickly, each with the same idea.

"The centre," said John.

"Yes, we just draw lines from the midpoint of each side to the opposing angle and where the lines cross, that's the place."

"We need a more detailed map. I'll get on the internet"

Thirty minutes later they were looking at a point, the intersection of three lines. John had performed the calculations using geographical coordinates and transferred the result to a street level print out.

"It's nowhere," exclaimed Mary.

The blue cross he had marked on the map was a short distance north west of a tiny village we will call Charwithdill in the county of Somerset, South West England.

34

After arriving in Birmingham late evening, Chris rented a car and found a nearby hotel where the three of them could spend the night before their journey to Somerset the next morning.

She was just leaving the shower when she caught the faintest knock at the door. It was sure to be John. She wrapped in a chastity towel, prepared her most pleasant 'not tonight' speech and then opened the door. Selena. Elegant as always and carrying a small case. She entered quickly, finger to her lips and guided Chris back to the bathroom. After turning on the cold taps and shower she finally spoke.

"Just making sure. You'll see why," she said with the vestige of a smile.

"I have a lot to tell you."

"I know but it can wait, I just have time to show you something."

Selena opened the case. The lid contained a screen while the base held a console.

"Watch this."

She pressed a button and the screen lit up, displaying a room, a hotel room. The picture was amazingly sharp and clear.

"That's this hotel," Chris exclaimed softly.

"And it's live."

Karmen and Katya were in the room, sitting at a table.

"You told him to come now?" asked Karmen, checking her watch.

The blonde nodded.

"He'll be here."

"You know we need to kill him when we have the formula."

Katya smiled.

"It's a pity, he is good looking. But when I first offered him the deal, after Catherine had killed Valla, he was completely naked. Definitely not man enough for me."

"His sexual urge is a weakness and we need to use it. Did you arrange the girls?"

There was a soft knocking sound.

"Yes, they're ready and here he is."

Katya opened the door, checking the corridor outside as John walked past her. He looked edgy.

"I'm worried we'll be seen."

Katya closed the door and smiled at him.

"Don't concern yourself, you're very safe with us. This is Karmen, you haven't met before."

He gave a nervous smile.

"Hello Karmen. We haven't spoken but I've seen you."

She attempted her most friendly expression, appearing almost human.

"I just wanted to confirm our arrangement. That devious bitch Jessica Crowne pays me but I've always worked for myself. I'll kill her before this is finished. We have guaranteed your safety and also a half share of everything in return for your assistance in finding the formula. Our agreement is still in place despite the difficulties in California. We may have failed to get the stock of your youth mixture but that's nothing compared to the money we'll make from the formula and this missing ingredient."

"Do I have a choice?"

"Yes. The only other option is that we kill you."

John didn't appear overly attracted to that alternative. Anxiety prospered anew.

"Look, I've already agreed. The only question I had was about Chris. I'd rather she wasn't harmed."

"She'd be a constant danger to you. After we succeed, I couldn't guarantee your safety if she's still alive."

John paused, eyes lowering.

"Okay, I understand. Do what you have to."

Karmen wrote on a pad and held it up.

"Memorise this number. You can reach me on it any time. Now I must go but Katya has a little reward for you."

She left, passing two girls waiting outside the door. They looked exactly what they were. East European budding B-movie actresses, one blonde and one raven-haired and specially selected for their chest size. Katya had learned from John's obsession with Catherine's assets.

She began to undress him while the girls quickly stripped and spread themselves on the bed. He joined them with enthusiasm as Katya shed her own clothes to make a party of four.

"I've seen enough," said Chris, eyes glistening.

Selena looked unemotional as usual.

"John is not trustworthy. Mary Duckworth doesn't know it but before he came to her, he was a confidence trickster who toured the beaches, fleecing rich women. He was on the run from the police when he turned up in Paraguay. Jessica had arranged for Catherine to abduct him in England to obtain his knowledge but you know how unstable she was. Instead, she killed Valla and ran away. Karmen had anticipated the possibility of the girl failing and had Katya waiting at the house."

"I didn't think he was a liar but it looks as if I was wrong," Chris murmured

"Karmen always had her own plans to take the formula for herself. Incalculable wealth and eternal life were understandably very enticing. When Catherine failed to kill John she told Katya to offer him a deal. The agreement was that John would locate the formula while Karmen eliminated the opposition. She had planned for some time to kill Jessica Crowne and sell the Blessing to the highest bidder."

Chris shook her head.

"I thought I liked John but there's someone else now although I don't think he's interested in me. Men can let you down sometimes."

"Women can be worse. Men have strings to pull but most women don't expose anything worth jerking."

"I'll make sure my strings are well tucked away."

Selena closed the case.

"Felix did a good job with the camera this time. I must leave now. Have a good journey to Charwithdill and no confrontation with John. I don't want him to suspect yet."

She picked up the case and was gone before Chris could speak again.

35

"We're making good time," observed Chris relishing the power of the Caballini as she skimmed through the English countryside.

"Next turning right," called John from his seat beside her. He rested the maps on his thighs and picked up a high resolution satellite location device that showed their position to the exact metre.

"We must be close now," Mary called from the back. After initial scepticism, her enthusiasm had intensified as they approached their objective.

The journey continued through rural country. Farms, green fields, sheep and hedgerows.

"Next left turn and it's under a mile away," called John.

They entered the little village of Charwithdill. About 30 houses, a church, a pub and one sell-it-all shop. Two women talking in the street turned to stare at them. This wasn't tourist country. Chris took the road out to the North that curled left.

"This is it," John announced, his calmness apparently growing in proportion to Mary's increasing excitement.

In front of them lay an old farmhouse and beyond it, a field with two stone barn buildings.

"If the point is exact, it's in one of the barns," John announced, checking the location finder.

Chris pulled into a grass driveway and turned to the others.

"Well, we can't just charge in. We'll need to talk to the farmer."

Mary opened a small case to reveal a stack of currency.

"I prepared for a situation like this. I will buy the farm," she announced.

A grey-haired man had left the house and was ambling slowly towards them.

"I'll talk," Chris said, getting out of the car.

She displayed her most friendly smile as the man approached.

"Good morning," he greeted her in a soft West Country accent.

"Hello. I'm sorry to interrupt your day but my American friends have a proposition for you."

"American, eh?"

"Yes, they're really big people over in California. They've been looking all over the area for a genuine English country place and they really like this one, Mr…?"

"Parkinson's the name. You want to buy the farm?"

"Yes."

"It's not cheap, you know."

Mary had listened in and jumped out of the car, opening the case.

"I'll pay you two million pounds. I have a deposit here of 250,000."

The man appeared totally unimpressed.

"That's a lot of money but I think it may be worth a bit more."

"That's at least five times the market value," Mary exclaimed.

"Well, you know, I would have agreed with you before yesterday."

Chris saw it coming.

"You've already sold it."

He laughed, his sharp blue eyes crinkling in the mellow sun.

"The new owner is waiting for you inside. Come and eat with us."

They followed him up the driveway and entered a steamy kitchen. A slim dark haired woman looked up with a glowing smile from beside a large solid fuel stove.

"This is my wife and the new owner here, Mr Jones."

It was the tall, lean Jerome Jones. He looked at them with a minimum of surprise.

"I was expecting you. Please sit and eat, the food's delicious."

Mary's anger was ill concealed.

"What's this about, Jerome?"

"It's about many things. An ancient group calling itself the Octagon, a number of dead people, a desire for power. We'll discuss it after the meal."

"Don't play words with me. I have sacrificed almost all my life for this and I will not tolerate interference from you now. Not now."

Jerome rose from his chair and walked towards her, his deep eyes glinting.

"I have saved your miserable life more than once. I am telling you to sit. Now sit."

Chris had never seen this side of Jerome and suspected no one argued with him in this mood, certainly no one still living. She moved him from her original Thinker categorisation and that strange feeling began again.

Mary was still for a moment. Then she placed her hands over her face and began to sob, the long blonde hair quivering as she sat down to cry. John moved alongside and put a sympathetic arm around her.

Food was served and the atmosphere lifted as they ate. Mary visited the bathroom, returning dry eyed. However determined, sobbing will stop eventually. As they sat drinking tea after the meal, the Parkinsons left the room, reappearing a few minutes later with suitcases.

"We're going on a long holiday thanks to Mr Jones here," the man said.

Jerome fumbled in his jacket. He pulled out a huge wad of notes and handed it to the farmer.

"I had a few spare dollars in my pocket, you'll need spending money."

Mary held up her case, a faint smile filtering through.

"Mr Parkinson, please drop this in the village hall as you pass. I noticed they need a new roof."

There was a silence as they heard the car drive off towards the road. Then Jerome spoke with a quiet authority, now uncontested.

"I will tell you a story, a little complicated perhaps. I think Chris is now well aware of the origins and procedures of the Octagon so I'll skip that part. All had been running smoothly until a short time ago when a gang of criminals attacked the house of the caretaker of your elixir. It was just a simple robbery and they were completely unaware of the real secrets in the house. Purely by unfortunate coincidence, one of my people was a dinner guest and Omasor became involved when she was murdered during the ensuing fight. It was only later that I saw the crest that the Countess had rather incautiously displayed in her room and found out that it represented a clandestine group."

"We guessed it was something like that," John interjected.

"Another person who already had knowledge of the Octagon also saw the crest. Perhaps it was on TV or maybe in a newspaper. That person was either Jessica or Martina Crowne of Velviva. I suspect they may be descendants of an original member of the group but the details are unclear and immaterial. From that moment, we competed to locate the rest of the Octagon and thereby find the secret youth formula. I understand that each member had been given a plaque at the inception of your organisation in the 17th century. Three of the plaques provided a geographical point, thus composing a triangle. We are now a few metres from its exact centre."

John interrupted.

"We'd worked that part out, but how did you find the location of the Primaries? No one was supposed to know where the others were."

"Betrayal, treachery if you will. Countess Pollan had her own agenda. She and her Secondary were planning to be the only current members alive in 2019. The scheme was to kill all the others at the last Renewals for each of you prior to your meeting in 2018. She had already chosen the poison to be used in your final drink. A toxic substance that would kill before the Blessing could react to it. I'm making an assumption that the Countess or her Secondary followed each of you to your residences after one of the annual ceremonies. When you were out of the way, she had already selected six others who would be invited to form her own new civilisation and she would naturally be the unchallenged leader."

"I can't believe you. Margaret was a close friend," Mary said.

"No one is close after 300 years. The complete project was encrypted and contained in a loose-leaf so-called cookery book among the Countess's papers. Fortunately, this book and her plaque were sold in the same batch at the auction and we were able to reach it first."

"The deciphering process was difficult in some ways. Each plaque has two sections. The top section is a coded message giving the location of the triangle points except on the plaque of the Countess, which simply shows the crest. The lower part displays a name bestowed on the recipient in the form of a Latin motto. The Countess was one of the original Octagon members and probably assisted Smith in producing the plaques so she knew the exact contents of each of them from memory. She used these mottoes as the keywords to decipher her papers."

"That's the part I couldn't work out," Chris said.

"Very understandable as it was a complex double helix code. The mottoes were used in two ways. One section of her cookery book was titled 'Lunch Recipes' and the phrase on her own plaque, 'Fideli certa merces', applied as a keyword to the first listed recipe gave us Wang Shu Island, the plaque we found there linked to the second recipe and gave us the Paraguay information and from there to California. The final one from California pointed back to Carney House."

"I've been trained in cryptology but I don't know this double helix system," Chris remarked.

"It's just about unbreakable, even by computer, unless you have the keywords. She used a similar encryption for her plan to kill the other members and take over the Octagon. This was hidden in the 'Dinner Recipes' section. The decipherment required all the mottoes to be combined in one long key phrase and then passed through another cipher to result in a new set of keywords that were then applied to the recipe text."

Mary sighed. "She always did like codes and ciphers. So she really did plan to kill me?"

"The prospect of ultimate power corrupts as much as the power itself. Which leads me to our current problem. Jessica and Martina are still alive, as is their main enforcer, a woman called Karmen."

A sudden, unpleasant thought struck Chris.

"I should have made sure we weren't followed but I think I'd have noticed."

"I had people checking out the airport. You weren't followed."

There had been a distinct change in Mary's attitude since Jerome's earlier admonition. Her voice now carried an element of appeasement.

"Have you found the Lifeblood?" she asked.

Jerome shook his head.

"Waiting for you. I thought you should be here. We can start now."

He led the group from the house towards one of the ancient stone barns. A small excavator vehicle stood behind it.

"It arrived just before you," he remarked.

Unfastening a heavy padlock that secured the heavy wooden doors, he pulled one open to reveal a virtually empty interior. Just a couple of bales of straw lay in a corner with a few tools leaning against the end wall.

"Who's driving?" Chris enquired.

"Done it before," said Jerome and walked to the excavator.

After two hours, well over a metre of topsoil had been cleared from most of the interior, exposing a patchwork of thick granite slabs. Jerome parked the vehicle outside and returned to the barn.

"I assume the smallest is the entrance," said Chris.

He nodded but as the four grouped around the slab, they were interrupted by the sound of a vehicle and moved outside to check. A car had pulled up near the farmhouse and the driver was walking rapidly towards them, waving as he approached. Jim Fischer.

"What the hell is he doing here?" Jerome asked angrily.

"I phoned him from the plane as soon as we identified the location. I thought he should be with us," said Mary.

"You are a stupid woman. Very stupid."

Jim was smiling as he reached them but his expression changed when he saw their grim faces.

"What's the problem? I'm here."

"So are they," sighed Jerome, gesturing at a van drawing up next to the car and disgorging a number of figures armed with automatic weapons.

Chris studied him. He must have suspected that Mary would make contact with Jim and in any case John would have told Karmen their destination. She didn't now underestimate Jerome and had a strong feeling that events were proceeding just as he had planned. He returned her gaze with an unfathomable expression.

"Sometimes it's better to wait," he murmured.

A few minutes later, the four of them sat against the wall of the barn guarded by five armed men. Jessica was talking on the phone, her eyes shining with elation.

"Mother, I've found it! I'm right next to the hiding place of the formula."

Mary stared venomously at her and for once Chris empathised with the anguish. Just at the final moment she had been denied. Still, it was pointless to dwell on misfortune.

Miss Fortune was one of the stage names of Melissa Anderson, the performing psychic mind reader. Her prosperity began following a one off wager with Chelmina Siggit the famous, if crumbling film actress. Melissa said they would each choose a place anywhere in the world, any place on this planet and together with two friends, Chelmina was to write a word on a piece of paper placed in front of them. Then the three of them should hold hands and concentrate on mentally sending the word to the psychic pathways in the ether. As Melissa emphasised, she could be in Australia or the North Pole and the communication would still reach her as she could attune to the signals from anywhere.

The amount involved was half a million dollars from each side, Melissa giving an IOU and lawyers acted as stakeholders. Unfortunately the legal experts somehow missed the word 'each', as in 'each choose a place'. Melissa chose to be in the same room as Chelmina, looking over her shoulder.

Chris glanced at Karmen. She didn't seem comfortable, eyes darting round as if expecting danger. What was she planning? She had said she would kill Jessica but when and how?

Turning back, Chris counted the opposition. Ten men, two of them outside on guard, plus Jessica and Karmen. Not good odds. She had faith in this Jerome Jones although still not confident of his skills in a fight. Now she began to doubt if events really were moving according to his plan. It wasn't too encouraging that he was currently sitting with eyes closed and apparently disinterested in proceedings.

Jessica instructed five of her men to pull up the smallest slab. They found some steel rods amongst the tools leaning against the end wall and began to use them as crowbars. Slowly the block of granite began to rise and the men swung it back until it stood vertically, exposing a dark cavern below.

"Lights, quickly." Jessica was trembling with excitement.

"It could be trapped," a voice said. Jerome was open-eyed again.

Jessica's eyes flashed. Knowing the devious nature of James Smith, it was a definite possibility and she couldn't take any risks now.

She pointed at Chris.

"You go first."

High-powered lamps revealed a wooden ladder down one side of the opening and Chris descended slowly, testing each step. The wood should have rotted away completely after all this time but the treads were still just strong enough to hold her weight. She was soon below the floor level of the barn and at the next step her foot crunched something. Twisting to look down she saw a gleam in the faint light. Bones. A mass of bones.

"Something dangerous. I need a lamp," she yelled up.

Important to emphasise the possibility of a trap as she didn't want anyone following her just yet.

"What is it?" shouted Jessica, throwing a torch.

Chris caught it and scanned the area. The shaft was barely wide enough for her to climb down and she could just see a doorway below her but it was almost completely blocked with skeletons. Shreds of colourless clothing still clung to the bones and she caught the reflection of jewellery on some of the figures. Fortunately, her body masked the view of those above.

"A blockage, I'll try to clear it," she called out.

Then she deliberately jumped down with a thundering crash. A jagged rib shredded her coat, just missing her chest. She deliberately gave a cry, waited for a few seconds then shouted, "Wait, wait, danger."

Chris was still stalling them, more time needed. Sliding from the pile of skeletons she entered the main chamber and surveyed it with the torch.

At first glance it was a disappointment. Two large wooden chests were positioned to one side and at the end of the room stood a large cube of granite that acted as a table or maybe an altar. On this block lay a leather covered book and next to it, a small, ornately carved metal box. The room was otherwise completely empty.

A sudden crash behind her as Jessica scrambled into the chamber.

"I don't trust you," she said, moving the beam of a halogen lamp around her.

It settled on the book. An embossed leather cover with a thick strap fitted with a lock that bound the pages tightly. Jessica gave a small cry and pushed past Chris to grasp it lovingly. Her eyes glittered in the torchlight as she ran her hands over the cover, gently caressing each line in the surface. Still clutching the book, she walked to one of the large chests and pulled the heavy lid open. It swung back easily as if it had just been oiled.

"Jeez," she exclaimed.

Chris stepped forward. The chest was filled to the top with a glittering mass of gold and jewels just like a proverbial pirate's treasure. Gold and silver everywhere, glittering ornaments encrusted with stones, rubies, emeralds and diamonds shimmered in the artificial light. Impossible to calculate the value but Chris estimated in the region of 5.1742 million dollars. The other chest was a duplicate of the first but this one also held a mass of gold coins in addition to the other treasures.

Grabbing a handful of coins, Jessica returned to the stone block to pick up the small box. Like the book it was locked, but there was no sign of a keyhole. As she languished in the enchantment of the moment, Chris briefly considered attacking her but dismissed the idea with her companions at the mercy of the armed men above. The moment passed and Jessica returned to her icy normality.

"You first," she said, pointing towards the entrance shaft.

When they emerged into the barn, she was waving the book triumphantly and held it in front of Jim Fischer.

"I have your secret, little man."

Chris could see his whole body quivering with fury that was headlined by the vitriolic expression on his face.

"It is not for you."

A burning anger in his voice but Jessica simply laughed.

"It is not for you," he repeated, louder this time. Then he sprang forward his hand grasping for the book.

"No, Jim," Mary screamed just as the first shot resounded. Then another and another as Karmen fired with cold accuracy.

Jim was still mouthing "Not for you" as he fell and lay very still.

"You people take some stopping. Anyone else?" Karmen spoke impassively as she loaded another clip into her gun.

"Murdering bitch," Mary shrieked, tears flowing as she rushed to kneel next to Jim's body.

Chris looked at Jerome and knew he shared her thoughts. Jessica's plan was that none of them would leave here alive. Another consignment of skeletons was destined for the chamber below. She glanced towards the nearest guard and he returned a grinning leer.

"When do we get the women?" he asked Jessica, his eyes still scanning Chris's body.

"Don't interrupt me," she replied, sawing at the leather strap of the book with a small stiletto.

The guard ran his tongue over his lips.

"Very soon, darling, very…" With a short gasp, he collapsed. One by one the other men rapidly followed his example, looking round in bewilderment even as they slumped to the ground.

A figure appeared in the doorway.

"Sorry I'm late," said Selena, brandishing a Kurcin dart pistol.

The unconscious men were quickly trussed and Chris picked up a fallen gun.

"Where's Karmen?" she shouted, looking round.

"She ran back to the car and is now driving away," replied Selena without concern.

"I'll stop her."

"No. Her time will come."

Chris considered pushing past Selena but felt a hand on her shoulder.

"Her time will come," repeated Jerome.

Jessica seemed oblivious to the events, slicing at the book strap with grim determination. Mary walked across and held out her hands.

"It's over now, give me the book."

"No."

"Give it to me."

This time it was a demand.

The strap finally split.

"No, it's mine now."

Jessica opened the book. A loud click. Then she screamed. Only once. Embedded in the centre of her forehead was a short stub of metal that hadn't been there before. She slumped backwards, the open volume falling open across her thighs.

Jerome ambled slowly towards the body.

"She wouldn't listen," he said, shaking his head.

He bent down, picked up the book and passed it to Mary without showing any interest in its contents.

"It's safe now. Just one trap for the uninitiated. I'm surprised it worked after all this time," he said quietly. Then he began examining the small metal box that Jessica had pushed dismissively to one side. He glanced at Selena.

"Perfect timing. Did you come by broomstick?"

"You know better. I have not used magick on this case," Selena responded.

Chris and John crowded round Mary as she opened the volume. The contents were amazingly well preserved with no sign of discolouration of the parchment pages and the black ink as dark as when written.

'A Testimonie To The Events And Occurrences During The Visitation Of The Spirit

On the eighteenth day of August 1585

In the hand of James Smith

On this day the Spirit did visit through the scryer Kelly and did bestow a warning upon us of a dire Event that will befall humanity in the Year Of Our Lord 2019 on the 20th day of the third month. By the Will of the Almighty, on that day will all men and women of this world depart their earthly existence.

Yet it did comforte us that in infinite wisdom we had been chosen to survive and begin the rebirth of a New World. And thus the Spirit did reveal a great and wondrous Blessing, an elixir conformed of ten constituents that will inure the chosen ones from the ravages of age and thus preserve our youth to eternity. This blessed state will preserve against all malefic disease and protect against the tragic Event that had been foretold. And nine of the constituents were revealed unto us with their due proportions declared.

And thereto the Spirit applied this counsel. That it was our duty to select from all mankind those others that would share this new civilisation and upon whom the Blessing should be bestowed. Our number in all should be no more than can be counted on our hands and the women and men shall be equal. By good will and grace this chosen few to go forward thence for we and our offspring to inherit as it was at the Beginning.

In finality did the Spirit speak unto us of one more magnificence, being the place of concealment wherein lay a treasure beyond the imaginings of mortal man. The Lifeblood. A most glorious gift, the tenth and final ingredient required to complete the wondrous elixir, the Blessing

Thus did the Spirit place upon us this onerous task and I trust we may be worthy of this great and momentous responsibility.

Appended hereto are the sole and perfect record of the words of the Spirit wherein the dire Event is described together with the form and constituents of the great Blessing granted in bounteous faith to we humble servants.'

Mary turned the page. A blank sheet. Then another and another, right through to the back cover. She thumbed through again and again.

Her expression melted like ice on a hot razor.

"It's not there!"

John took the book from her and quickly leafed through it.

"Four pages have been cut out," he said, displaying the narrow stubs.

Mary began to sob again and John looked ready to join her. Chris shared their disappointment. The cuts were old and the pages must have been removed before entombment in the chamber. She was certain that they had been the first visitors since its construction.

Jerome continued to examine the box and still showed no interest in the book.

"This is clever. There's a hidden lock somewhere. It'll take time to solve it," he said quietly.

Selena came up from the chamber, having completed her own search. She held out a hand.

"I'll have that and also the book, assuming you've finished with it."

Mary nodded sadly and passed her the volume.

"You and John will stay at a hotel tonight and return to California tomorrow. You can take the treasure chests with you. Jerome will arrange transport."

It wasn't a suggestion, it was an instruction. Chris noted that Jerome was included in her orders, confirming her suspicions. She was now certain that the real Jerome Jones did not exist.

"What do we do with these men and the bodies?" asked John.

"We will arrange everything."

Chris walked over to her.

"And what do I do?"

"You'll join me and Jerome. We'll be staying here tonight."

36

Selena arranged for Mary and John to spend the night at a hotel a couple of miles away. Jerome made telephone calls and within an hour an Omasor team of twelve had arrived and the farm was buzzing with activity. Then he began supervising the loading of Jessica's men, still unconscious, into a large van.

Chris and Selena had returned to the farmhouse.

"Where will you take them?" asked Chris.

"They're just mercenaries. They'll disappear when they find out that Jessica's not alive to pay them. I'll get our people to dump them somewhere in Africa."

"And what about Jessica's body?"

"We'll make sure she has a good send-off. I think a high-profile cremation in Switzerland would be appropriate. The certificate will say she died in a car crash."

"Should we tell her mother?"

"She is being visited shortly."

Some hours later, Jerome returned from the barn.

"Everything is done. We've just replaced the entry slab and re-covered the floor. You wouldn't know anyone had ever been there. Jessica is on her way to Geneva and her men will be out of the country before tomorrow."

Selena smiled. "We will stay here tonight. Is there any food in the house?"

He nodded. "I was ready for three guests. I'd like to cook dinner for you if that's agreeable."

"I accept with sincerity," said Chris, the culinary arts not being in her CV.

After dinner, they relaxed around the table. Two coffees but Jerome preferred tea. Chris sipped from her mug, questions still running through her mind.

"So the Octagon is now down to just two members and one of those is a traitor. What will we do about John?"

Selena looked across at Jerome before replying.

"We'll sort that out tomorrow."

"And Karmen, what about her?"

"Same answer. Tonight we can relax a little before finally tidying everything up. We should be clear by tomorrow, unless we're killed in the process."

"That's a cheering thought. If we're relaxing, I'd like to ask more questions. I can't switch off when I haven't got all the details."

"You can ask but you may always not get an answer."

"You said something in the barn. If I heard correctly, you apparently have a knowledge of witchcraft."

"I was a witch. A real witch, not one of those black eyed schoolgirls with a little spell book but a genuine practitioner."

"Dancing about naked? Skyclad I think they call it."

"That's exactly what I didn't do. You'll learn a lot about real magick working for Omasor. Your right to joke about the fictional versions but the real thing is very different."

"I'll have to discover that. And you, Jerome, are you a warlock or a wizard?"

"Neither and I know only a little about the subject."

Selena's phone rang and she wandered out of the room to answer. Chris immediately felt very comfortable with the tall, lean man.

"Where are you from, Jerome? What do you do before Omasor?"

"I was an academic."

"Can't imagine you drinking in the students bar."

"A professor," he added with zero pretence.

"What was your subject?"

"Knowledge and clarity don't always cohabit."

She smiled.

"Our brains contain many strange bedfellows. Maybe you'll tell me sometime."

Chris couldn't suppress the tingle she got from him, so very different from the feeling she had with John. That had been just a frothy entree and this started to feel like the main course. He remained inscrutable and she had still never seen him smile but the deep-set eyes seemed to hold so many secrets. For some reason she enjoyed looking at him, not a habit she was used to with men.

Habits can be addictive. However, the old saying 'when the nuns lose the habit, the monks start celibating' is patently inaccurate.

"What happened to Jessica with the book?"

"A little trap. It was simply a pointed iron bolt with a spring mechanism that triggered when it was opened. I expected it as James Smith was an extraordinary man. He appeared to allow for most contingencies and ensured the uninitiated paid a heavy penalty."

"Despite that, the Octagon is nearly finished," remarked Chris.

"That's true but it's taken a long, long time. Without the misfortune of the murder and attempted robbery at Countess Pollan's house, it's quite possible they would never have been discovered. I appreciate the frustration of the members of the group. To crumble and fall now, so very close to the end of all other humanity. That is if the spiritual prophecy is correct."

"I just can't believe everyone is going to die in a few years. There have been so many predictions of the end of the world and none of them were correct. The only thing I can think of that will kill everyone without destroying the earth is some sort of plague but however virulent it may be, some people will always survive. Isolated communities where it just couldn't reach."

"There is no precedent in our current civilisation but who knows if an event like this has not occurred before?"

"I think I'll just have to make the most of the time until 2019 and then see what happens."

Selena returned from her telephone call.

"Change of plan, I need to go. I'll be back tomorrow morning at about ten to pick you up, Chris. You know where you're going, Jerome?" she enquired.

He nodded. "All arranged."

They sat in silence after her departure. Jerome sank back in his chair, looking into the crackling coal fire. Alone with him, Chris felt that strange sensation growing again and this time it wouldn't be denied.

"So you're leaving tomorrow?" she asked.

He turned his dark eyes to her.

"Yes. I expect we may meet again."

"Au revoir, perhaps?"

"Perhaps."

Then the feeling became irresistible force. She walked in front of the fire and undressed down to her underwear.

"I don't do this every day," she said softly.

His expression didn't change.

"No, I wouldn't make a habit of it."

"Well, are you going to do something?"

"I'm giving it some thought."

Then he was holding her, kissing soft and deep.

"I thought and made a decision. You are a very exceptional woman."

"Last time I was with an academic we talked Socrates all night."

"He'll have to wait until tomorrow."

Chris woke later than usual the next morning. For once she didn't feel like running, the night's exercise had more than fulfilled her training requirements for a week. Jerome was a wonderful lover, showing imagination and energy far beyond her previous horizons. When she reached a pinnacle, he took her to other levels she didn't know existed. It was the best night of her life.

Chris studied him, sleeping in sunrise tranquillity.

"I'd like to spend every night with you," she whispered.

He raised an eyelid.

"You want to talk Socrates now?"

She swung a palm at his chest.

"I thought you were sleeping."

For the first time she saw him laugh. And it was beautiful.

37

Martina Crowne was more than pleased. Jessica had phoned her from the barn in England and told her she had found the secret. It felt like the climax to Martina's life, a life she now believed was just about to begin anew and then last forever. First she would resolve some outstanding problems.

She punched a button on her desk console.

"This is Martina. Come to my office immediately."

Hony Pammican replaced the phone. She knew the woman despised her and constantly sensed disapproval of her relationship with Jessica. The vindictiveness has so far only extended to minor insults and veiled threats but she had made it clear that Hony was very expendable unless the formula was discovered quickly. Hony walked to the laboratory security room and opened the double locks. With a lemon smile, she filled a syringe from one of the bottles.

Martina had a 24-hour security guard outside her door and the current shift raised a muscular arm as she approached.

"ID please."

"I am Hony Pammican, everyone knows me."

He sighed.

"ID please, Ms Pammican."

She pulled out her company ID card and held it in front of his eyes.

"Satisfied?"

He stepped back, pressed a button and the door slid open. Martina was seated as usual behind her large desk but Hony noticed an unusual glint in her eyes.

"About time. I have some unfortunate news for you."

Hony ignored that.

"I've just produced a new compound using an ingredient we'd never tried before."

The old woman paused, relishing the moment. Her face was coated smug.

"You're too late. I'd called you in to announce that Jessica has found the missing ingredient."

Hony was stunned.

"So you know the formula?"

Martina sat back in her chair and placed her fingertips together.

"Not yet. I'm sure she'll phone back soon. Then I don't think we will require your further services."

The thought of this apology for a woman achieving perpetual life made Hony shudder.

"Why not try my new compound while you wait? If you have the real formula, you won't want to reveal it to too many people and there would be massive demand for a downmarket version."

Martina paused and Hony saw she recognised the validity of the proposition. There was no way that the true elixir would be shared with anyone. Just herself and Jessica.

"What is the effect of your new mixture?"

"I can absolutely guarantee it will stop the ageing process."

"I won't get older?"

"No."

"Then I can remain at this age until we have started to produce Jessica's discovery?"

"Yes."

"And how long does it take to be effective?"

"It's almost immediate."

Martina glowed with excitement. She walked round the desk and leant over it, pulling up her dress. Hony jabbed the syringe into her crinkled buttock, emptying it completely and then helped the woman back to her chair.

"I feel a little dizzy."

"It won't last long you miserable crone."

"What have you done?"

The face was already contorting.

"An enhanced essence of curare. The new added ingredient. You won't age now, your evil old hag, just as I promised."

Martina died as she had lived, in misery and resentment. Her eyes became glazed windows overlooking the bitterness in her soul.

"Saved me a job."

Hony whirled round. The guard had entered and was standing just behind her. A chunky, square faced man.

"Who are you?"

"I'm Jerome Jones."

"The detective?"

"Sort of."

She regained a little composure.

"You're the guy no one's ever seen."

"You're looking at me."

"So, am I arrested?"

He looked at his watch.

"No. You have exactly 16 minutes to get all the staff clear of the building. Only people may leave. Anyone trying to take papers, chemicals or other stuff will be shot. I have people outside to make sure."

Thirty minutes later they stood in the street watching the fire services surround the blazing building. Hony turned to Jerome.

"Jessica, is she all right?"

"She had options and decided to go wait for her mother. This is your choice."

He handed her an envelope then disappeared into the gathering crowd. Hony was surprised she felt no shock, no grief. The affection had long gone. She knew Jessica had been using her and her only feeling was a sense of relief it was over. She opened the envelope. Inside was a job offer, the head of a new free medical institute in one of Rio de Janeiro's poorest suburbs. Hony made her choice without hesitation.

38

On a bright late afternoon, the county of Somerset pleasures the spirit like a lingering soft kiss. Its embrace plays tranquil chords as Nature deigns to sacrifice a few moments to entertain her errant fleas. In the midst of this beguiling assignation, a silver grey Caballini wound its way along the turning country roads like a rampant squirrel in a nuttery.

Chris sat in the passenger seat puzzling over the box. She had already checked through the book several times and was satisfied that it held no other secrets. But something else was nagging at her, something about the text. Something not right.

The box was a real enigma. It was about 20 centimetres long and half that size wide and deep. Exquisitely carved with a detailed panorama of swirls and waves that almost imparted motion to it. The crest of the Octagon was embedded in the design on the top. There was no keyhole and no apparent join where the lid should be. If it hadn't sounded hollow when she tapped it, she would have assumed it was a solid block.

She looked across at Selena.

"Where did you go last night?"

"I stayed at the same hotel as Mary and John."

"To watch him?"

"Partly."

"Who phoned you before you went?"

"I triggered the call myself. I hope you enjoyed your evening?"

"Yes, I did and you're as cunning as he is."

Selena smiled.

"To save you asking, the answer is no, I've never slept with him."

Chris wouldn't have asked but liked the answer. She returned to the box.

"I give up. Do you know how to open it?"

"No."

"So what do we do now? Are we going back to the office?"

"I thought we'd take a little tour first to absorb this beautiful country. And there are still some loose ends."

"Karmen, Katya and John."

"Yes."

"John's going to California with Mary. Shouldn't we be looking for the two women?"

"I think the word no summarises the answer. Mary is en route to America but John made an excuse to follow later. He's in a vehicle about 600 metres behind us with his new friends."

Chris turned to look but the twisting roads limited the viewing range to a much shorter distance.

"How do you know?"

"Felix tagged their car."

She nodded towards a flashing light on a small screen stuck next to the steering wheel.

"Why not stop and ambush them?"

"Yes, we might do something like that."

They passed through another group of houses. This one had a small village green with a duck pond in the centre. Selena followed the road for another kilometre and then stopped the car.

"Bring the box and the book," she instructed, handing Chris a backpack.

They walked to a wooden fence and surveyed the scene. Sun speckled rolling green hills formed the backdrop to the perfect picture of England. A meadow of lush grass stretched in front of them and nestling just to their right, at the edge of a small forest, was a farmhouse. An uncultivated area lay to the left where a mass of tall bushes grew out of control.

"You go left and I'll go right," said Selena and disappeared rapidly and silently towards the farmhouse.

Chris reached the cover of the bushes and waited, gun in hand, watching for the chasing car. It was a short wait.

"Drop your gun and turn slowly," a woman's voice said.

Cursing herself for focusing her attention on the road, she dropped the weapon and turned.

Karmen held a pistol with John standing unhappily at her side.

"Can't trust a surfer," Chris said acidly.

"Look, there's no need to kill," he said, avoiding her eyes.

Karmen didn't lower the gun.

"Yes there is. We don't need her, the other woman will have what we want."

Chris searched desperately for a stall.

"Did you enjoy the four in a bed, John?"

He looked aghast and Karmen loosened her finger on the trigger.

"How did you know?" he mumbled.

"I also know they're going to kill you."

Karmen's reptilian eyes shone with hatred.

"That's a lie," she yelled, aiming the gun directly at Chris's forehead.

John jumped at her, screaming something unintelligible.

He hit her as she was squeezing the trigger, pushing her arm around. The bullet channelled into his heart but his momentum knocked the gun from her grasp. Chris leapt forward but as she moved, something fizzed past her ear, hitting a bush just in front. Then Karmen was gone, disappearing into the thick mass of foliage behind her.

Chris started to follow.

"No!" shouted a voice.

She twisted round and saw Selena standing with a pistol in one hand and Katya's body draped over her other shoulder.

"Why not? I can take her."

Chris was angry. She didn't enjoy being rescued like some helpless bimbo and John had been shot trying to protect her. She badly wanted to repay the debt.

"Unnecessary risk. She'll have another gun and plenty of cover."

Selena dropped the blonde's limp body near to John.

"He's dead. Sorry."

"At the end he was trying to save me."

"The world is infested with people who are applauded for doing one good thing in a life of evil. It's called public relations."

There was bitterness in her voice that Chris didn't want to challenge.

"What about Katya?"

"Just unconscious. I'll tie her up and collect her later. It would be a shame to kill her now. I still remember Florida and I also saw the rest of the foursome video. She's terrific in bed."

"I'll never work you out."

"I sincerely hope not."

After binding Katya, they walked down past the farm. A ruddy-faced old man was tending a rose bush and Chris waved idly at him. He gave a friendly smile.

"I'm just making tea. Would you ladies like some?"

Selena shrugged.

"We might as well. I can tell you more then."

The old man showed them into the tiny lounge of the stone cottage and they sat on old wooden chairs at an ancient round oak table. He brought two steaming mugs of tea.

"You ladies take your time, I'll be on the porch."

He sat on a wooden bench outside the open front door and started to light an antiquated pipe.

"Okay, you've kept me in the dark long enough," said Chris, draining her cup.

"You could say it's a trust thing. Need to be sure about you."

"Have I passed?"

Selena nodded.

"I had to be convinced."

"You're not good with praise are you?"

"Praise is transient. If you can't operate without it you can't work at Omasor."

"Talking of Omasor, I've worked out that you're the boss. How do you run the organisation? And how do you control all those Jerome Jones fakes?"

"Maybe the box has the answer."

"What?"

Chris had placed it on the table alongside the book. Selena examined it and began to press and push the top and sides. She shook her head.

"Beats me. Ever seen one of these before?" she called to the old man.

He returned slowly from the porch and took it from her.

"That's a nice box."

His fingers quickly moved over it and the end slid open.

It took a lot to astonish Chris. This was a lot.

"How the hell did you do that?"

"I don't think you've been introduced. This is Jerome Jones." Selena said.

"What?"

Chris looked at the old man, unkempt grey hair straggling across his face. His skin was weathered like an ancient galleon.

"But you don't exist."

"Chris Darmant. I almost didn't recognise you with your clothes on."

The voice had changed, younger and vibrant.

A plug fitted in Chris's brain.

"You were the guard who helped us on Wang Shu Island."

He shrugged. Then for the first time she noticed the look in his steel grey eyes. It caught her, bounced her a few times then threw her in the air. Chris knew she had been wrong. This really was Jerome Jones.

"I suspect your actual appearance is not as it is now."

"Your suspicions are correct. I think Selena may want to leave before we talk."

He nodded to her and she moved quickly outside. Then he turned back to Chris, holding up the box.

"Do you want to see the contents?"

She took it. The centre had slid out from one end. It had a deep carved recess that was covered with pure white bunched silk. She pulled the silk back to reveal a small silver flask.

"I'm guessing this contains the secret ingredient of the eternal youth mixture, the Lifeblood."

"Another good guess."

He didn't offer so she asked.

"And what is it?"

"I don't think you will believe me if I tell you"

"Nothing will surprise me now. Is it frog's livers or bats wings?"

He didn't smile.

"You recall the Christian Bible?"

"A little from school."

"You know of Lazarus?"

"The man who rose from the dead?"

"The one who entered his tomb made a small cut in his finger and allowed one drop of blood to fall into the mouth of Lazarus."

"I don't remember that bit."

"It's not in the Scriptures."

Chris paused.

"You're going to tell me this flask contains more of that blood."

"It's clear. Looks exactly like water."

Chris vaguely remembered a spear entering a body and water emerging instead of red blood. Jerome unscrewed the cap and began to turn the flask in his hand.

"Careful, you'll spill the stuff," Chris called.

"Like this?" he asked, inverting it completely. The clear liquid splashed on the floor, disappearing between cracks in the stones.

Chris jumped to her feet.

"Why did you do that? No one can make the Blessing now."

Jerome didn't respond. He screwed the cap back on and then replaced the flask in the casket. He turned to the table and Chris saw he had positioned the box and the book next to each other. Then he looked expectantly at the door.

As if in response, it burst open. Karmen didn't look pleased. Her eyes, usually darting like a snake, were sharp and steady. The automatic she was holding didn't waver a millimetre.

"What's all this then?" said Jerome, back in the farmer's voice.

"Shut up old man."

Then her gaze moved to the book and the box.

"If you take that box you will die," he said casually.

Karmen laughed and pushed Chris next to him.

"Sorry, no witnesses."

A shot from a silenced weapon makes very little noise and the automatic appeared to fly from Karmen's hand by magic. Selena stood in the doorway, one hand on her hip, the other holding a gun.

Karmen crouched like a vampire under a sun lamp. Then spinning, she kicked a leg towards Selena's face. The blow never reached its target. Selena swayed just sufficiently to avoid the leather boot.

"Let me kill her, Jerome," she asked placidly.

He shook his head and waved her from the doorway. For a second Karmen looked at them, uncertainty in her eyes and then she grabbed the book and box and headed for the door.

After two strides she screamed, the hand holding the box dripping with blood. She looked back to see Jerome shaking his head. Then she fell. Motionless, peaceful and very dead.

"I did warn you," he murmured quietly.

Chris knelt by the body and could see two jagged wounds in the palm of Karmen's hand. She reached for the box, now stained red.

"Don't touch it," said Jerome.

"But I was holding it."

"No. That was this one." He pulled an identical box from his coat.

Then an innocent smile crossed his old farmer face.

"I had three of them made. The second one has two little spikes loaded with Vraskian, not something you should have in your bloodstream."

It took exactly four seconds to register in Chris's mind.

"Did you say you had three made?"

Silence. Jerome glanced briefly at Selena.

"I believe I did. Look in the sideboard drawer."

She opened it. Inside was a plaque, a fifth plaque. A crest with 'The Octagon' inscribed below it. The upper text was not in code. It simply said

'The Church Steeple at Mowden-In-Lucay'.

The lower part had an inscription.

'Virtus Pretiosior Auro'. Virtue is more precious than gold.

Chris tried to focus.

"A fourth marker. Not a triangle but a quadrangle. So the barn was not the centre point."

"I'll save you the time. Draw diagonal lines to join the opposite corners and they meet here."

"And the missing pages of the book?"

"I have them."

Her head was buzzing. The world had lost stability.

"I'm getting lost here. So you're another who has been taking the Blessing? How old are you?"

"Shall we say I was born over 400 years ago."

Chris ran fingers through her hair.

"I can't believe all this. It's just like a fantasy."

"Not difficult. I was alive when the spirit visited and have taken the Blessing every year since then."

A pause as Chris gathered her thoughts.

"Well, let's start with the book. If you have the missing pages, you read the details of what will happen in 2019?"

His steel grey eyes softened a fraction.

"Do you really want to know?"

"I think so."

"Then perhaps I will tell you at some time, but not now."

"Why not?"

"Trust me. You don't need that knowledge yet. But you can believe that all human life will end on the twentieth of March 2019, except for those taking the Blessing."

She nodded but noted the 'you can believe' in the statement. He wasn't actually saying it would occur.

"What will happen to Mary Duckworth?"

"She has lived a long time. We won't harm her."

"Perhaps she'll recruit more people, start a new Octagon?"

"No. The supply of the Blessing is no longer in California. I arranged to procure the complete stock and have it safely hidden. Mary has told Selena that she now desires to grow old normally or at least until 2019. Perhaps she will die then, if not before."

Chris turned to Selena.

"So I guess that you're also a bit older than you look?"

"I've already told you some of my history but without the dates. I was born in Morocco in 1729. A gang of cutthroats murdered my parents when I was three. I married at 18 and had a young son. He was killed in a fire and my husband died trying to save him. Jerome found me in Madeira. I was 22 then."

"I'm sorry. I didn't know all of that."

Chris was surprised to see her smile.

"I can't change history. But soon I'll have more children."

"After 2019?"

"Yes. I'm planning a large family."

"So are you and Jerome married?"

"No. We're not a partnership."

Chris couldn't identify the emotion behind her sharp reply and jumped off that subject before it bit. She looked back at Jerome.

"Why not just release the formula to the world and ignore the stupid restrictions."

"In 1756, I attempted to give the Blessing to an additional person, a young child who was dying of an incurable disease. It acted as a poison and the girl passed away shortly after."

"That is weird. How can a liquid keep a count of numbers?"

His eyes were averted.

"I also doubted but I was wrong. However, the child would have died within hours with or without the Blessing."

"I'm sorry, I'm really sorry."

"Selena is correct. We can't change history, but we can improve that part of the future we are able to control."

"So you're one of the Octagon members?"

"No. But I knew James Smith."

Connections were clicking into place in Chris's brain.

"I've just realised the thing that was bothering me in the book. It said count on two hands. Using thumbs, that's ten not eight. Ten people could take the Blessing."

"I reserved two places and allowed Smith to allocate the remaining number amongst his little group."

"You emptied the flask from the box in the barn but there were three boxes. It really was water, wasn't it?"

"I did say that's what it looked like."

"The second box had the poison spikes and the third, with the real flask was hidden here. You always had the remainder of the tenth constituent, the Lifeblood."

"The spirit visited in 1585. Within a week we found the hiding place of the Lifeblood. From this, I made a supply of the Blessing, more than sufficient for ten people until 2019 and gave four fifths to Smith. Much to his chagrin, I insisted that I kept the remainder of the Lifeblood. Then we parted and went our ways for 65 years with very little contact. In 1650, Smith told me of his decision to kill himself and establish the Octagon, the eight who he believed would inherit the earth after 2019."

"Plus you and later, Selena. Surely you wanted to know who these others were? Just the ten of you on the planet?"

A quiet smile on the weathered face.

"A final agreement with Smith was that he would ensure his entire group met together one year before the event."

"Yes, at Canterbury Cathedral on the twentieth of March 2018."

"Knowing this, I would therefore be able to meet them at that time and make a decision."

"What decision?"

"An assessment of their suitability and the replacement of any that I found inadequate."

"How? You mean kill them?"

He shrugged.

"Of course. These recent events have simply brought the judgement forward."

"Then you intend to be the leader after 2019?"

"Resentment festers in that statement. You question what right I have to assume leadership?"

"There should be a vote, something democratic."

A pause. Chris watched as Jerome Jones sat back in his chair and raised his eyes to her. Like a physical blow. She was stunned for a second and then he spoke.

"Do not make inferences about me. This is not a presumption of power. I was told that I must lead. Smith's account does not include all the statements of the spirit."

Chris found speech impossible. She had never lacked courage but this was different. A feeling of insignificance in his presence. Then he lowered his eyes and she was suddenly very aware of her surroundings. The old cottage, sunlight on green fields outside and an old man facing her. The moment had passed but she was never going to forget it. Finally, she spoke.

"The book. Yes, the book said we and us rather than I and me. That means Smith wasn't alone when this spirit came. Now I see it. You were there with him."

"A logical deduction. I was present for the whole time. We were both transcribing the words but the occasion overwhelmed him. He fainted and missed the final four minutes."

"Then the Octagon's history was wrong. You were the primary choice of the spirit, not Smith?"

"Perhaps you could interpret it that way. I was the one to arrange the session with Kelly and employed Smith as an independent critical witness. As I mentioned, he fainted before the end of the Spirit's pronouncements and was unaware that I had been chosen to lead. In the final part of the message, I was told things normally beyond mortal knowledge."

Some seconds before Chris could speak.

"I still don't understand the arrangement with the plaques. If you were working with Smith, why didn't you always know what they said? Why was it necessary to get photographs of them?"

"I will tell you more but not all. Smith was a bitter man. He had lost his wife to illness just a few years before the visit of the spirit and if he had known the information earlier, he could have saved her life. By 1650, he had taken the Blessing for 65 years and wasted that time by bedding an infinite number of women as he fruitlessly sought one who could replace the one love of his life. He increasingly began to resent my refusal to tell him the words of the spirit after he fainted and my insistence on retaining the Lifeblood. These concerns seemed to unbalance his mind."

"He was mad?"

"I did not say madness. He had made the decision to kill himself in the belief that it would allow him to rejoin his wife in the afterlife. In 1650, we met in secrecy and he described a plan to appoint four others to receive the Blessing, in addition to myself. Each of us could select one other as assistant and that was likely to be our future spouse after 2019. Back at that time, I felt sympathetic towards him and agreed to the plan."

"So you were a part of the original group?"

"That was his original proposal. However, I insisted on keeping the tenth constituent and the book with his account of the visitation. He had already fitted it with a lock and the bolt that killed Jessica Crowne. I made a supply of the Blessing for myself and allowed Smith his four pairs of people until 2018, knowing I would make a judgement then. Then Smith requested a final meeting at his house, asking me to bring the Lifeblood and his book. I recall us seated around the dining table and on it I placed the book and the box with the flask inside."

"I assume he tried to take them from you?"

"He had four men hiding outside the room. They burst in and held me while he took the box and the book. As he left, he told the men to kill me with a dagger in the heart."

"My wild guess is that they didn't succeed."

"I didn't do anything until he departed. Then I killed the men."

"A sword fight?"

"I entered their minds using certain trivial magickal abilities that I possess. Instructed the four to kill themselves. I had been ready for Smith's treachery. The flask in the box contained only water and I had removed the four pages from the book."

"I suppose life was full of backstabbing at that time."

"No more than now. I had concealed the real flask and the missing pages in the cellar of my residence and was content not to pursue Smith. He could give the Blessing to whoever he wished and I would appoint another to receive it. His eight would still meet together at Canterbury in 2018 and then be subject to my approval."

"So why didn't you know where the flask and pages were?"

"A few days after the meeting, I decided to check the hiding place. It was empty except for a plaque. You noticed that it carries not only a location and the motto but also the crest with the words 'The Octagon' beneath it."

"So who took the items?"

"No human had entered the cellar."

"So you're saying that the box and the missing pages were spirited away from your cellar and hidden here?"

"Spirited away may be correct."

"And in their place, a plaque was left for you that gave a location."

"Yes."

"Meanwhile, Smith had hidden what he believed to be the real Lifeblood and the book at the centre of a triangle. The points of the triangle were indicated on three of the four plaques he had made and the centre was in that barn at Charwithdill."

"Yes."

"But you found another plaque, not made by Smith that converted the triangle to a quadrangle to give a different centre point. That is this cottage."

"Yes."

"You're telling me that something supernatural took the Lifeblood and the pages, hid them here and then created a plaque of the same design used by Smith. This gave another location but you had to see Smith's plaques before you could find this place. You couldn't call it uncomplicated and it's hard to believe."

"An excellent summary but if you had been present when the spirit visited, you would not be in doubt. That which was revealed in the four minutes after Smith fainted was as much as any human could absorb. Knowledge that can not be shared, even with Selena. That may help you accept but you will never understand."

Chris began to feel the reality was slipping away.

"Why didn't you chase after Smith and stop him?"

"I saw no necessity to follow him, he did not have the Lifeblood and his book was incomplete. I also understood that it was not intended. At that point, he had not yet created his set of plaques. If his Octagon plan had been prevented, I would never have found the hiding place."

"So you didn't know exactly what Smith had done until you saw the plaque of the Countess?"

"No. He buried what he thought was the complete book and the genuine flask for his Octagon people to locate when they got together in 2018. That was in the barn at the farm."

Silence for nearly a minute before Chris asked another question.

"I assume that you're planning to form your own Octagon?"

She saw a smile developing across his elderly face and then realised that somewhere underneath must be the body of young man in his early twenties.

"Perhaps a Decagon. Selena and I are the first and I have decided you will join us."

"I'm still a little concerned about taking this Blessing."

"Did you enjoy your tea?"

She sighed.

"It was in the tea. I might have agreed but you had no right to do that without asking."

"I understand why you say that. However, it was my decision. You don't know me well and perhaps never will."

She saw his gaze fix on her again and shuddered.

"Chris wants to recommend another member," Selena said innocently.

"Really? Who would that be?"

Now Chris smiled.

"As if you didn't know."

"You have never been told his name."

"No I haven't and I've never felt the need to ask. I'll call him Jerome Two. He's one of your Jerome Jones copies or at least he was. How many do you have?"

"As many as necessary, sometimes more."

Chris barely heard the reply. She stared into the magnetic grey eyes.

"So who are you?"

"The records say that I died a long time ago. I've had several names since then."

"Yes, but your real name?"

Jerome Jones walked to the door, turning briefly to speak as he left.

"Surely you can deduce that by now."

www.ingramcontent.com/pod-product-compliance
Lightning Source LLC
Chambersburg PA
CBHW030242200626
46816CB00002BA/474